'Myth, magic and supers
and mesmerising novel of w
I loved both *A Jigsaw of F*
this is Badoe's
Fiona Noble, *The B*

'Badoe's breathtaking prose weaves a heart-thumping tale… *Lionheart Girl* is deeply atmospheric, stunningly original, and sizzling with ancient myth and magic. Utterly unmissable.'
Sophie Anderson, author of *The Castle of Tangled Magic*

'Fierce and thrilling, *Lionheart Girl* delivers on the promise of Badoe's debut, and then some. I loved this original, lyrical, dark fable.' Kiran Millwood Hargrave, author of *A Secret of Birds and Bone*

'Vividly imaginative, brave, passionate with an original heroine. A different kind of magical adventure that draws on West African myth for a story of universal interest.'
Amanda Craig, author of *The Golden Rule*

'Loved it! Yaba's best so far – a wonderful tale of magic and family.' Catherine Johnson, author of *Queen of Freedom: Defending Jamaica*

'Yaba's writing is a rich feast to be savoured. Filled with unforgettable images that leave you breathless, it is about the strength of love. It shows us that we are many things, never just one, and that truth often has many different feathers.'
Sally Gardner, author of *Invisible in a Bright Light*

'Unlike anything I've ever read. Mythical, vivid, unsettling and utterly page-turning, *Lionheart Girl* explores bonds of blood, friendship and the power of being true to yourself. Both unique and brilliant.' Ele Fountain, author of *Melt*

LIONHEART GIRL

Also by Yaba Badoe

A Jigsaw of Fire and Stars
Wolf Light

LIONHEART GIRL

YABA BADOE

ZEPHYR

An imprint of Head of Zeus

First published in the UK in 2021 by Zephyr, an imprint of Head of Zeus Ltd
This Zephyr paperback edition first published in the UK in 2022 by Head of
Zeus Ltd, part of Bloomsbury Publishing Plc

9 7 5 3 1 2 4 6 8

A catalogue record for this book is available from
the British Library.

ISBN (PB): 9781789540864
ISBN (E): 9781789540871

Cover artwork by Leo Nickolls
Designed by Heather Ryerson

Printed and bound in Great Britain by
CPI Group (UK) Ltd, Croydon CR0 4YY

Head of Zeus Ltd
5–8 Hardwick Street,
London EC1R 4RG
WWW.HEADOFZEUS.COM

For my dear 'dead-departed':
Uncle Kaku Aka, Auntie Irene, Uncle
George, Charry, Nana Nyima and
Keith Shearer, with love and gratitude.

And to the next generation of
Lionheart Girls, Holly and Fara, may
you be as brave and determined as
your grandmother, Julie, and your
great-grandmothers, Beryl and Edith.

I

THE FIRST TIME I ran away from home I was seven.

Instead of turning right outside the family house and going to school as I was supposed to, I turned left in the direction of the river and forest. Left, to find my father.

Ma had confessed days earlier that he was a creature of the forest; a creature she met in a woodland grove on a day she was harvesting wild honey. One kiss and that was it. The thought of me had seeded in her mind and I took root in her womb.

'One kiss and you made me?'

Ma had nodded.

'What's his name? What's he like?' I'd asked. 'Is my father an animal or a bird creature? A human being or a chick like me?'

Ma laughed. That's what she called me, you see: her little chick, half-hidden in the feathers of her wing.

'Tell me!'

She'd laughed again, a golden peal that spun me in circles as she tickled my ribs.

'I want to know!' I'd squealed.

'Come closer.'

I'd backed away, reluctant to touch her, to feel that fizz in my fingers, which frightened me. 'Tell me!'

'I don't recall his name. Or what happened in the forest after he kissed me. What matters, my dear, is that you're here and you're mine.'

'I'd like to meet him, Ma. Just once. *Please...*'

She'd smiled. 'Have you ever wondered if what you want is what he desires? Best not wake a sleeping snake, little chick. Best forget him!'

In truth, I couldn't. It was this, and the fizz in my fingers whenever I touched Ma's hair, that spurred me on a quest to find my father.

Two days later, after my mother's off on her travels again, as soon as I'm dressed and ready for school, I run.

If I find him, I decide, I'll ask my father his name. If he tells me, I'll tell him mine. 'They call me Sheba,' I'll say. 'I'm your daughter, Sheba, named after a queen in a big book. A queen as black and beautiful as I am, and every bit as wise as Nana says I'll be one day.'

I inhale a whiff of river, the one that flows through

farmland to the forest and
resolve to follow the
scent. I'm confident
that the moment I
invoke the name of
my great-grandfather,
Nana Gyata su, I'll find
a tree, a special tree, which'll
point me in the direction I need to
go. With the help of my ancestor, the last
chief of our village, brave as a king of the
forest, I can do anything! I know, because
last night he came to me and changed into a
lion. One moment, there was an old man
in a kente cloth at the door. I blinked,
and a lion was at my feet. 'I'm Sheba,'
I'll say to my father. 'Sheba, a girl who
walks with lions.'

I skip down the track, sidestepping a street vendor,
a woman roasting plantain and groundnuts.

'Small girl, shouldn't you be going that way?' The
vendor points to the cotton tree at the centre of our
village where we assemble for school.

Even as my uniform betrays me, I shake my head.
'Today I'm going to the forest.'

'Small fry like you? Go back to school.'

I shake my head a second time. 'The forest won't
harm me,' I assure her. 'That's where my father lives.'

A question stirs on the woman's face. 'Aren't you the child who sleeps in the big house over there?'

Before I can answer, before I can shake my head, she replies: 'You're Nana Serwah's granddaughter, aren't you? Sika Prempeh's last-born.'

'My mother's gone travelling. If you see Nana, tell her I'm on my way to the forest to look for my father.'

The woman lumbers forward, an elephant about to drag me home with her trunk.

I dodge.

'Aba!' the woman cries. 'Someone, anyone, help me!'

There's no one else around, only the dark silhouettes of kiosks, a splash of pink in the sky as the moon gives way to the sun.

I race down the track. When I dare look back, the woman is at her stall once again.

My nose for the river takes me through fields of sugar cane and maize. The plants sway, fluttering and rolling in wind-dance. I wave at them, arms whirling in a welcome song of my own.

'I'm going to the forest,' I tell earth, wind and sky.

Up high, a cluster of clouds shadowing the sun peeps at me.

I grin in reply. 'Today's the day I meet my father! I'm going to tell him about Ma!'

'What?'

Another adult. This time a farmer, his skin dark as pitch after hours labouring in the heat. In a basket, he carries tubers of yam and a machete.

'Which way is the forest?' I ask.

'A lot further than those short legs of yours can carry you, girl.'

I smile, clicking my tongue to stop laughter spilling from my mouth. The man has no idea how strong I am! I'm sturdy, and yet, light as a balloon scudding through the sky, I'll duck and dive to reach my destination. 'Which way to the forest?'

'Go home, girl,' the man says. 'There's mud ahead, a bridge to cross and then wetlands to tramp over before you reach the forest's edge. If you get there, beware of snakes.'

'Snakes?'

'This is the season of snakes,' says the farmer. 'But snakes are nothing compared to Sasabonsam.'

'Sasabonsam?'

'Ha! You mean to say you don't know about those blood-sucking monsters in the forest?'

I step back, shaking my head.

'Those creatures have tongues of fire.' The man waggles his tongue, slurping, as if getting ready to gulp me down. 'Their eyes are red, flame-red; their bodies are covered in hair and they dangle from trees to catch small girls like you.'

I lift my head high. 'I'm a creature of the forest too. I'm like my father. I'm not scared of snakes or monsters.'

The man looks me up and down. Takes me in, and then spits me out like an orange pip he's swallowed by mistake. 'Turn around,' he says. 'The forest is no place for a girl alone.'

'Where my father lives, so shall I!'

'Small girl, don't make me walk you back.'

Face set, legs apart, I stand my ground until the farmer, towering above me, lowers his hand to grab mine. Quick as a flea, I turn and run into the cornfield crying:

> 'Cornfield! Cornfield! Watch over me!
>
>   Form a ring of protection and hide me!'

I sing my grandmother's song. The song she's taught me to use when danger is so close, that not only can I smell her breath, I can see her baring her teeth as well. In an emergency, Nana says, I am to call for help from every living thing around me and then run and hide.

I hear the farmer behind me, thrashing about, pushing back stalks and breaking them. Stomping up and down, beating the crop with a stick. The charm I've muttered, combined with the goodwill of the plants, unite in frustrating him. A row of corn, sensing my haste and panic, responds by shifting, rearranging itself in a circle that shields me from view.

The man curses. Three times he curses, before trudging to the footpath. He picks up his basket and leaves.

When I'm sure he's gone, I step from the corn circle to be met by laughter.

Crouching in the undergrowth ahead of me is a boy. He flings back his head and cackles, a finger pointing my way. The more the boy laughs, the more my mood sours, until all I can do is glare. No one laughs at me, not if I can help it!

'Small boy, has anyone told you that you have a laugh like a hyena?'

'Are you talking to me? Are you calling me small? A hyena?' The boy unpeels himself, stretching to his full height. 'Now tell me I'm small.'

He's a head taller than I am and older as well. Wiry, long-limbed, his coppery complexion is almost as red as the ground we're standing on. His features are not as rounded and plump as mine, but sharp, thin. He looks familiar. Even so, I don't recall where I've met him before.

'What's your name?' I stride to his left, then his right – the way my teacher drills us in class one.

'Maybe.' The boy smiles and his eyes, dark as molasses, sweeten the bitter taste on my tongue: the taste that floods my mouth when I'm angry.

'What sort of name is Maybe?'

His eyes crinkle as he smiles again. This time the sweetness in him tumbles out, spilling over me. My mind empties while my face mirrors his. A grin spreads to my cheeks, flickering over my lips as my dimples dance.

Perhaps this was what it was like for Ma and my father. One smile and that was it. One kiss and they made me.

'Come, let me take you to the river. It's on the way to the forest,' the boy says. 'Follow me and I'll tell you the story of my name.'

Side by side, his hand brushing mine, the lure of water beckons while he tells me his tale.

'My mother gave me my name to cheat mischief-makers and soul-eaters,' he explains. 'Before I came along, none of my brothers or my sister survived. Within a week, *peh*, they were gone. Number one. Number two. Number three. Come and see my mother crying. Every day, crying!' The boy traces tears down his cheeks, and, wrapping his arms around his head, he rocks from side to side to demonstrate his mother's grief.

My mouth opens in sympathy.

'At last, she goes to see a mallam, a wise man, and asks for help. All she wants is a child. A living, breathing child! The mallam tells her that the best way to confuse masters of mischief and death is to give her next baby a name they won't understand. A name that will make it impossible for them to know if the child is a girl or a boy, an animal or a plant, dead or alive.'

'Truly?'

'True, true,' he replies. 'As soon as I was conceived my mother called me Maybe and I've endured up till now because my name confuses those who wish to destroy life. I am the first of my mother's children to grow tall!' Head high, he grins.

'Maybe,' I murmur. 'My name is Sheba.'

'I know. I've seen you under the cotton tree with the small fry at school. I don't always bother with school myself...'

We've walked far enough to hear the river's call: the splash and gurgle of waves amid the chatter of women washing clothes. Downriver, a gaggle of girls are fetching water. Buckets filled, they lift them on to their heads while children laugh and play. Amazed it's taken me until now to find my way here, I stop and stare.

In that moment, time freezes as, one after the other, heads turn to meet my gaze. A woman whispers. Another laughs. There's a murmur of sighs before a buzz unfurls and I catch snippets of what's said:

'That's Nana Serwah's granddaughter.'

'The old woman in that house without men?'

'Those witches in the former chief's palace who keep us hidden?'

'We're all outlaws or runaways here...'

I've been warned not to listen to gossip, not to search for approval on the faces of my neighbours.

Those who smile at you today may condemn you tomorrow, Sheba. A wise woman closes her ears to speculation and finds her own path.

That's Nana talking. She's raised me as a daughter of the royal house of our village. A princess in our line, I'm used to being petted and pawed – a cub among lionesses. Yet what I've heard unsettles me.

Stomach churns. Legs wobble.

Maybe and I have walked for miles. There hasn't been much mud to speak of, just raised beds of yam and cassava that we tramped over to get to the river. The wetlands are on the other side. Beyond a sprawl of mangrove bushes, on the rim of the horizon, is the forest. Remote and distant as a star, it shimmers in a haze of heat.

I remember the farmer's words, how legs as short as mine would struggle to walk so far. The sun, already high in the sky, beads sweat on my brow. A trickle runs down my back. My school uniform clings. I'm wilting, and as my hands grow clammy, my throat dry,

I sink to my knees.

Maybe sits beside me on the riverbank. He's hot as well. He must be, because he plucks a frond from a broad-leaved plant and, cupping it in his hands, scoops up water. He drinks and then dribbles the rest into my mouth.

The water is cool, earthy, yet instead of reviving me, tiredness crawls through my body.

'Do you have to go to the forest today?' asks Maybe.

'I have to look for my father.'

'Can't you search for him another time? I'll come with you.'

'Will you?'

His eyes say 'yes'. That's when I touch his head.

While his eyes probe mine, delving deeper and deeper into the heart of me, while he turns me inside out as he rustles through the truth in me, I caress his hair. I fondle it, savouring its softness, the crinkle-twist of each curl. I touch, and as I do, pictures in his mind slip into mine.

I see his mother's smile, hear yelps of delight in his

little brother's laughter, and flowing through him I taste a lake of kindness as full as the river at our feet; a kindness that tickles my soul.

'You have the heart of lion,' he says, 'a heart that's strong and true.'

I flinch, reminded of why I turned left outside our house. I wanted to confide in my father, tell him about the fizz in my fingers and then ask him if I'm a creature of the forest too.

My father will know what to do. He, more than anyone, will teach me how to quell the fire that rages in my mother; the fire that burns me when she lashes out. He'll show me the way. He has to.

'We'll find him soon,' says Maybe. 'With my help, we'll track him down!'

I nod, hoping that what he's said will come true.

2

MA AND I live at the outer edge of Asante-land. Our village can't be found on an ordinary map. It's half-hidden, a blur in the distance you'd never reach unless you're with someone who comes from here.

Our village has no name, a decision taken by our ancestors who, needing a place to hide from war and traffickers in human flesh, performed rituals to shield us from view. Like other communities close by, it is home to old people and children. Most of those in-between left long ago to find work in the city because unless you're a farmer, there's not enough work; not enough gold and money to earn – not enough sika, my mother's name.

There isn't much to boast about here: a few cement houses, a school and clinic and on the outskirts in Zongo, where outsiders live, a scattering of mud-and-thatch houses. Water we fetch from the river or draw from a well. No matter where you live, the first thing you smell on waking is the river; and the last thing you feel at night is its lick on your face as you fall asleep.

This is my home, yet I have to tell you plain-plain, my corner of the world is an inside-out, upside-down, twist-in-time place where strange things happen. A place with eyes and ears everywhere. Eyes watching in the sky and on the ground. Eyes unblinking as stones at the bottom of the river, while tongues cluck and peck like hens.

'I told you to go home, but no! You ran away! Now look at you!'

'Aba! Small girl, big trouble!'

That's what people are muttering as I walk home with Maybe and his mother, Salmata, either side of me.

I keep my eyes lowered to avoid the scorn on the roast-plantain-seller's face. Keep them lowered to stop glowering as she gestures to other vendors and chats. My hands balled in tight, angry fists, I shove them in the pockets of my school uniform.

Eyes fastened on my feet I hear gasps of: 'Oh! Small girl like that? *No!*'

I hear lips squeezed at my gidi-gidi behaviour. Listen to them whispering my name: 'Sheba, Sika Prempeh's last-born. You know, Sika. Madam High and Mighty. The trader who refuses to marry and no one likes. Well, do you?'

I raise my head, keep my mouth zipped as the taste of lemon on my tongue sets my heart on fire. Shoulders hunched in shame, I take one painful step after the other, as my companions escort me to my family's compound.

Not far from the village centre, the only dwelling with an upstairs and downstairs, a whitewashed mansion looms ahead of us. Ma and I sleep in a room in the living quarters, next door to the wisest of our relatives, my grandmother, Nana Serwah.

'Ago!' Salmata cries, knocking on our front door.

'Amie,' comes the reply. 'The door is open. Come in! Come in!'

My companions follow me across a courtyard to an alcove, an outdoor sitting room where my relatives are seated: Nana, head of our household of women; her daughter, Ruby; and squatting on a stool beside Nana, her youngest sister, Grandma Baby, with her only child, the last in her line, Aunt Clara. Aunt Clara holds a comb, my comb, and on her palm are strands of my hair, while on Aunt Ruby's lap is a dress I wore the day before.

I begin to wonder if others in my family can 'see' with their fingers as I do. Why else would they be touching my things as if to harvest clues from them? What's more, they appear calm. There's no hint of anxiety on their faces, no worry whatsoever. That's what I believe until Nana exhales, releasing a sigh so deep that, as her breath mingles with mine, it rattles my bones.

Nana sighs. Aunt Clara drops the comb, and tears begin to leak down Aunt Ruby and Grandma Baby's cheeks. Before their tears turn to sobs, Maybe's mother, Salmata, introduces herself. She explains what's happened. How, after her son found me on my way to the river and took me to their dwelling in Zongo, she decided to bring me home.

My aunts and grandmothers thank her, insisting she stay and sit with us. I do too. I need the presence of strangers; anything to delay the tongue-lashing I expect from my family.

'Thank you, Madam,' Salmata replies. 'But I must get back to my youngest. Madam, this is not necessary,' she says as Aunt Clara brings her a basket of cassava and plantain. 'Anyone would have behaved as I did. Any mother would do the same.'

The more she resists, the more Aunt Clara adds to the basket: okra, garden eggs, tubers of yam, while Aunt Ruby fusses over our guests, patting Salmata's shoulder, straightening her blouse, before cupping Maybe's chin in her palm. Until now, I never noticed how *touchy-touch* my aunt is.

'You've returned our daughter to us,' says Aunt Clara.

'We'll never be able to thank you enough.'

Countless thank yous and goodbyes later, after hands have been squeezed and shaken and backs patted, the front door finally closes. I am alone with my family, their eyes pinning me to the spot. Probing, demanding I tell them what happened, four pairs of eyes clear as river-washed stones peer at me. They pinch and pry while I shift from one foot to the other.

How can I talk about something I don't understand? How can I explain the need to speak to my father about the sizzling in my fingers that puts pictures in my mind? I gnaw on my tongue, hunting for words.

'Why?' asks Nana, a hand on her sister's arm.

Baby, still tearful, sniffs as she plucks at a lace handkerchief. 'I smelled trouble in the wind, and when I looked you were gone,' she laments, before Nana says:

'Why did you leave, child, without telling us where you were going? We waited and waited for you after school. When you didn't come home, Ruby and Clara went looking for you.' Nana pauses.

Aunt Ruby takes over. 'We spoke to your teacher, questioned your friend, Ama, next door.'

'We were distraught,' Grandma Baby continues. 'Nothing has passed our lips. Nothing has entered my stomach since you went missing.'

Now I understand her tears. Though she's the smallest of the adults around me, light and nimble on her feet, her appetite is huge. For her to be too upset to eat, too upset to allow the aroma of Aunt Clara's food to titillate her nose, shakes me as much as Nana's sigh.

'Come here,' says Nana.

I inch to where she's sitting on a brass-studded chair. Her late father's ceremonial seat, higher than others in the alcove, is her favourite. Made of mahogany with a crest of a lion at its centre, its arms are carved in the shape of lion's paws, claws and all. This is the chair she uses at family meetings in the hope that the good sense of our ancestors will flow through her as she speaks. Nana Gyata su was the wealthiest man in our village and Nana, the first and brightest of his children, stands head and shoulders above his sons and nephews. That's why none of them stay with us for long. After a night, two at the most, they're gone, and the house becomes a coven of women once again.

'Come,' Nana says, urging me closer.

I creep towards her. Opening her arms, she pulls me to her chest. The warmth and scent of her, that mixture of nutmeg and cloves that reminds me of the cakes she bakes, releases my tears. Nana hugs me closer, tighter. So tightly that words I couldn't find moments before, leap off my tongue.

'You won't tell Ma, will you? Please don't tell her. Please, Nana.'

That night, after I've eaten and washed the dust of the day away, Nana sits on my bed, cradling me. I still haven't told her why I bolted. I mumbled something about trying to find my father and that was it.

It's not until Aunt Ruby has left us that Nana asks: 'Were you running away from all of us today, or one of us in particular?'

'I wanted to get away from Ma.'

Nana nods, and for a moment, I think she understands.

'Your mother will be gone a week or two at least.'

A trader of fabric and jewellery, Ma comes and goes, leaving me in the care of Nana, Grandma Baby and my aunts. Ma can be gone for weeks at a time. No problem. It's her coming back that worries me.

I pull away, squeezing my hands to calm a tornado circling my heart. I pummel my palms, and then, twisting one hand over the other, wring them again and again. If anything can dampen the squall rising within me, if anything can keep it hidden, this is it.

Nana eases her fingers into mine. 'What's happened between the two of you? What did your mother say? Tell me, child.'

I close my eyes.

Nana's grip tightens. 'Tell me, Sheba. I saw you born,' she says. 'I introduced you to Mother Earth at your outdooring. I've watched you grow, grandchild of mine, and if I'm lucky, you'll be with me when I die. Nothing you say frightens me.'

My eyes open. 'Nothing?'

Nana nods. 'The roof of this house protects you as much as it does me. For our family to stay strong, we have to talk to each other.'

Outside, the clatter of pots and pans as Aunt Clara tidies up the kitchen, the swish of her broom as she sweeps the floor, reassure me, giving me courage to speak. 'I asked Ma who my father is. She said he's a creature of the forest.'

Nana's ancient eyes clear, as a circle of blue glows around ebony-dark irises. 'That's what she told us when we begged her to name the man whose seed was growing in her. Whether she was telling the truth or not–'

'Then, Ma said...' I speak quickly, so quickly words tumble out of my mouth before I can claw them back: 'Ma said I should forget him. Another time, she said I wasn't to do what my sisters did. I mustn't leave her. Mustn't let Aunt Lila take me away. And if there's any hint that I'm going to behave like my sisters, Ma says she'll shrink me and seal me in her locket.'

I say the words and see a fingernail the colour of blood, tapping the gold locket around Ma's neck. The nail taps, and bit by bit, I shrink into Ma's shadow.

Nana sighs, shaking her head.

'Aunt Lila's a thief, Nana! She stole my sisters and now she's slicing them up, eating them small-small day after day!' I make the gobbling sound Ma made of a hog gorging food.

'Sika, *paaah*! My baby-last came into this world angry and is still angry. Grandchild, your Aunt Lila is doing no such thing!'

'She isn't?'

'No,' Nana insists. Then, to silence whispers of suspicion on my face, she adds: 'Your Uncle Solomon and his wife have done everything they can to help us, to help your mother especially. No brother could have done more for his twin sister.'

'But Ma says Aunt Lila is coming–'

'No one is coming to take you away, Sheba. I won't let them! What's more, your mother can't shrink you or seal you in her locket, I promise.'

Unsure whether to believe her or not, I touch Nana's hair.

I've always enjoyed playing with hair, always loved trailing my fingers through it, letting them linger on stray strands before twisting them together. I do so again, but this time as I dip into Nana's truth, she realises something vital is leaving her.

My fingers sizzle as light flickers, forming pictures in my mind.

A face.

A gesture.

The smile of a woman I haven't yet met.

Beside her, my uncle, who I recognise from visits long ago: my Uncle Solomon, Ma's twin; Solo for short.

'You too?' Nana asks, removing my hand from her braid. 'You too have the touch?'

'What, Nana?'

'The touch: a gift some of our family have. Is that what frightened you, child?'

'Does Ma have it too?

'No,' Nana replies. 'Your mother looks elsewhere for her power. Is that why you ran away?'

I half-nod, before shaking my head. There's something else, something I can't recall: a memory just beyond my reach. I feel its tread, sense it lurking in the shadows. Dig deeper, rummaging in the hope that whatever I've forgotten will leap out and surprise me. But before I can catch it and claim it, light as a puff of wind, it slips through my fingers.

'Is it to do with your mother?' Nana asks.

I don't reply. Not knowing baffles me.

I try again to remember, but the effort sets my heart racing, cramping my chest till I'm gasping.

Stroking my back as she rocks me, Nana sings an old-time song, the song she used to sing to lull me to sleep. A song of love from a far-away place across

the sea, her 'Lullaby of
Broadway'.

Gradually, as my heartbeat
settles and I'm able to breathe
once more, she murmurs: 'We'll keep
what you've told me to ourselves, Sheba.
There's no need for your mother to know, no need
for her to worry, OK?'

I sigh with relief.

'When you're old enough,' she tells me, 'your Aunt
Clara will show you how to make the most of your gift.
In the meantime, I shall try to teach you to remember.
I moulded your head to shape your destiny. Now, I
shall help you fulfil it.'

3

IN SEARCH OF my father, I found Maybe.

Next day, before he arrives, I know he's coming. He doesn't knock at our door, doesn't call my name or stand on the porch waiting for me to come out. There's no need to. Like a river whirled by wind, the current between us glimmers when he's nearby. It reels me in and sings as I smile.

I run, open the door. In his arms is a crate of sobolo, a drink his mother makes from hibiscus petals and ginger.

Cackling with glee, Aunt Ruby relieves him of his cargo. 'Sheba! Walk to school with your friend! Krachi,' she says to Maybe, honouring him with the title of 'young man', 'be our eyes and ears today. Look out for our daughter. And on your way home, pick up the money I owe your mother.'

The two of us head in the direction of the cotton tree. I'm wearing shoes while Maybe, barefoot, walks with the tread of a leopard about to leap on its prey: poised, alert, hushed. Between the pad of his footfall, I detect the patter of feet.

I hear it again: a shuffle like the rustle of seed pods in a breeze. The sound scatters, and then settling on Maybe, changes into pinpricks of light on his skin.

I freeze.

'Aren't you coming?'

I nod, even as I stare. The more I stare, the more the sunbeams on him glitter, then fade, only to brighten moments later. They shiver and blur, forming shapes that shimmer. Three of them; shifting, retreating.

The curve of a cheek.

The smudge of a lip in a play of shadow and light.

Three mouths cup in smiles as Maybe turns to me.

'Are you frightened?'

I shake my head. I've seen such things in our house. Spirits of the dead-departed who watch over us. I've listened to Nana Gyata su walking down our corridors. And when Ma's away, I've heard his ghost purring in my ear before I fall asleep. Spirits are everywhere, Nana says. And of those of us who glimpse them, it's usually children who see them most. Our eyes haven't yet set, so we're likely to see more of the world we came from than adults.

'They wanted to meet you,' Maybe explains. 'They

waited for me to be born to delight in this.' His arm circles our village: the splendid cotton tree at its centre; steam rising from banana leaves at the first kiss of the sun; the coo and gurgle of nesting pigeons. 'I'm their everything,' says Maybe.

'True, true?'

He nods. 'Meet my brothers, Musa and Jebril. My sister, Moona.' Shadows flit through him, accentuating the shine of his skin.

My mouth opens. 'They were with you in the cornfield?'

'Of course! That's why they wanted to greet you.'

'Does your mother see them?'

He shakes his head. 'She's suffered enough. Some things are only for those of us who are still close to where we come from.'

Maybe grins, and as he does so, I hear the tinkling of those around him; their chuckles as they escort us to school.

From that day on, Maybe is my forever friend, my closest companion. He's not as frightened of me as most of the children at school are. He isn't bothered that I'm Nana Serwah's granddaughter, or that I hail from a house of royal women.

If I'm not following Maybe or imitating his leopard prowl, we're side by side, walking in step with his classmate, Gaza – so called because every once in a while, his father thrashes him within an inch of his life.

One afternoon, when the three of us go home for a snack, Aunt Ruby sucks her teeth, enraged at a bruise on Gaza's cheek.

'Krachi, your mother was a friend of my heart. I loved her,' she reminds him. 'Next time your father touches you, tell me, and I'll deal with him.'

She turns Gaza round. Lifts his shirt. Touches the marks on his back and recoils as an ocean of hurt sears her fingers.

Ancient welts quiver beside tender new ones.

My aunt is furious – so incensed that as she peels sugar cane with a cutlass, disgust clamps her lips. Doesn't speak. No! Not a word escapes her until her fury, unleashed in the slash and thrust of the cutlass, is spent.

Aunt Ruby severs the stalk in three: a piece for each of us. Then, in a voice that rumbles like thunder, a voice that makes everyone who hears it sit up and listen, she says: 'Krachi, what my poor friend endured, you shall not! As long as I'm here, a man who drinks kill-me-quick liquor, morning, noon and night will not obliterate you as he did her! You hear?'

Gaza nods and Aunt Ruby turns to Maybe and me. 'If you're ever in a situation where this boy needs my help, make sure you come and fetch me.'

We promise to do so, while Gaza, who hasn't talked much since his mother died, wheezes his thanks on a harmonica, a gift from his ma.

The instrument sneezes and a tune soars from the ocean within him: a serenade to his mother's love, a sad song with a melody so sweet, it entices her to reveal herself. Those of us able to see, watch as she emerges, drifting closer. Three steps. Two and the scent of neem flowers circles us as her hand flutters over the bruise on her son's cheek.

She tries to touch it, kiss it, fondle his hair. But hand, face and lips dip into him and disappear. Frustration illuminating what was once her face, she steps away. 'Please help my boy,' she says. 'I won't be able to rest until he's happy again.'

I nod, and so does Maybe.

The serenade complete, Gaza puts his harmonica away and retrieves a gecko from a pocket of his school shirt. He gives the lizard a strand of cane to eat. Uh-huh. Gecko doesn't relish sugar as much as we do. We're chomping and sucking, spitting out cane. Once we've guzzled the last drops of sweetness and there's nothing left but shredded strands on the floor, we sweep it up and go back to school.

'When we finish pick fruit, mek we visit Ama's house.'
I'm dangling from a bough of the mango tree in our
back yard. Dangling while talking to Maybe.

'Ama? Huh!' He scrunches his face as if he's eaten
something rotten. Scrunches it, and then shakes the
tree to grab Gaza's attention.

Above us, hidden by foliage, Gaza's dozing while
Gecko feasts on fruit-flies.

I throw a mango at Maybe. He drops it into Aunt
Clara's hamper. Eager to create a relish she craves,
she's asked us to fill it with green mangoes. Climbing
down, I perch beside my friend.

What Maybe decides, Gaza
usually agrees to. Sure enough,
Gaza swivels his eyes in a
signal that encompasses
all of us. He wants us
to stick together and
keep away from
Ama.

'But I want to see
her,' I insist.

Maybe shakes his
head, counting Ama's
flaws on his fingers. 'One.
Your friend is too *know*.'

'How?'

'She thinks she knows everything. Two. That mouth of hers! She's the queen of name-calling, and three, she takes up too much space.'

My next-door neighbour, Ama, is clever and doesn't bother to hide it. Even when boys say she's weird and yell 'Ama *Smart*! Ama *Smart*!' at her because she knows so much more about the world than they do, she pretends not to care. In fact, she wears her nickname as a badge of honour and shrugs, a smile on her face, while she mutters insults under her breath. Insults she thinks only I can hear, such as: 'Look at your nose, you son of a rat.' 'Ah! Those ears of yours are the size of an elephant's.' Her favourite insult is to call those who offend her nincompoops. At times, I've felt the burn of her ant's-bite tongue as well. It can be brutal, I tell you! I don't mean brutal like the bite of black ants, but those red ones with stings that make you shriek.

She can be nasty, I admit it. But *take up too much space*? I pucker my lips at such foolishness. 'You want us to take up less space than you do?' I say to Maybe. 'How possible?'

Gecko back in his pocket, Gaza clambers down to our branch. 'Her tongue never tires,' he grumbles. 'Even when she's old and her teeth fall out, she'll yap, yap plenty.'

Maybe nods. 'That girl is like cow dung. Hard on the outside, slippery inside.'

'What?' I talk with my lips again, this time in horror. 'Are you saying my friend is *shitty*? Aba!' I lip-talk some more. Nana says it's vulgar when people resort to lip-talk. But sometimes you have to be vulgar to make a point.

'No one is perfect!' I confess. 'Not even you!' I fold my arms, disgruntled.

'OK, OK,' Maybe concedes. 'If you girls can beat either Gaza or me in a tyre race, she can join us. But if we win, she stays away.'

I twist his words in a way I hope will benefit me: 'Why not – if one of you defeats us in a game of ampe, you join us?'

'But ampe is a game for girls,' says Gaza.

'And tyres are for boys!'

'But you want Ama to join us,' Maybe replies.

Seeing the logic in his argument and the mistake in mine, I take up his challenge. We pump fists. But then, annoyed at the insults they've heaped on my sister-friend, I lob a mango in the basket and lip-talk to myself.

4

THERE ARE THREE of us in our gang: Maybe, Gaza and me. Today, if I get my way, we'll become a gang of four. Despite the boys dragging their feet every step of the way, today's the day of our race.

Not so long ago, Ama's mother, Auntie Esi, was close to Ma. They ate from the same bowl and shared so many stories that when they were pregnant with us and their sister-love grew, they swore that we'd be friends as well. Friendship by force! Huh! Come and see Ama and I quarrelling! Quarrelling. Then laughing. Up and down. Down and up. Gidi-gidi, day and night.

Only this morning, after reminding me yet again that in our village, girls do not play with boys, and certainly not a nincompoop who lives in Zongo, I tell Ama plain-plain, 'My friend, your ant's tongue tires me! How many times must I tell you, that I, Sheba Prempeh, do not care for "they say, they say"! And if you're foolish enough to think I do – you don't know me!'

'You want everyone to see *you* – a chief's great-granddaughter – playing with a pauper who behaves like a *bush-boy*?' She pulls a face, her pupils specks of black ice. 'Look at him!'

I glance at Maybe, trying to see him as she does, but before my vision adjusts, my heart heaves and, reminded of the day I first met him, I'm back at his home in Zongo once again.

We've tramped over ground marshy as pounded palm nuts oozing oil. Fought our way through a forest of reeds, across rice fields to a patch of dry land where Maybe lives. In a hut on the edge of our village: a simple dwelling of mud-and-thatch that's quickly put up, easily pulled down.

Maybe's father has yet to visit him. Unlike me, he knows his father's name.

'He's a hunter and herdsman up north,' he says. 'He's looking after cattle. My mother travelled south to build a business and keep us safe.'

Aware that most outsiders go round in circles, never locating the path to our village, I ask, 'How was she able to find us?'

'We were running for our lives,' Maybe explains. 'When you're fleeing from mischief-makers, a path opens up in front of you that brings you here.'

'Truly?'

'True, true,' Maybe assures me. 'But we won't stay forever. One day soon my father will take me back to our people. First, he'll come for me, then, when my brother, Better Life, is older, he'll collect him. We belong to his line.'

The idea of having a father willing to embrace me and include me in his family, tunnels like a weevil to my heart. That's what I want: a father with people of his own. Distracted, dreaming of a life away from Ma, I'm mulling this over as I step inside Maybe's home. One moment I'm outside, eager to find my father. Next, I'm inside, and as the breath of Maybe's soul warms my skin, I decide there and then that wherever he goes, so will I.

Aunt Clara says that's what it's like for some of us with the 'touch'. We understand the future before it occurs. We know exactly what's right for us; what's meant. And once we've fingered the hair of someone we love, there's no turning back.

'I used to be the same,' she says. 'But then look what happened to me, Sheba.'

Aunt Clara didn't have my ear that day. The only voice I hear, the only voice that matters, is Nana's.

'*The heart is stronger than the mind,*' she whispers. '*In all things, listen to the beat of your heart and move to its rhythm.*'

My feet are tapping, unfazed by the difference

between my home
and Maybe's. We
have tables to
eat and write off,
beds to sleep on, chairs
for sitting and dining. Our house
is large, with room after room to
walk through and sleep in – a salon
for lounging and chatting during
daylight hours, and at night,
an old gramophone player to
sing and dance to. Our house
without men is a place of plenty.

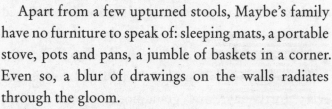

Apart from a few upturned stools, Maybe's family have no furniture to speak of: sleeping mats, a portable stove, pots and pans, a jumble of baskets in a corner. Even so, a blur of drawings on the walls radiates through the gloom.

I step into the shadows. Step over a sleeping mat. Duck beneath a line of clothes before I'm able to see that the pictures are of a village with homes like his: mud-and-thatch. A village laden with fruit trees and in the distance, gigantic baobab trees with bulbous trunks.

'That's our village,' he murmurs. 'And these are some of the baobab trees that grow in the savannah close by.'

He's drawn the trees again and again. Sometimes

in flower, sometimes old and hollowed out with flickering, ghostly shapes beside them. Or with zebras and antelopes munching underneath.

'We call it the tree of life,' he tells me. 'There isn't a part of it we don't use: bark, leaves, fruit and seeds.'

As he talks, I feel Maybe's breath again and tremble. 'Your pictures are alive.'

His figures dance and sing, while his animals quiver in motion.

I walk to the biggest and best of them, a drawing of an ancient tree, luminous shades around it. 'What's this?'

'Sometimes, where I come from, when the wisest and best among us die, we bury them inside a wizened baobab. The tree can become a place of healing. A good place; a happy place, like the cotton tree here.'

I'm not so sure about that. What I do know is that every forty days, my grandmother and Grandma Baby talk to our ancestors by pouring libation at the cotton tree and river. They say it's to help our village prosper and to keep it hidden. They do what they can, I suppose, and yet the fact remains: everyone with an iota of ambition leaves for the city quicker than a flea can bite you twice.

Nonetheless, I've never seen anything like Maybe's creations before. We gaze at his drawings. Behind his village are grasslands full of trees. Above them, a brilliant blue sky illuminates the nooks and curves of

Maybe's home.

'Will you draw me one day?' I ask.

'One day, one day.' He nods.

'Good. I'll pester you, *ahhhhhh*, until you keep your promise.'

'Sheba, can't you see what I'm seeing?' asks Ama.

Maybe's torn shirt is jostled by gusts of harmattan wind. Laden with dust, it scuffs his shins grey while he and Gaza wheel tyres up the track. Up to the top of the hill they trundle, while Ama and I roll a tyre between us.

Behind us, at an upstairs window, Grandma Baby, her lace handkerchief at the ready, is poised to signal the start of our race.

'His shirt is basaa basaa,' Ama whinges. 'Would you wear a shirt like that? No! Your boy is Zongo through and through. Because over there, there's no money for shoes. No money at all!' Ama wrinkles her nose. 'And he *smells*!'

You see what I mean about her ant-bite tongue? Before the tang of citrus scours my mouth and I lash out, I begin to wonder if jealousy has curdled her brain and made her sour. After all, since I met Maybe I've been spending a lot of time with him, and his swagger has entered my walk.

37

I'm tempted to turn my back on her but somehow, I stay put until I'm able to say: 'Ama, if you don't want to race with us, if you don't want to befriend a boy from Zongo as well as be *my* friend, why don't you go home?'

'You want to lose? Without me, those boys will defeat you as breezily as I greeted you this morning!' She snorts to emphasise her point.

In the space of a few weeks, the four of us have built a kite of turquoise blue, and releasing it one balmy afternoon, we watched it soar in the sky over the hill to the river.

We've discovered Video Man's van, where, perched on benches, a sheet as a screen, we take in the latest Nollywood films: diabolical ju ju movies about witches which we laugh at, or romances with too much kissing, which make us gasp for air.

Thanks to Maybe, I'm able to catch tilapia, gut it, and roast it with breadfruit, pepper and yam. Now, having mastered the art of manoeuvring tyres, depending on who reaches the bottom first, we're going to find out if Ama will join us; no questions asked, no insults traded.

When the four of us are in position at the top, I

wave to Grandma Baby. She drops her handkerchief and we're off.

Maybe surges ahead, Gaza a hair's breadth behind. Each of us, a stick wedged inside the tyre controls it as best as we can. Its direction, its propulsion as we launch rubber over pebbles and ridges. Too far to the left, the tyre tips over. Too much to the right, you'll tumble. Too fast? Too slow? Ditto. Balance and speed are vital. To be swift but nimble of foot, an added bonus.

Gaza stumbles, falls into a ditch, as step by step, Ama and I gather speed.

I shall always be smaller than Maybe, and my legs will remain shorter than his. But I'm light, fleet of foot. Indeed, sometimes being short is an advantage, for, like an arrow in a bow, as soon as I'm released, there's no stopping me.

'Small Girl Danger,' I yell.

Ama wheels the tyre with the palm of her hand, while I use the stick.

We've practised creating momentum yet keeping pace with each other for days. Down, down, we run, faster and faster until we're almost where we need to be, almost neck and neck with my forever friend.

He propels the tyre forward.

Lunges. Leaps. Zips ahead. Ama's resolve quickens and we push harder still. So hard that with our feet scarcely touching the ground, we're nearly flying.

Three feet. Two palms. A hand apart. A finger, and then, *crack*!

A stick snaps and we're overtaking Maybe.

There's no looking back now.

Bounding over spikes, avoiding sticks and stones, we whizz to the bottom of the hill and braking, tumble on top of each other, screaming.

Ama may hiss and spit about my forever friend from Zongo. She may dismiss Maybe as an outsider, a Fulani, who wouldn't know how to wear a kente cloth if he had money to buy one. She grumbles continuously, and yet her joy in winning is every bit as bright as mine.

'Yah! Yah!' she shrieks. 'Women warriors!'

'We did it!' I reply. 'We destroyed them! Smashed them!'

'Life is sweet-*ooh*!' Ama cackles. 'All hail, women warriors! All hail to Ama and Sheba! And to Nana Gyata su, a chief brave as a lion, whose spirit lives forever!'

We do a war dance. And as we roll our hips and bottoms, stamping our feet, we hoot at Gaza and Maybe, arm-in-arm, limping down the hill.

5

I'M A TEENAGER when my aunt starts teaching me to plait hair.

'You're now my apprentice,' she tells me. 'What I'm about to show you is work. Work to explore your gift is not something to play with, Sheba.'

I nod, while Maybe, watching us, finds a sheet of cardboard and, using crayon and a chunk of charcoal from our stove, begins moving his hand on the packaging. The sound he makes is like that of a cockerel scuttling on a zinc roof. Crayon soothes, charcoal squeals. Scraping, scratching. He pauses, stares at me, his eyes darkening before his scratching and scraping begins again.

'You do it like this,' Aunt Clara instructs.

She gives me three lengths of twine – the sort Aunt Ruby uses to make the necklaces Ma sells on her travels: polished balls of amber, each stone held in place by cord. Although I know how to plait already, I follow my aunt's instructions, while Gaza, harmonica

in his mouth, Gecko on his shoulder, hovers beside
Maybe, who delves, rootling deeper and deeper to pin
me down.

'Do it again,' says Aunt Clara. 'And this time, keep
the twine flat. You don't want your clients to have
lumps in their hair.'

Gaza's mouthpiece hoots, delighted.

'You think you can do better?' Indignant, my aunt
quivers like a cane of sugar in a breeze.

The harmonica squawks.

'I thought not!'

By the time Aunt Clara is satisfied with my work,
Aunt Ruby, drawn to the motion of Maybe's hand on
cardboard, the smudges of charcoal and gold crayon
on his fingers, has manoeuvred herself into a space
behind him.

Ruby's eyes move from the cardboard to me, back
and forth until she gawps, astonished.

My aunt is a large woman. She walks tall and if she
favours you, you'll walk tall as well. 'Sheba,' she says,
'your friend has magic at his fingertips. He's captured
you. Come and see.'

How can I, when I'm clamped between Aunt
Clara's thighs?

Her fingers wrapped around mine, she's now
showing me how to plait with black cotton thread.
She guides me, tightening cotton as it circles a sheaf of
weave attached to a chair.

'Not bad,' she says, eventually. 'If you practise every day, you'll get better.'

She turns me around, clasps my hands and, rubbing my fingers between hers, blows on them. 'Time will tell. But if my instinct is right, you'll soon be one of us.'

I flex my fingers, stretch my back.

By then, Maybe has so many fans, he's the star of our compound. Gaza, Aunt Ruby, Grandma Baby, everyone in the house, even Nana and Ama are riveted by what he's doing. They cluck at him, patting his back, clapping their appreciation as they look from the cardboard to me. At last, Maybe holds it up. In a bound he's at my side.

'Here,' he says, his promise from years before kept.

I recognise impressions of my nose and mouth delivered in dark, bold strokes. My face, my shoulders – but is this really me? Before me is a picture of a girl on fire. Eyes aflame, crinkly hair circles her head in jagged waves, as if blasted by thunder and lightning. The portrait glows in black and gold, for at the girl's core is an outline of our family emblem: a magnificent lion.

Maybe's gift pulls me in. Yes, that is indeed my face. And my hair, when unplaited, is every bit as wild as the image in front of me. Forced to look at myself afresh, my heart stirs. 'Yes! This is "me". When I'm grown, this is the "me" I want to be.' Me, a lionheart girl. Me, a lion purring in my ear.

'Take it,' says Maybe. 'It's yours.'

'Take it?' Ama barges between us. 'My friend, you should sell it.' Ama rubs her fingers implying that with guile and brain power there's money to be made – lots of it.

Maybe shrugs. If there's one thing I know it's this: he wears his talent as lightly as the broni-wawu clothes his mother buys for him. Second-hand clothes, which my mother scorns, are no big deal to Maybe. That's the way he is. 'I want you to have it for free,' he assures me.

I hold the cardboard up in the fading light of dusk. The portrait twinkles, hinting that one day, one day, I too will be as tall as Aunt Ruby and as patient and deft-fingered as Aunt Clara. Best of all, the portrait gives me hope that perhaps, with time, I too will know the name of my father. When I do and I'm able to claim him as my own, I resolve that this will be my first gift to him. Because then he'll see me as Maybe does: a girl on fire with the heart of a lion.

She wanted me to remember, she said. Remember when I first became aware of the sensitivity in my fingers.

Remember what happened to make me wary of my mother.

'Grandchild of mine, where are you?'

I close my eyes, hear Nana's call, and I'm seven again, running as quickly as my legs can carry me to the faint grumble in her voice.

'Sheba, find my slippers, child.'

I burrowed under Nana's bed, sneezed at a tickle of dust in my nose and re-emerged, triumphant, leather slippers in each hand.

Her smile was my reward; a smile bolstered by warmth at the back of my head as her hand cradled it.

'What would I do without you?' she said. She smiled a second time, and brim-full of glee, I was off.

Half an hour later, the air quivered. 'Grandchild of mine, come!'

I paused between claps in the game of ampe I was playing with Ama; a game in which the quickest, smartest girl wins. Maybe and Gaza were keeping count of the score. By my reckoning I was about to thrash Ama when Nana summoned me again.

'Later,' I told my friends.

I dashed to the quadrangle,

dived beneath clothes drying in the sun and found Nana sitting on a stool with the women of our household. Nana may have looked old, but to me she was all-powerful, a giant baobab surrounded by flowering neem trees. Aunt Ruby, glistening, fat; slender Aunt Clara and, beside her, a mistress of oils and lotions because of her discerning nose, Grandma Baby.

On Nana's lap lay a splendid yellow and black kente cloth. In her hand, a needle. 'Will you be my eyes today, child?'

I took the needle from her. Baby passed me a strand of pale cotton. Within seconds, the needle was threaded.

'My treasure,' said Nana. 'Your eyes are not yet dim and for that I am grateful.'

A skip and a jump and I was gone.

Not for long though. Another shout and I returned to locate Nana's stick and then unpick plaits in her hair: lots and lots of tiny cornrow meticulously fashioned by Aunt Clara.

My aunt and teacher is a dresser of brides. She bathes and adorns them on their day of triumph and tears. She plaits their hair and then decorates them with necklaces: precious coils of aggrey beads – flecked, glass beads, which Aunt Ruby assembles. Clara matches these with love-beads that she arranges around the bride's waist.

Aunt Clara creates a style for Nana's hair, and

within a fortnight I'm unpicking it.

'You're my girl with deft fingers,' Nana tells me every time.

Today, a teenager perched on a chair, I focus on disentangling hair white as the inside of a coconut.

'You unravel me,' Nana murmurs. 'You tease out my thoughts, child.'

Nana always says what she feels. I didn't understand her before. Not fully. Now that I'm older, now that I'm Aunt Clara's apprentice, after years of trial and error, after meandering, guided voyages into my past, I realise that something inside me is shifting.

What I picture in my mind, I glimpse through Nana's hair: the touch of my fingers on it, the rub of my hands on her scalp. The more I touch, the quicker I unpick Nana's cornrow, teasing strands apart with a silver hairpin, the more vivid the colours that shiver through my mind – colours that mingle my thoughts with hers.

Her curls tingle with music as well, a tune I find myself humming. Nana's song, my long-ago lullaby. She chuckles, then sings along with me, swaying in time to words she whispers: her song of love.

'Do you remember?' she asks, encouraging me to follow her back to a moment in time.

Her question is more a command than a query. A command to plunge deeper into her thoughts and uncover a memory she's mulling. I concentrate by placing my hands on the crown of her head.

Little by little, as the warmth of her scalp radiates through my fingers, the colours and images flitting through her glide into me. They blend into a scene in which I hear someone singing *that* song. Nana's memory-thread spins me back further, to moments before the singing begins.

I see a doll, a child as well.

Then, *whoosh*! The doll flies through the air and shatters.

Head and arms smashed.

The child inhales, then shrieks.

I hear her and tremble. My breath catches. Spine tingles. The hairs on the back of my neck rise as fear prods my heart.

'Do you remember?' Nana asks again.

I shake my head. 'My heart won't let me.'

'Breathe, Sheba,' she says. 'Grow your gift and thrive. Try again.'

What Nana Serwah calls my gift scares me, especially at times like this, when I wish I were more

48

like Ma: born without this weird tingling in my fingers, this itch in my palms that Nana calls 'the gift of touch'.

Aunt Ruby has it for a fact. She can read a person's destiny and mood by brushing her hand on whatever they're wearing. Whether it's a heavy kente stole or silk slip, she's able to sense their passion and grief by fingering crumbs of unhappiness and joy that cling to clothes. That's why, when I ran away, she sat with one of my dresses on her lap. And following my return, was all over Maybe and Salmata. She got the measure of them quickly and, after doing so, encouraged our friendship.

Aunt Ruby delights in Maybe's skill as an artist. But what pleases her most of all is the way he looks out for Gaza. 'That Fulani boy of yours is kind,' my aunt often says. 'Keep him close, Sheba, because a kind man is worth his weight in gold. Believe me, I should know.'

Aunt Ruby touches, while Grandma Baby has such a talent for smell, she can sniff trouble in an instant. Smells it on the wind, she says, and on skin. There's so much strife in Asante-land, so much truth rubbing against her nostrils that, sometimes, for her peace of mind, she smothers her gift with perfume. Either that, or she blends oils and lotions to ensure the wellbeing of her clients and herself. In fact, Grandma Baby can guess someone's state of mind from a whiff of their pores.

Aunt Clara, on the other hand, is like me. Hair is our medium, our way of seeing what most people can't. My aunt's story is one of love and heartbreak.

That's why she counsels the brides she dresses not to make the mistakes she did. 'Far better to marry for friendship and security,' she tells them, 'than for love alone. For love can be cruel and bitter as the grave.'

Adept at using the 'touch', she's not as wary of it as I am. Nana's gift is that of wisdom. When she sees a problem, she tries to solve it, even if it means returning to its source, years later, as she's doing now with me.

The reassuring croon in Nana's voice eases the skittering of my heart. My mind clears and I touch Nana's hair once again – only, this time I close my eyes to see better.

There's that broken doll.

The crying child.

And then screams of: 'Sika! Sika! What's happening?'

Screams followed by the slip-slap of footsteps.

A door swings open. Shadows dangle in the door-frame, rush forward.

One of them looms over me as I once was. I recognise Nana Serwah, behind her, Aunt Ruby.

Aunt Ruby restrains my mother while my grandmother, lifting me off the bed, gathers me in her arms. Once she's checked I'm unharmed, she starts singing that song – her 'Lullaby of Broadway'.

It calms the hammering in my chest, and from the

distance of time, I grasp the memory that's eluded me for years. Ma hit me. She hit me.

'She wouldn't stop crying,' Ma sobs. 'No matter what I do, she cries and cries. Why won't she stop?'

Aunt Ruby folds Ma in her arms, wiping tears from her face. Then, smoothing her clothes, she says: 'It's OK, my sister. We know you're doing the best you can.'

I watch the child squirm. Watch her screech.

Her screams rip through me, jangling my nerves.

'Hush,' I say to the child that's me. 'Hush. You're safe.'

Her sobs settle into whimpers as she blinks back a tear.

'Hush,' I tell her again.

Sensing my presence like a shadow in a dream, she turns.

I gaze into the eyes of a younger version of myself. My gut clenches as I become convinced that something other than a smack terrified her.

Unable to touch, I do the next best thing. My hand hovers over her body.

Waves of terror roll off her skin. My hands shake. I delve deeper, fill my lungs with air, and then slowly exhale as I slide in a spiral of memory to a place where another scene unfurls. I go back in time beyond Nana's song to Ma putting me to bed.

She was in a hurry as usual; distracted. That didn't

stop me wanting to hug her before she left. I raised my hand and touched her face that seemed as luminous as the moon outside.

Face, hair, and then, *zing*!

A tremor zipped through my fingers.

Startled, I touched Ma again and gasped at the searing sensation racing down my arm. A sensation somehow linked to her.

I had no idea skin and hair could talk louder than mouth-talk. Wild talk. Blistering talk. Talk hot as boiling water.

Fingers sizzling, tears salted my eyes and I howled.

In a way I couldn't understand, I'd slipped beneath Ma's skin and touched something that burned within her. I'd opened a pit of restlessness that seeped through her pores in hisses of smoke. Traces of it circled her head. Smouldering, twisting, it sparked, speckling my face with ash.

Moon-bright eyes gazed at me.

I looked on transfixed as tears dropped from my mother's cheek to my face. In that instant, as her tears merged with mine, flecks of ash turned silver and a trap snapped shut around me.

'Ma! Ma!'

Unable to witness my distress, she turned away,

while I was thrust into a realm of shadows, where darkness engulfed me. Darkness saturated with a perfume so thick I could almost stroke it. It smothered me until another sensation took hold. Dread. Unabated dread, as, plunged into the open mouth of the ground, the earth swallowed me. Someone smoothed soil over my head, patting it into my nose, my throat.

I screamed.

It was then Ma hit me.

Seconds later, Nana and Aunt Ruby came to my rescue.

6

TIME SLIPS.

Another scene ripples, splashing memories through me as I unpick Nana's hair.

On Aunt Ruby's advice, Ma was getting ready to travel again. She needed time, her sister said, to fulfil the promise of her name. Time away to pursue what she loved best: buying and selling material and jewellery.

Aunt Ruby helped my mother pack, dumping two suitcases on the bed in our room. I hadn't slept on that bed for over a week. I hadn't dared to in case shadow darkness swallowed me again. But, drawn to Ma's glow of excitement, the chatter of adults inside the room, I tiptoed to the door and watch.

On the bed were bundles of cloth: bales of dyed indigo beside a jumble of smocks and stoles. There were multi-coloured kente cloths as well. Aunt Ruby selected the best of her stock, while Ma packed it.

'Indigo from Kano,' said Aunt Ruby, hoisting a

dark blue bale on to what's already stuffed inside.

Ma managed to squeeze it in. Just. She lowered the suitcase lid, Aunt Ruby tugging and pulling while Ma wrestled the lid down with a knee.

Once the suitcase was fastened, my aunt remembered: 'Asemane! I almost forgot to show you my latest necklaces.'

She hurried out, tickling the crown of my head.

Ma flung open the second suitcase. Half-hidden behind the door, she turned to me and said: 'Would you like to come travelling with me, Sheba?'

I shook my head.

'You don't want to be with me any more?'

I let out a sob. Of course I want to be with my mother! She's Ma: my sun in the morning, my moon at night as she guides me to bed. Ma of all people must realise that after the explosion in my hand, after her tears turned to silver and ensnared me, I can't touch her any more.

'Bone of my bone, come to me!'

I recalled that sizzling in my fingers, that crackle of heat.

Ma leaned forward, beckoned. 'Come, little chick…'

The possibility that if I didn't touch her too much, I'd be OK flitted through my mind and before I knew it, I was running. I stopped in front of her and gazed into eyes black as the feathers of a crow.

'Good girl,' she said. 'I've missed you.'

She lifted me. My legs straddled either side of her hips as her nose nuzzled mine. She kissed both my cheeks and happiness streamed through me, for, like a river coursing to the sea, I've found my way home to her.

'Blood of my blood,' said Ma, 'be good to your aunts while I'm away, you hear? Listen to Nana and take heed of every word she says.'

I nodded.

Her skin rubbed against mine and I noticed that her body-talk today was hushed, her scent musky; the smell of earth after it's rained. I was tempted to touch her hair to see if her hair-talk was silent as well.

I hesitated, and catching my drift, Ma said: 'I'm sorry about the other night. I didn't mean to hurt you, Sheba. Sometimes…'

She sighed, unable to find the right words to soothe her tongue. She put me down beside the open suitcase and making space for herself, said: 'Listen, my baby-last, sometimes I'm so angry my head hurts.'

She tensed, shuddered and her hair, scraped in a twirl at the top of her head, shivered like a horse flicking its tail. Ma has a lot of hair – tight crinkly curls that fall to her shoulders when she wears it down.

'My head hurts,' Ma said again.

I stretched my hand and stroked a curl. It wasn't as hot as before, but the burn was still there.

'I always feel better when you're close to me.'

Folding my hand in hers, Ma placed it on her heart. 'Will you promise me something, Sheba?'

I nodded.

'Whatever happens, don't do what your sisters did. Promise you'll never leave me.'

The fierce urgency of her words planted a seed of disquiet in my chest.

Even so, she repeated her request. 'Promise me you won't let your uncle Solo's wife steal you like she did your sisters. Promise!'

I nodded again, confused by emotions shimmering over her face like sunlight on water; rearranging her features, distorting them until they settled in a scowl.

'Thanks to Lila, your sisters think they're better than me. Those girls don't know what I do. If the trunk of a tree dies, its branches wither as well!'

'Are you going to die, Ma?'

I touched her hair and my fingers were singed in a blast of heat.

I was about to start crying when Aunt Ruby returned with a basket full of necklaces and beads.

'Here you are, Sika,' she said, 'trinkets to sell on your travels. We're going to make a fortune, you and me. A fortune.'

Ma winked at me, put a finger to her lips, and then smiled at Aunt Ruby.

7

'ARE YOU SURE?'

I've finished describing revelations the waft and weave of Nana's hair have uncovered.

'Nana, that's what I saw. Tears, wisps of smoke, and then...' I clap my hands, a crocodile snapping its mouth shut. 'Come and see! I'm caught in a vice and the ground swallows me.' I stroke the varnished concrete beneath my feet, performing the sensation of being buried alive.

Her hair white as the feathers of an egret flutters in alarm. To begin with, I think Nana's agitation is directed at me, but when she sighs deeply and my bones tremble in response, I realise that I should be concerned as well.

'This cannot be,' she murmurs. 'Who would do such a thing?'

I shrug.

'I always wondered... but this? No!' Nana dismisses a thought and shudders. She picks up a comb and, dragging it through her hair, bunches her curls in a topknot. 'There,' she says. 'We're going to sort this out, child. We're going to track down whoever's meddled with your fate and stolen your future.'

'How so, Nana?'

She doesn't answer. No more is said. No one is blamed. But as Nana sets her plan in motion, Ma's presence looms in her absence. I feel it growing as the kernel of disquiet she planted in me long ago sprouts and seeds others. Tangled, spindly, they stifle my breath, sowing confusion in my mind.

That night and next, I wake up gasping from a dream: a dream of fear and flight as crows dark as midnight circle the roof of our house. I watch, convinced that if a bird lands, tragedy will befall us. The foundations of our house will crumble; our lives will change forever.

I fling stones at the birds, crying: 'Sa! Sa!'

Undeterred, they fly closer and closer, wheeling and cawing: 'Death is coming! Death is coming!'

Their screeches rip through my dream until a

scrabble of talons on the roof prises me awake.

On the afternoon of the third day, Grandma Baby's nose twitches, sensitive to a change in the air.

'She's coming,' she says. 'Your mother will arrive soon, Sheba. Prepare yourselves, children.'

Maybe and Gaza wolf down what's left of our lunch of waakye – rice and beans – then disappear. *Poof!* As if they'd never set foot in our house, never strolled along our corridors or sat at our dining room table to do homework. 'Cowards! Quitters!' Ama and I tease them. Mockery doesn't stop them. They're off faster than a pair of antelopes at the first sniff of a predator.

Not long ago, my mother happened on us in Grandma Baby's boudoir. Her 'boudoir' is what my junior grandmother calls her bedroom. It's where she keeps a music box and sleeps on a four-poster bed from Lamu island in Kenya. Grandma Baby's husband was Kenyan, you see. 'Things didn't work out between us, so I returned home with Clara,' she once told me. 'He was a nice enough man, but our love didn't last. The trade winds scattered it like petals and then he died, just like that.' She blew in my face.

'How?' I asked.

She wouldn't say.

Anyway, the four of us were in her boudoir practising our dance moves to one of Grandma Baby's all-time favourite songs – 'Shame, Shame, Shame'. I'd twisted the boys' hair into Bantu knots. Ama had put lipstick on our mouths, I'd rubbed kohl around our eyes. Grandma Baby had lent us some of her old disco gear – sequinned tops and glittery T-shirts – and was teaching us a dance from her youth – the Bump. Ama and I quickly got the hang of it. Gaza, in a groove of his own, clapped his hands, moving to the beat of the music as he waggled his torso, while Grandma Baby, reliving her days as a Disco Queen of Nairobi, rocked her bottom against Maybe's hip. We'd already played the song twice. We were dancing to it a third time, belting out the chorus. We were shrieking and hollering: 'Shame, shame, shame,' waving our arms in the air, when the door opened.

Grandma Baby was having such a glorious time in days-gone-by that she didn't catch a whiff of danger.

I turned around.

Grandma Baby followed, and there she was: Ma in her travelling clothes; a loose-fitting kaba, a matching head wrap tied around her hair.

'Sheba?' she said. Then, catching sight of Maybe behind Grandma Baby, '*with your friend again.*'

Coal-bright eyes flitted from Maybe to me. Braced for Maybe's welcoming smile, Ma's face glazed with the zeal of someone determined to crush a cockroach.

'Huh! You think you can charm me with that smile? Me?' She thumped her chest. 'No, Fulani boy. I know who you are and what you're after. Empty bellies smile the most. They have to, to chop small.'

Maybe hadn't felt the slash of Ma's tongue before. He bristled as a sensation of a scorpion on the verge of biting me crawled over my skin.

'No, Ma! No!' I wanted to shout. 'You can't talk to my friend like that!' That's what I wanted to say, but no words came out. Paralysed, speechless, I only watched as Ma's tongue cut again.

'I lie? Not me. I know what you're after. I know your game.'

Maybe was dumbstruck as well.

Grandma Baby winked at him, hugging him, massaging his shoulders to ease his distress. 'My friend, don't mind her! Sika's always angry when she returns home because she's hungry. '*A hungry man is an angry man*,' she sang. 'Come now. Downstairs. Let's eat. We've earned it.'

That was Maybe's first taste of Ma.

Today, forewarned by Grandma Baby, the boys flee, while she hurries upstairs to her boudoir to douse herself in lavender. 'To soothe my nerves, dear,' my junior grandmother explains.

The boys gone, only Aunt Clara and Ama – whose hair I'm about to plait – remain. And only Ama has a tongue brave and fast enough to withstand Ma.

'Are you ready?' I ask her, after washing my hands.

Ama nods.

The first rule of Aunt Clara's guide to the gift of touch, is to work with clean hands. 'A client's hair,' she says, 'deserves cleanliness and should be treated with tenderness and respect at all times, especially if our aim is to give solace to the person we're working with.'

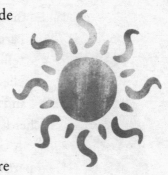

Having taught me the basics of plaiting in cornrow and twists, how to plait with weave extensions and black thread; having shown me how to create styles to suit the shape of a girl's face and character, today I'm using Ama as my model from start to finish.

I sit on a stool, her body nestled between my thighs, my grip on her head and hair firm. Ama giggles, revealing a gap in her front teeth.

Her laughter tickles my heart, but as I chuckle in reply, Aunt Clara tuts-tuts.

'This is no laughing matter, Sheba. Be sensitive to hair-talk. Allow hair to speak to you. Is it dry or greasy? Brittle as leaves falling from the cotton tree or soft as a baby's bottom?'

I touch Ama's crown. Her hair is silky, light. I say so.

'Good,' my aunt replies. 'Now, remember that the style you choose has to be much more than adornment. Hair is the soul's flame. It reveals what

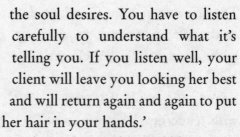

the soul desires. You have to listen carefully to understand what it's telling you. If you listen well, your client will leave you looking her best and will return again and again to put her hair in your hands.'

A design in mind, I quickly trace a parting on Ama's head.

Aunt Clara hovers, watching my fingers, my face. I'm about to start plaiting with black thread, when she says: 'Have you worked on her scalp yet?'

I haven't. I spritz Ama's hair with water to soften it. Then, after dipping my fingers in a pot of shea butter, I begin rubbing my friend's scalp.

My aunt has taught me everything I know: how best to moisturise hair with a combination of shea butter and oil of jojoba; how to soothe strands splintered dry at the tips with a remedy of coconut or castor oil. She's taught me how to massage the scalp to stimulate growth, and then rub it to ease tension.

Ama's still giggling as I knead the crown of her head; giggling and wriggling at the same time. There's me, my friend and Aunt Clara. No change, no big wahala, nothing. Everything, same as usual.

'Aba!' I say. 'You and your coconut head!'

'You think my head's bigger than yours? Small head, no brain inside.'

I chuckle, feel a faint itch in my palms, and in my fingers, a flutter light as a butterfly's wing. The tips of my fingers tingle. Blood rushes into my hands and *wham*! My connection with Ama deepens. So much so, that in an instant I'm in another place and time, looking on as Ama teases her brother.

Yao's dribbling a ball.

She tackles him, snatches his plaything, runs and hides.

He sobs. In a heartbeat, huge heaving howls turn to shrieks.

From the kitchen, a voice yells: 'Ama! Stop harassing your brother!'

'I am not!'

'Lawato! Don't lie to me!'

'Ma! Can you see me?'

'I don't have to! Go and buy me a few tomatoes. And Ama, don't go playing in that house without men. Don't put your snout in their ju ju matter. And if Madam High and Mighty Sika Prempeh shows her face, promise me you'll leave straightaway.'

'But Ma!'

'Daughter, do as I say.'

I remove my fingers from Ama's scalp and shake them, perplexed.

My intention is to do her hair, nothing more. I have no desire to observe scenes from her soul's flame or to spy on her. Under my aunt's guidance, it seems my experience of hair-talk is taking me to places where not only do I witness my past, but it also allows me to eavesdrop on conversations. This is new.

Aunt Clara, still hovering, nods before she blinks three times – a family gesture that signals: *I know. We'll talk about this later.*

She says out loud: 'Well done, Sheba. You're ready to start plaiting now.'

Ama's face is round and her spirit, despite her ant-bite tongue, is, for the most part, in sympathy with mine. Above all, she's my friend. Why else would she defy her mother to come to our house? I part her hair and then carefully wrap portions of it in spiky sheaves of black cotton until, within an hour, her hair sticks out like the quills of an angry porcupine.

'Onigi,' Aunt Clara says, naming a Nigerian style she's taught me from her time there. 'Sticks. My dear, you've captured your friend's rebellious spirit perfectly.'

After kissing her fingers as if imagining the very best pepper soup, my aunt passes me a large mirror, which I hold in front of Ama. Ama smiles, a smile of such intense satisfaction it warms my face as much as standing in sunlight does.

I grin. 'Big head, beautiful hair.'

A hand to her heart, Ama bows. 'You, my friend, are good at this hair-talk matter.'

She says those words and Ma walks in.

Hips rolling, sandals clattering. *Kapa. Kapa. Kapa.* A woman in motion, strolling, all eyes on her. Larger than life, skin alight with a molten glow that heralds her name: Sika, gold, a woman of great wealth and good fortune. Wouldn't you stare at a well-dressed woman in a village as small as ours? And when that woman struts with the confidence of a catwalk model, head high, shoulders back, while wearing the best Nigerian sheda that no one else can afford to buy, people stare even more. I certainly do!

The sheda gleams russet-red. A blazing sky at dusk, her bou-bou is matched by an elaborate head tie that resembles an orange crane: long-necked, wings outstretched. A bird swooping and diving in perpetual flight.

Ma sweeps in and a chill enters the house. A chill so cold, even the walls seem to flinch. They shrink, turning inwards as surely as I do.

I hear a scrabble of talons and, reminded of my dream of the night before, I shiver. My vision dims and for a second, instead of the head wrap, a halo of crow's feathers shimmer around Ma's head. I shut my eyes. When I open them again, the feathers have disappeared, and Ma is lacing her lips in an expression I know well.

Half-way between a sneer and a laugh, it's guaranteed to clear our house of friends and strangers. No one wants to stay where they're not welcome; no one wants to react to a face that weighs you up before you speak.

'What did you say?' Ma asks Ama.

Ama doesn't know that Ma hasn't a clue about 'this hair-talk matter'. That she has no idea I have a gift and Aunt Clara is helping me grow it. My friend, still mesmerised by her reflection, wriggles hips and shoulders in a dance of joy. Arms open, Ama spins around gleeful at her new look. 'Auntie Sika! Look how beautiful I am!' she cries.

Irrepressible, a balloon bobbing up and down, she spins a second time.

Not even a curled lip can dispel Ama's delight today. Putting an arm around me, she hugs me. 'Thank you, Sheba! Thank you, lionheart girl!'

'Are you calling my little chick here lionheart girl? This girl?'

Ma's never seen Maybe's portrait of me. I keep it hidden in Grandma Baby's boudoir for safekeeping as I would a lucky charm. I blink twice at Ama. Don't tell her! Don't say a thing!

'Sheba did my hair, Auntie. Am I cool or what?' Ama, shoulders shimmying, boogies her way back to the mirror Aunt Clara's holding.

Ma steps closer to inspect my handiwork. A finger prodding my friend's forehead, she tilts her head up and down and then swivels it from side to side.

I hold my breath.

'Hmm!' Ma sniffs. 'It's almost impossible to make a head shaped like a coconut attractive, but I'll say this for you, Sheba, you've tried. Indeed, you've tried.'

Aunt Clara winces. 'Sika, if you can't find something good to say, don't say anything.'

'Tell me, Clara,' Ma replies, 'how is it that a childless woman such as you, dares tell me, a mother of three, how to speak to a friend of my daughter?'

Aunt Clara lowers her lashes while Ama's shine, vivid as a firefly moments before, flutters and fades.

Ma pokes Ama's forehead again. 'It's the shape of your head that worries me, child. I advised your mother to ask Nana Serwah to mould it when you were born. Nana did my head, Sheba's as well. That's why we Prempehs look so much better than your lot.'

It's at times like this that I want to hide. My innards quailing, I squeeze Ama's hand, and as I do so, her mother's words return to me: *If Madam High and Mighty Sika Prempeh shows her face, promise me you'll leave straightaway.*

Ama should have followed her mother's counsel.

YABA BADOE

Quills quivering with rage, her pupils shrink to sparks of anger. Chin out, she pulls back her shoulders and ready to bite, puckers her lips. 'Auntie Sika, Sheba here is my bestie-best. Where she goes, I go. Where she stays, I stay. One day, one day, we're going to leave this village and open a salon in Accra. And when we do, we'll work on all sizes and shapes of heads: coconut heads, pineapple heads, pea heads, all of them. Won't we, Sheba?'

I nod, wary of what my friend will say next.

'Auntie Clara will be our inspiration because she knows how to dress hair better than anyone else. Best of all, we'll even do the hair of people with no friends whatsoever. People like you, Auntie.'

Revealing a glint of teeth in a rare smile, Ma replies, 'I wish my Sheba had half the spirit you do.'

And with that, she turns and saunters up the stairs, chuckling.

8

'GRANDCHILD OF MINE? Come talk to me!' A few days later, when Ma is on the road again, Nana's summons slashes the air like a whip.

My heart tingles, immediately alert.

I'm with Maybe and Ama, about to go down to the river. Maybe clutches a breadfruit, a gift from Aunt Ruby. We intend to swim, then treat ourselves to a barbeque of fish and breadfruit spiced with Aunt Clara's mango relish. I can smell the fish already, almost taste it, when Nana calls me again.

'Grandchild of mine, where are you?'

'Later,' I say to my friends. 'I'll catch up with you and Gaza later.'

Maybe frowns. 'Sheba, let us wait small.'

'Go,' I insist. 'Family…'

Sensing my unease, Maybe inhales. His eyes lighten, a sign he's sensitive to tension in the air, tension seeping from the pores of my skin. He notices shadows beneath my eyes and a question clambers to his throat. He pushes it down. 'Later,' he agrees. 'Tell me later.'

I climb upstairs and walk along a white-washed corridor that leads to the sitting room. The most formal room in our house, it's dusted and cleaned every day, its floorboards polished to a shine once a month. This is where Nana calls family members when she has something urgent to discuss. Disputes are settled here, family cravings satisfied, so it is not a place to enter lightly.

I take a deep breath, for as I open the door, I appreciate I'm stepping into my family's past.

The first thing I see, the first thing that strikes anyone who enters, is a huge portrait of my great-grandfather in the regalia of an Asante chief. The ancestor I never met in the flesh, but see once in a while pacing our corridors at night, bears an uncanny resemblance to Nana. They share the same forehead in faces framed by manes that give them the air of lions in repose. Regal, relaxed. Look again, and you'll see a glint of steel in their eyes.

Nana Gyata su – a chief with the courage of a lion – was the overall leader of our community. Everyone in the family calls him Nana Gyata su, so I do as well. And like Nana, I nod as soon as I catch sight of him, acknowledging his authority displayed by his attire and a brocade umbrella over his head.

Heavy gold chains roll from his neck over a kente

cloth woven especially for him. On his feet he wears
a pair of ceremonial slippers to ensure his soles never
touch the ground. He bristles power. I meet his gaze
and a smile quickens his lips.

I grin in reply, using Nana's words to greet him:
'Good morning, Nana Gyata su. How are you today?'

'Come here,' says my grandmother.

A wave of sadness swirls off her and splashes in a
sigh as she pats an empty space beside her.

The day before, Grandma Baby and Aunt Ruby
had been about to leave for the funeral of Nana's
oldest friend. My grandmother had packed her bags
too, and was about to set off, when she had realised
that her bones had grown so stiff and weary with
age, her travelling days were over. She would grieve
for her friend at home, she said. She would do what
our ancestors advised us against: she would weep for
a friend alone.

I felt the weight of Nana's sigh yesterday. Today, I
feel it again, and glimpse fragments of her pain, bright
as seashells on a shore. I sit down, my blood warming
her bones, my thigh against hers.

'I've spoken to my friend, Maanu, about what you
told me,' she says. 'Maanu is a diviner I've consulted
before. She's willing to see us at daybreak, six days
from now. Before and after we see her, Sheba, I want
you to remember that our problem is a family matter.
It stays under this roof. You do not discuss it with

your friends, and certainly not your mother. Do you understand?'

I place a palm on Nana's thigh. She covers it with her fingers, gently garlanding my wrist. Once again, her sadness seeps into me. I feel the tug of it, the inky blackness of its depth as I'm dragged to its centre. Something twitches, flickers. A minnow terrified of light dives to a place beyond my grasp, where only Nana can reach.

Turning my palm upward, lacing my fingers in hers, Nana looks me in the eye. 'Every family has its secrets, and this will be ours, Sheba.'

I'm about to nod, when I remember Maybe. Only moments before, without a word being exchanged, he had appreciated how anxious I was. What goes through my mind, enters his as easily as sunlight licking skin. To shut him out would be as useless as trying to stop breathing. 'But, Nana, what if…'

'Not a word to *anyone*,' Nana insists. 'What happens under this roof stays here. For all our sakes, don't be an okra mouth, child. Don't indulge in foolish, konkonsa behaviour by spreading gossip. Keep your lips sealed or the people of this village will start pointing fingers. And when they do that, no one can predict where it will end.'

Nana's warning hurts. How can she suggest that our secret may slip out unbidden, when for as long as I've lived, I've listened to her voice above all others?

I am *not* an okra mouth. Never have been, never will be! And to imply that what I've uncovered may bring shame to our family tightens a noose of dread around my neck.

My hand still in hers, Nana looks past the portrait on the wall to the cotton tree outside. Planted by the earliest settlers, it's about to flower for the first time in years. Its leaves, stirred by an afternoon breeze, rustle, while thorns that protect its trunk strum in reply.

The tree sways, its branches clap, as leaves and thorns begin humming. In a swish of a lion's tail, its song will pad to the river before ambling to the forest beyond. But first, it slinks into our house in a tangle of sound: the purr of buds opening, high-pitched creaks of wood, followed by tremulous, low notes. 'Weee,' the cotton tree croons. 'Weee.' Over and over. The tree sings, and a musky smell of river, moist as earth after rain, nuzzles my face.

The song tears open my heart, for as I listen, a crow circles the tree. Three times it circles, before banking and alighting on to a branch. The bird twists its neck and seeing us, hops closer, pebbled eyes blinking.

'Sa! Sa!' I want to cry. I listen instead, because the tree's song and the crow remind me of my dream; my dream and the grief in Nana's sigh.

'Can you hear it?' she asks. 'Whenever that tree's about to flower, it sings. It sings to prepare us…' She hauls herself up.

I take her hand and walk her to the window where she catches sight of the crow. The glint in her eyes dim as she steadies herself, clutching my shoulder.

'Before the week is over, grandchild of mine, I shall take you to Maanu. She sees what other people can't. She'll tell us what to do.'

'But Nana…'

'Keep your questions for Maanu,' Nana says. 'Only a fool describes a calabash no one can see or touch. All I can tell you, grandchild of mine, is that in all my years on this earth, I've never heard of such a thing as what you described to me the other day. Never!'

As chance would have it, the afternoon before we're due to visit the diviner, Ma returns home to stock up on merchandise. As soon as I sense her presence, I freeze.

The four of us – Maybe, Gaza, Ama and me – have spent the day running errands for my aunts: delivering material to a seamstress for Aunt Ruby, taking pomade to a client of Aunt Clara's, a basket of snacks to an ailing relative. Having bustled up and down, from the top of the hill to the river, we stop at the cotton tree for a bout of Kung-fu boxing.

It's our current obsession after watching yet another of Video Man's movies. In the film, a gang of street children wage battle against the Bandit Queen. A queen of bandits by day, she's a fraudster, stealing children with every breath she takes. At night, she becomes the Fire Queen, a raging inferno that whirls from village to village consuming people and homes. Entranced, we decide to play the part of street children who, using a combination of Kung-fu skills and guile, pummel our version of the Fire Queen – Queen Sasabonsam; the Devil Queen – to death. *Pow! Zap! Keerching!*

The boys show Ama and I how to kick with our feet and hands, block assailants with a slash of our palms and then slay them in a frenzy of elbow and knee jabs. We perform. And when he feels like it, Maybe sketches on a special pad – a gift from Aunt Ruby. Before he draws a line, we stand and – legs apart, ready for combat – we practise our war cries, screaming: '*Hi-ya!*' Chinese-style.

Gaza, mimicking shrieks on his harmonica, echoes us while Maybe, a hand to his ear, encourages us to scream louder.

'Queen Sasabonsam is crazy-bad,' he says, 'an

elephant on the rampage. Release your trumpet call.'

Legs astride, I inhale, allowing a tornado to gather in my lungs before hurling it in Ama's face.

She roars: '*Hi-ya!*' in reply.

I spin around, kick a leg in the air.

Ama and I are preparing to spar again, when street vendors either side of the track flap their arms, waving cloths at us. 'Enough of this *hi-ya!* nonsense! Don't you *hi-ya!* people know that some of us rest on a Saturday?'

We scramble home, a pack of hungry hyenas chasing each other, to be rewarded with a mound of Aunt Clara's tatale: plantain and chilli pancakes cooked in palm oil. Tatale, my favourite, downed with sobolo, the drink Aunt Ruby buys from Maybe's mother.

We feast while the adults in the house retreat to their rooms for their afternoon naps. Then, as we start fighting again and Maybe sketches our Kung-fu kicks, the air around me changes. It bristles like the fur of a hissing cat.

Goosebumps fleck my arms. I listen, sense my mother at the door. Sweat moistens my palms. Heart skitters. Flips. Lands with such a thud, I can scarcely breathe as Ma, dumping her bags in the hall, saunters into the courtyard. Instead of speaking, she watches us, arms folded. Eyes glittering, an eyebrow arched, she stiffens, an incarnation of Queen Sasabonsam on the verge of unleashing her rage.

Maybe, sketchpad on lap, turns to see who's erased my dimples, placing pinpricks of terror in my eyes.

Ma glares at him. Scowls at me, and my heart shrivels to a puddle.

Years before, I would have run into her arms excited by the rub and kiss of her nose, the tickle-lick of her lashes and those gifts she brought me from Lomé, Bolgatanga, Ouagadougou: faraway destinations the sound of which thrilled me.

Today, her stare spikes my skin and I cower as if the thorns on the cotton tree outside, having pierced the walls of our house, have filled the air with barbs.

I hold my breath.

Unfolding her arms, Ma harrumphs. 'Nowadays, this house no longer feels like home,' she remarks. 'No one welcomes me. No one, not even my little chick here.'

Unable to fill my mouth with words she'd like to hear, I begin to stutter. Mouth, tongue, lips, no part of me obeys my command.

'You see!' Ma cries, triumphant. 'Even my baby-last can't greet me as she should.'

I try again. My throat clenches.

Gaza smooths his hand over mine. He too, finds it difficult to talk at times. He too, on occasion, stutters, making his harmonica do most of his talking, while Gecko soaks up his love.

The thought of Gecko zips through me, and the

lizard perks up. Basking in a pool of sunshine, he flips his tongue at a fly. Gobbles it, then begins the long journey back to Gaza. Meanders. Pauses. Flicks his tail, picking up a hint of danger as Ma, following my eyes, catches sight of him.

Ma sniffs and Gecko scrambles from one end of the courtyard to the other.

As he runs, as Maybe slips his hand in mine, Ma raises her foot, and, quick as a snake strikes, she stamps.

I gasp. All of us do, even Ama. All of us except Ma.

A smile greases her mouth as Gecko, his tail trapped, flees, dumping his appendage as only lizards can. Diminished, he scuttles up Gaza's leg and into his hip pocket.

No one moves.

Seconds pass.

Ama, behind me, touches my shoulder.

Maybe and Gaza hold on to me. Bit by bit, disdain, a magnet in Ma's eyes, clamps on me, dragging me to her, head bowed, until I'm in her shadow.

Ma laces long fingers around my neck. The noose tightens.

'Welcome home, Ma!' says Ama, and grabbing one of my mother's bags, she hauls it to our bedroom.

'You two, out!'

Maybe and Gaza, about to take the rest of Ma's luggage, pause.

Ma jerks her chin at the door. 'You heard me! Out!'

The taste of lemon stings my tongue. 'Wait!'

The noose stifles my breath. Gagging, I force Ma's fingers apart and then pulling away, bundle what's left of our feast into a parcel I thrust at Maybe. 'Tomorrow?'

'Tomorrow,' he replies. 'Welcome home, Ma,' he adds as Gaza trails him to the door.

'Ma? Ma?' my mother cries. 'Young man, don't you dare "Ma" me! I am not your mother. I am not your aunt, and I am certainly not your friend. If you must call me anything, call me *Madam.*'

Maybe winces.

Flecks of light dart over his face. His skin flames, and for an instant I'm aware he's gazing at Ma and me with more than his own eyes. Ma may not realise it, but four pairs of eyes are inspecting us: burrowing, probing, uncovering our beginnings and endings. Maybe and his departed-dead. They surface. Flicker. Fade.

Maybe glances at me, baffled, and then turning again to Ma, he says: 'Sorry, Madam. Welcome home.'

9

AFTER WHAT SHE did to Gaza and said to Maybe, I don't want to be anywhere near my mother. That's what I tell myself. Never again! I say this, yet I know in my gut that some things are easier said than done – especially when my heart, big as a lake in the wet season, shrivels to a slick of water in the dry.

This is what happens when Ma is home; this is what it feels like. Every spark of defiance in me splutters. I become a ghost. Ensnared by her shadow, I'm unable to touch or feel in a way I recognise to be true. Like a child in thrall to Queen Sasabonsam, Ma hijacks me to do her bidding.

For the rest of the day, I'm at her beck and call. I'm her little chick. 'Fetch this for me, Sheba. Fetch that... Unpack.' I trot up and down the stairs retrieving a purse, a glass of water. Sweets, which she munches as she sorts out clothes that need washing.

I wash and hang them in the quadrangle. Between hanging and ironing her clothes, between my comings and goings, my replies of 'Yes, Ma!', 'Of course, Ma!' to her cries of 'Sheba! Sheba! Where are you?', I deliver Ma's gifts to my aunts Ruby and Clara. A present to Nana, then, a smaller one to Grandma Baby: a fan from Abidjan.

'I thought she was on her way back. Sniffed her on the breeze this morning and now here she is.' Grandma Baby dabs a scented handkerchief to her brow. Frangipani this time, to refresh her soul.

She anoints herself hourly when my mother's in the house. Her neck, her wrists, behind her ears. Dabs lavender or frangipani and sighs because resentment between Ma and her is engrained in the blood that flows through their veins and in the air we breathe when Ma's home.

One of them says 'yes', the other says 'no'.

Black? White!

Ma can't stomach Grandma Baby's favourite meal of palm-nut soup with fufu.

Grandma Baby loves fish. Ma never touches it.

If one of them wears red to a funeral, the other will opt for black.

They're blood rivals in a ruthless battle of baby-lasts. As different as fufu and gold dust. That's just the way it is with them.

'Do whatever your mother asks of you, dear,' Grandma Baby whispers in my ear. 'Then she'll soon be gone. Within a day or two she'll…' She flutters her new fan, a bird flapping its wings as it flies away.

'Stop it, Baby,' says Nana. 'Allow Sheba to enjoy her mother's safe return.'

Grandma Baby rolls her eyes. 'Sister, please! Our granddaughter is not a fool. She knows as well as we do that while Madam Sika is home, she'll be the shoe that doesn't quite fit. She'll pinch our toes till she's off again.'

The room Ma and I share is the one we were born in. The story goes that when Ma and her twin brother tumbled into the world, she was so furious that my Uncle Solomon arrived first, she's been enraged ever since.

'Some people are like that,' Nana confirms. 'For a reason no one fully understands, they have a spirit that's angry from the moment they draw breath.'

Grandma Baby snorts. Snorts a second time. Louder. 'What you mean, my dear sister, is your last-born is *cantankerous*!' Her mouth lingers on the word, relishing its rough edges like a bone she's sucking to the marrow. 'Sika can't help herself. The truth is, there's nothing she enjoys more than a good fight. Our daughter *delights* in quarrelling.'

Ma certainly enjoyed squabbling with Maybe. That night, the questions I heard when his eyes probed mine, torment me. They gnaw at me as I slip into the bed I share with my mother. We occupy the same room, when she's home – an occurrence so rare these days, I don't usually mind.

I'm at the edge of the mattress, as far away from where she's curled up as possible. I stiffen, straighten my back. Whether it's my mother's presence or the moonlit night that disturbs me, I can't say. But within seconds, the insidious sensation of being buried alive steals over me.

Windows and walls close in. My skin crawls, and for precious moments that become an eternity, I imagine I'm not in the room my sisters and I were born in, but sealed in a coffin.

I gather the bedsheet beneath me, gripping it to smother fear, to steady my breathing.

Chest heaves. Lungs expand as from one moment to the next, I reassure myself that I'm not in a tomb, but lying beside my mother in the room that cradled my sisters.

Myma, the eldest, so called because Ma named her after Nana, and rather than have two Serwahs under the same roof, my aunts chose to call her My Ma.

My second sister, Sweetie, arrived in the season of harmattan wind and dust; a season teeming with tiny, black ants. Sweetie, named for her craving for sugar.

Three of us. Each with a father Ma refuses to name.

I inhale deeper still, and as my breathing settles, I dwell on the puzzle that binds me to my sisters.

What is our mother hiding from us? And why?

I've wheedled and needled her, been deflected so often that in Ma's absence, I've searched her belongings for clues: a photograph, a letter, some token or note from a former boyfriend. I've found nothing. Not a scrap that links me or my sisters to anyone but her.

To withhold information from one of us might be what Nana calls mule-headed stubbornness. To withhold the names of our fathers three times over is beyond my understanding. Even in a household of women who've run from their husbands or been dumped by them, Ma's behaviour is weird. I don't have a word to describe it, but this I know: Ma doesn't want our fathers to have anything to do with us. And after her behaviour today, it seems she doesn't want me to have any friends at all. No wonder my sisters don't visit us!

Your mother is not correct, Maybe's eyes told me. *She's crazy-mad. Crazy as a dog afraid of water.*

And then again, as he turned and looked at me: *What's happening to you, Sheba? Where do you go when your mother's here? Where do you disappear?*

I toss and turn. And yet, slowly, slowly, I'm drawn to a nook in my mother's spine between her shoulders. This is where I end up sleeping when she's home. My head below hers in the space she carried me as a baby. On her back. Today of all days, I try to resist a pull that lulls me to a place before memory; to a time when her body sheltered mine and, attuned to the beating of her heart, our blood flowed as one. I try, but little by little, as my nose lures me to the muskiness of her scent, the space between us contracts.

As the rise and fall of my breath begins to harmonise with hers, my eyes close.

What is wrong with your mother, Sheba? Where do you go when your mother's here? Maybe's questions pester me until I sit up, exhausted.

'Ma! Ma! Why do you hate my friends? Why do you humiliate me in front of them?'

'Aba, Sheba! Can't you see I'm sleeping?'

She rolls over. In the shadows her body shifts beneath a sleeping cloth. She raises her head, pillows it on an arm. I feel the cold slither of her smile as she scans my face.

'Why, Ma?'

She chuckles, amused.

Her laughter goads me, so that even as the tang of lemon scours my mouth, my tongue retaliates: 'You embarrassed me, Ma!'

'Enough of this nonsense.'

'You enjoyed hurting Gaza and Gecko. Enjoyed insulting Maybe.'

'Why bother doing anything if you don't enjoy it?'

Her admission stuns me. I've always recognised that Ma's not quite the same as other mothers. Other mothers name the fathers of their children even if they want nothing more to do with them. I appreciate that not all mothers are loving and patient. No way is Ma patient. She's secretive, canny, her likes and dislikes immediate. But to gain pleasure from hurting others? This goes against everything Nana has taught me. And to admit it openly, as if a liking for cruelty is as commonplace as cracking an egg? I shake my head, bewildered.

'Don't be a fool, Sheba,' Ma spits. 'All I did was step on a lizard. I didn't step on you.'

'You might as well have done. Gaza loves Gecko. We all do. He depends on him.'

'A lizard is just a lizard,' Ma replies. 'You'll be telling me off for killing mosquitoes next.' Eyeballing me, she adds, 'I don't hate your friends. Wayside characters can be useful at times.'

'They're my friends, Ma.' I cross two fingers on my right hand, squeezing them skin to skin. No space in-between, inseparable. *'Friends.'*

Ma sucks her teeth. 'You're so *naïve* you have no idea how the world outside this village operates. Never forget, Sheba, you're a child of royal descent. I

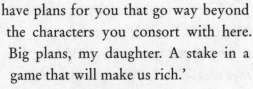

have plans for you that go way beyond the characters you consort with here. Big plans, my daughter. A stake in a game that will make us rich.'

'Ma, I know what I want.' I can't say it any clearer than that. Can't allow her to belittle me by bad-mouthing my friends. My resolve hardening, I clench my fists. 'I know what I want, and there's nothing you can do to change me. *Nothing*.'

'Are you sure?' Speaking slowly, deliberately, as if revealing the facts of life to small fry in class one, my mother asks: 'Haven't you ever wondered, Sheba, why there are no men in this house? And why it is that when they do come here, none stay long?'

I shrug, wary of where Ma's heading with her questions. What I do know is what my junior grandmother told me: only the bravest of men is able to spend more than two nights in Nana Gyata su's old room – where our male visitors stay. Because on the third, his ghost appears. And unlike the women of our house, our men are terrified of ghosts.

'Don't believe a word that old curmudgeon tells you,' says Ma, catching my drift. 'I'm talking facts here, Sheba. There are more women than men in our village, no? Have you ever wondered why that may be? Or why the father of your Fulani boyfriend hasn't set foot in our village since he arrived?'

I have wondered. Of course
I have! Yet I shrug, preparing
to be unfazed by whatever Ma
says next, even as panic prickles
my skin.

A haze of cloud darkens the
moon. It glides away and, in a heartbeat,
the room shivers as Ma's complexion glows.

Threading her fingers through coils of hair, dangling
them in a knot, her eyes glisten; her cheeks shine like
burnished gold.

The moon hides again, and the night air thickens
with shadows.

'Listen carefully, Sheba. I'll explain.'

IO

WHAT MA TELLS me is more vivid than a waking dream that follows me wherever I go. It echoes within, playing its song again and again, so that every once in a while, I'm taken to a place of dread: that moment when I understand that what's about to be said is going to change earth, river and sky – the world as I know it – forever.

There's a cloying heaviness in the air, as if I'm swaddled in an ancient kente cloth, struggling to breathe. Heaviness and smouldering heat: a sign the season of rain will soon be with us.

I'm suffocating.

A finger caresses my forehead, and the waking dream begins.

'We royal women are special,' Ma tells me. 'Our blood is enriched by generations of ritual and magic. Magic flows through us, Sheba, and whether we like it or not, it trickles out of us. Let me show you.'

The scent of her breath muzzles my face.

Eyes won't open.

Neck can't turn.

Foreboding scuttles up my spine. 'Ma!' I cry. 'Ma!'

'Trust me, Sheba! I'm your mother.'

Her hand covers mine as she holds it to her chest. I hear her heart's song and yield to its beat.

'That's better. Don't fight it, child. Hush, Sheba, hush.'

I obey her command as half-singing, half-chanting, my mother weaves a spell:

'Where your sisters have failed, you will succeed.
Run wild, my child, wild as the wind.
Be the beating heart of every storm
The calm eye of a hurricane
The fiercest flame of a forest fire
Run wild, my child. Run!'

Ma sings and in a blink of an eye, we're out of the house in the night sky. She's a bird. I'm a feather on her wing.

'The moon! The moon!' I shriek, dazzled by the sickle moon above us. 'I'm flying!'

I scream. Cry. Yelp. No sound emerges.

'You're flying because of me, my daughter. I am Crow. Your

mother, Crow. I feed on carrion and unless
you do as I say, I shall drop you. Lose you.
Ditch you in darkness. Is that what you
want?'

Unable to reply, I twitch. Arms and
legs bound, feathered in flecks of
hair, all I can do is twitch. *Twitch*,
I tell you.

Can't run.

Can't sing a song of
protection. Can't bargain
or cajole when danger has me.

I twist and turn till it dawns on me that if I am
to endure, if I'm to escape this bird and beat her at
whatever game she's playing, I must bide my time.

Think, Sheba! Think.

What would Nana Gyata su do? Or a girl who
walks with lions?

A hunter listens and watches, waiting for the
moment to attack.

Alert, I listen with my senses as Mother Crow
swoops and dives in an ecstasy of movement. Gliding,
she tilts as currents of air sweep us over prekese
and neem trees. At this time of year their fragrance
saturates our side of the village, almost smothering
the marshy scent of wetland and river. Prekese and
neem – barks and fruit Nana uses for healing.

I think of Nana and the bird caws, her thoughts

rushing through me in a torrent that tosses me aside.

'Nana? Your precious grandmother, my mother, the high priestess of righteousness, is not who you think she is, child. She's the biggest hypocrite of us all! As is that hyena sister of hers, Grandma Baby. One day, one day, you should ask them both how they got rid of their husbands. Three children your Nana gave my father and then, *whoosh*! The man's gone. Out of our lives forever. Ask your Nana exactly what your great-grandfather Nana Gyata su possessed that made her cleave to him more than her husband. Even in death, he has power, Sheba. Power he's passed on to her.'

Her feathers ruffle, indignant, as more of our story unfolds. 'Ruby, that sister of mine, has the hide of an elephant and a mind so sharp she'll cut you with a glance if you're not careful. Cut her husband dead the moment he broke his promise and married another wife. That man wouldn't let her leave with even *one* of her children. Not one, *peh*! Huh! One day, one day, Ruby's going to take her revenge on all men; her husband and Gaza's father especially.

'Aba! You don't know? Smart girl like you? That drunkard did away with Gaza's mother. How your aunt loved that woman! And as for my cousin Clara, let me tell you her story.'

I already know about Aunt Clara. Nonetheless, Mother Crow shoves her tale down my throat. 'My poor cousin married a Naija man – a Yoruba man. I could have had him just like that!' She clicks her beak in anger. 'Is my face not prettier than Clara's? Is my skin not lighter? Don't I have more flesh on my bones, more curves on my body? Clara meets her Nigerian at a wedding and after she touches his hair, come and see my sister running. She chases him from Kumasi to Accra. Accra to Lomé and then Lagos. My sister is happy-oh! So happy she learns how to cook his food, his favourite, pepper soup. Then she learns how to plait Naija hair, how to sew long, flowing agbada – matching gown, trousers and cap. Two years of pepper soup and sweet palm wine, that's how much they love each other.'

Mother Crow cackles as she ducks and dives in the air, whooping. 'Ha! After two years, pickney no come. So, the man's mother knocks on the door of their marriage and says, "Madam Daughter-in-law – mek you go home to Ghana. Mek you leave my boy quick-quick, so he mek pickney with Naija woman while I still have breath. Clara, pack your bags and go."'

Mother Crow screams, swooping with delight at the thought of my aunt's anguish. 'The first time his mother comes, the man stands his ground. Second time. No can do. To stop this "no-baby, no-baby" wahala, Yoruba Man gives in to his ma. Clara packs her bags and comes home. But with every step away from her husband, her heart breaks until bit by bit, piece by piece, it scatters, and she has no heart left to love again. Ha!'

Mother Crow quakes with laughter as, talons extended, she settles on a branch of the cotton tree. The air is warmer here, the wind softer. She flexes her wings and power surges through the vane and shaft of each of her wing feathers. The bird struts, black tail bobbing, bib glimmering in moonlight.

'And that is our Clara!' she squawks. 'Limp as a rag and barren. Useless as a mat everyone steps on and no one wants to keep. Let this be a lesson to you: Naija man be the same as Ghana man. No pickney, no marriage. Poor Clara! Nobody loves her! Nobody cares.' She laughs as if her song of scorn to moon and stars, a song leeching tenderness from earth and sky, has everyone cackling with her.

I love Aunt Clara. I love her kindness. Nothing pleases her more than–

Snuffed out, my thought flaps away as colours pulse. Sounds and smells surge as instinct throbs in bark and heartwood, in every creature roosting in the boughs of the tree. Crimson-petalled flowers, stamens stirring, turn to the moon, while clouds of bats and moths guzzle nectar.

Mother Crow is the only one of her kind here. She hops along the branch, the same one, I realise, where only days ago another crow spied on me and Nana while the cotton tree sang.

'Yes,' she says. 'I keep a close eye on you when I'm away, Sheba. I know what you're up to, my daughter. I know your back and front, your comings and goings. I know it all, because you're mine.'

Anger crackles through me as I think of my father.

It took two of you to make me, not you alone. One day soon, my father will come for me!

'No, he won't. I took his seed and that was it. Your father will never claim you, my chick! He'll never lay a hand on you.'

Silence gathers. I listen, sensing an idea winding its way towards me until, mind outstretched, I grasp it and remember. Feathers and human hair are similar. Made of the same substance, they serve the same purpose and more.

My mind darkens the better to hide my thoughts; the better to tease truth from the plumage around me.

I sink into Mother Crow relishing the warmth of her feathers, the gentle curve of vane, the flexible strength of shaft. I drop down, down, through sinew and gristle, beak and bone. Down, beyond thoughts she wants to share, to those she keeps hidden. Then, deeper still, till I'm in her heart's shrine, the flame of her soul.

All is quiet here, calm. So calm, it bears no resemblance to the voice that rattled through me moments ago.

I listen, heart to heart; flame to flame.

The hush thickens as possibilities bloom.

One falls and is crushed straightaway. 'I took what I needed. Then I let him go.'

She says the same thing again and again. Switches to: 'I took his seed. Nothing more.'

Her caw echoes, reverberating through the cotton tree. '*Nothing more! Nothing more!*'

The flame in her heart flickers, releasing smoke in a trail of letters.

I read them and quail.

Read the words that reveal the breath of my mother's soul: *I lie.*

And the truth slaps me.

I taste blood on her beak.

His blood.

Feel the stony stare she fixed on him, when having taken what she needed, she was done.

True as the feathers on her back, on her wings and tail, a scene unfolds: my mother gorging on my father, drinking him dry as the light within him is snuffed out.

'Don't you *dare* judge me!' Mother Crow screeches. 'I haven't met a man yet who didn't betray me. Even my brother Solomon deserted me for his wife. There's no man alive able to give me the freedom I crave, Sheba. No man generous enough to let me fly free and burnish my throat in bird-song. No, my daughter, living with a man is like living with a rat. Better to eat a man than marry him. Better to have just a few in our village than too many. We women are wonderfully, gorgeously made, and men fear us because we give birth to them. You and I deserve more, my daughter. Much more. I've made sure of that.'

My mother the crow.

I now know where I go when Ma is near. I hide in the darkest corner of my heart because she terrifies me. And unless I take time to prepare, she'll sup on my soul and destroy me as she did my father.

11

NEXT MORNING, I wake to Ma's fingers caressing my brow. Her breath fills mine and as my eyes open, I stay still. I don't recoil. No, I marshal every morsel of strength I possess, every shred of will that's in me and yawn.

My innards are quaking for sure, yet as I arch my back in a welcome stretch to the sun, I pretend today's the same as yesterday and the day before.

Ma cups my chin. Rubs my nose. Hugs me, saying: 'Sheba, you've grown so much since I last saw you! You're quite the young woman now.'

She pinches my nipple. Laughs when I shriek and run to bathe.

Seems she can't get enough of me this morning. She calls me: 'My chick. My precious one. My darling. My princess,' before spreading two kaba cloths on the bed. One for her, one for me. Mother and daughter in matching tops and skirts.

'It's made from the best fabric,' she insists. 'Dutch

wax print is perfect for church.'

After putting her kaba blouse on, after hauling the bottom half to cover her toma, the waist-beads she wears to accentuate her figure, Ma preens in front of a mirror stroking hips garlanded with flowers in a jungle of leaves.

My up and down may be cut from the best cloth, but the skirt, tight as a chicken's gizzard, crushes my legs into a mermaid's tail. So much so, I almost topple as Ma twirls me around.

'Head high. Back straight,' she instructs. 'That's better. All eyes will be on you today, Sheba, dazzled by your beauty, the glow of your skin and the mother who made you!'

'But this is too tight, Ma. I can barely walk!'

'Don't be silly. And don't you dare be a queen of sighs today,' she adds, wielding a blade in her voice. 'Just don't.'

No amount of sulking on my part can change her mind. She's going to show the world that we're mother and daughter, even if it means squeezing my flesh into a sheaf of blooms.

Over breakfast of eggs and avocado, pawpaw and pineapple, Ma coddles and pets me in such a way that my aunts glance at each other, puzzled. They stare.

Grandma Baby's nostrils flare, while Nana blinks, confused by what she's seeing: not only are we dressed in identical clothes, but Ma's lavishing me with affection as well. The spectacle is so bizarre that as Nana's mouth opens, Aunt Clara shuts her eyes – a signal to keep our lips zipped.

The oldest in our family obeys, but her little sister, oblivious to nudges and hints, brushes a hand over my forehead. Feels a burn on my brow, for Grandma Baby then lifts my chin.

I hold my breath, knowing full well that though my junior grandmother is small, though she spends much of her time obsessing over which oils to use to soothe the day's anxieties, when she decides to speak her mind, no one can stop her.

She smooths a palm over my shoulders, and after sniffing repeatedly turns to Ma. 'Sika, what have you been doing to our granddaughter?'

My aunts gasp.

A blast of wind clatters at the windows. Gusts coil around curtains, shifting then lifting them as charcoal clouds block the sun.

The room darkens and Ma, baring her teeth, replies: 'What are you insinuating, old crone?'

'Haba! I'm an old crone today, am I? All the better to detect mischief-makers,' says Grandma Baby. 'I sniffed it. Suspected it. You've dipped your beak in her, haven't you, Sika?'

Grandma Baby glares at Ma, then touches my cheeks, my shoulders and arms. 'Sheba, are you all right?'

I nod, shivering at the sensation of
fingers on skin.

'Sheba, what's happening to you?'

Grandma Baby shakes me and
instinct tugs, reminding me that
to outwit my mother, I have to
convince everyone present that I'm
fine; that today is the same as any other
day. While Ma's with us, I can't let Grandma
Baby scuttle my plan.

*I am a girl who walks with lions. I am not a feather
in my mother's wing. I am here. Here!*

Grandma Baby leans in. Inhales. Comes closer still
until her nose nestles at the base of my neck. The base
and back of the neck, she claims, are places where
encounters with danger leave traces of distress.

She sniffs again, and as her fingers lick a slick of
sweat off my arm, I flash my eyes:

Grandma, don't say a word. Not a word. Please.

Her pupils spark. To my relief, she smiles before
saying to Ma, 'Sika, forgive me. I'm like a mouse
lost in a hole when that cotton tree's in bloom. The
perfume of its flowers plays havoc with my mind.'

For as long as I've been able to distinguish left
from right and right from wrong, Grandma Baby
has never apologised to my mother. In their battle of
baby-lasts, for one of them to ask forgiveness of the
other is unheard of.

Ma raises an eyebrow, tilting her head from Baby to me. 'Are you sure you're all right, Sheba?'

'I'm tired and hungry, that's all,' I reply.

Naïve, she called me last night. I'll show her!

I follow Grandma Baby's example. Spoon egg and bread on a plate, add a slice of avocado and eat, while those around me continue talking without words.

Shoulders sag, buttocks shift.

Eyes sparkle in accusation, glitter in defiance, and as faces glare and frown, as they kiss their lips and grunt, they forget that I'm no longer the child I once was. I learned to decipher their body-talk years ago. Indeed, they taught me how to perfect those winks and blinks we use the moment outsiders are in our midst. They taught me, yet today I'm the stranger here.

As I eat watching them through lowered lashes, they silently scream at each other.

Nana's seething.

Ma stares her down.

Aunt Ruby tells them to stay calm, to think of me. Not now, she keeps telling them. Let's talk this through later.

The child can understand what we're saying, Aunt Clara reminds them. Too late, Nana's fury is incandescent.

'Haven't you eaten enough?' grumbles Aunt Ruby.

She wants me gone. They all do.

I ladle more egg on my plate. Take another slice

of bread. Tuck in as the room writhes in unspoken conversation.

You've dipped your beak in her, haven't you? Grandma Baby said.

From what I can gather, from the hush, they know about Ma. They know, yet did nothing to prepare me!

I'm tempted to set my plan aside, stand up and shout, 'How could you? Why, in the name of Nana Gyata su, in the name of all that's good and honourable in our family, why didn't you tell me?'

The moment passes. The room crackles with emotion and I find myself looking at my family with the unblinking gaze of a huntress.

If they knew, why didn't anyone warn me?

I begin to wonder and, bit by bit, thoughts surface, pooling into a lake of memories. I dive in. Untangling stray words and phrases, I recall asides that should have told me that others suspected what I did not.

The big house without men.

Those witches in the former chief's palace?

Madam High and Mighty.

I taste the disdain in a nickname given to Ma by her fellow traders, their reluctance to have anything to do with her. I recall Ama's mother's hostility to her:

If Madam High and Mighty Sika Prempeh shows her face, promise me you'll leave straightaway.

I remember Nana's advice that instead of listening to gossip I should find my own path. Perhaps if I had taken heed of what other people were saying, how they were behaving, I wouldn't be surprised at the scene before me now: the voiceless tussle between Nana and my aunts on one side, Ma on the other. I watch them as more of my past emerges.

'Does Ma have the gift of touch?' I'd once asked Nana.

'Your mother looks elsewhere for her power,' she'd replied.

Nana's words rise to a crescendo as memories slip, revealing clues I haven't noticed before: assurances to Ma that no matter how far she travels, I'll be well looked after; that she should do what pleases her best, pursue her destiny and make money. I remember a plea from Aunt Ruby that Ma should follow her heart.

Perhaps my aunts and grandmothers were trying to keep Mother Crow away from me. Perhaps they were doing their best to protect me.

I look again at the puzzle that's my family. The more I stare, the more I try to slot pieces together to find out where I fit in, the more clearly I see at their centre the secret they've tried to shield me from. I watch it burrowing out of its hole, as, looping and sliding, it slithers on the table.

That's the thing with secrets. Once they give off a scent, you want to see it: muscles, sinews, scales and skin. Its body ripples and flexes, coiling and uncoiling as it gives off a whiff of prekese and a trace of something else.

Grandma Baby's nose twitches. I sniff, almost gagging at the metallic odour of blood and decay oozing from its flesh – a stink of carrion to attract scavengers such as Mother Crow. Yet Ma doesn't seem aware of it. Busy insulting Nana and my aunts with the steel tip of her glare, she sees nothing but her anger at them.

Grandma Baby, sensitive to a reek in the air, inhales, attempting to find its source. She can't make it out either. To my horror, only I can.

'Every family has its secrets, Sheba. Let this be ours,' Nana had said.

As the snake's head rises, as it flicks its tongue and then opens its mouth revealing fangs, I watch transfixed.

Befriend it, a voice tells me. *Quickly.*

Head shaking, I recoil.

Emerald-green eyes ablaze, the snake strikes.

I push back my chair at the same time as Grandma Baby seizes my hand. Grabs me and before I have time to resist, we're out of the room, racing across the courtyard up to her chamber.

Behind us, Ma bellows, 'Sheba, we're going to church. I want you back here! Now! This instant!'

My knees buckle.

Grandma Baby hauls me forward. 'We're almost there, Sheba. Hurry!'

I try to follow her example, placing one foot in front of the other, but I double over, lassoed by the fury of Ma's voice in my head: *Come back, Sheba! Come back!*

'Look at me! Look into my eyes, child.'

I do as Grandma Baby says and discover that if I focus on the light in her pupils, Ma's power recedes.

'Now touch my hair and walk.'

I caress her silky pelt, warming myself in her soul's flame. Images in her mind tickle my fingers, radiating through my palm until I glimpse what she's seeing. I'm a toddler once again and Grandma Baby, encouraging me to walk, is repeating words she used to coo at me: 'Ta ta,' she says, as, her hand in mine, she urges me to put one foot in front of the other. 'Ta ta. Good girl.'

I obey her command and, over what seems an eternity, we stagger upstairs.

My limbs may be cumbersome, my feet unwieldy as tree stumps, yet bit by bit, she drags me down the corridor to the safety of her room.

12

'ARE YOU ALL right?'

We're in Grandma Baby's boudoir. The doors locked, the windows shuttered. Outside a squall hurls leaves in the air, dashing them against the house. The cotton tree is singing its song: that high-pitched refrain of splintering wood and fading petals. '*Weee*,' the tree hums. '*Weee*.' Over and over as the moist scent of river licks my nostrils.

'What's the matter with you, child? What's she done?'

I try to explain, but as soon as I open my mouth to describe the night before, no sound emerges. Shivering, determined to talk, I close my eyes.

Once again, I open my mouth. But this time, from the depth of my throat, Ma's chatter gushes, tangling my tongue, until I'm tweeting helplessly, her little chick.

Tears glide down my cheeks.

Cradling my body, Grandma Baby guides me to her bed. 'You don't have to say anything, dear. Don't talk. She's tied your tongue to stop you sharing her secrets. Calm down, Sheba. I've got you.'

She undresses me, peeling me out of my new kaba cloth. Then, smoothing her fingers over my arms, legs and body, my junior grandmother anoints me with oil.

'Ginger and lavender to revive and calm your soul,' she murmurs. 'And now orange to warm the sweetness in you.'

Her fingers pummel and squeeze, rub and tease. When she's done, when my breathing is more relaxed, she wraps me in a cover cloth and easing me on to her lap, rocks me back and forth. The motion, soothing as a long-ago lullaby, steadies my pulse.

'There,' Grandma Baby says. 'That's better. Don't speak, child. Not yet. Not until we understand Sika's hold on you. Breathe. Keep breathing.'

A sob jolts my chest. *What's happening to me, Grandma?*

I want to tell her that this is worse than anything my friends and I imagined in the scenarios we created in our battle with Queen Sasabonsam. In fact, this is a nightmare; a dream that refuses to release me.

Snuffling a necklace of fear from around my neck, Grandma Baby loosens it by drawing me closer. 'Fear in small doses can be useful,' she tells me. 'It sharpens your wits and whets your courage. Always remember, Sheba, your gift is the breath of your soul. Learn to use it, and I promise, you'll save yourself.'

She places my hand on her head. Nana braids her hair while Grandma Baby shaves hers, leaving bristles sleek as a seal's skin on her scalp. I finger them, and as my palm tingles with the throb of her love, she says:

'Sister told me she was planning to take you to see her old friend, Maanu, today. Sika must have got wind of it somehow. Don't be afraid, Sheba, we've got you. We've looked out for you and your sisters from the moment you were born. Nothing is going to stop us now, I promise.'

Feeling as fragile as a snail without a shell, I gulp down tears. Never felt less safe in my life than I do now.

'Go to sleep, child. You need sleep to gather your wits. Sleep. These old bones of mine are still strong enough to carry your weight. Close your eyes.'

Lulled by the tenderness in Grandma Baby's voice, my lashes flutter, then fall, as sleep gathers me in her arms.

I wake up alone. Outside, the silent tussle at the breakfast table has turned into cries of: 'Sika, you promised! You promised!'

I try the door. Still locked. From the outside, this time.

I place an ear against a mahogany panel. Too thick for eavesdropping, it fails to block the tornado of rage rampaging through the house. Red-hot, it flings me away.

I tumble to my knees and a vision of Snake, emerald eyes glittering, flashes before me. I reel as terror jangles my bones. Every bit of me, inside and out, trembles petrified of the Snake and Ma.

And when Nana shrieks: 'Sika! Sika! How could you?' as if Ma's name is a curse she can no longer live with, I taste fire and bile in my mouth.

Run Sheba, run.

I dash to Grandma Baby's wardrobe. Right at the back is Maybe's picture of me – his portrait of the girl on fire with the heart of a lion. Though faded now, it still speaks to me, hinting at the person I want to be – courageous, defiant. *Me.* The very best of me. I touch the girl's face and her eyes sparkle, reassuring me that if I can only hold my nerve, all will be well. I return the portrait to its hiding place, fish out one of Grandma Baby's nightdresses and pull it on as I turn to the windows. Flinging them open, I lever myself on to the ledge outside.

Just below is the tree I climb to pluck mangoes for Aunt Clara's relish. Never climbed it from top to bottom before. Never leaped from a window into its arms.

I am a girl who walks with lions, I mutter to myself. A huntress. With the help of Nana Gyata su and all that's good and true in me, I shall use my arms and legs to swing and jump.

I can do it. I have to, because the best kind of magic, Nana always tells me, is belief in myself and my ancestors.

I repeat my mantra. After saying it a third time, with my hand clasping the ledge, I extend a leg to the nearest branch.

It groans. Twigs splinter. I test it again.

Won't hold longer than a second; two, at the most. Desperation gnawing at my gut, I edge towards the tree, head, soul and heart crying loud and clear: *better fall and end up limping than stay here a moment longer.*

Stay, and sure as the sweat on my palms, my elders will crack Ma's spell and interrogate me. Then, they'll force me to take sides in a battle I can't yet win.

I seize the moment and lunge at the tree.

Branch snaps. Arms wrapped around the trunk, I cling on, my foot probing foliage beneath.

Soon as I find a limb sturdy enough to support me, I twist and turn, and within minutes I'm perching on it. Then, looping an arm around it, I clamber down, until I'm close enough to the ground to jump.

13

THE SECOND TIME I run away from home, I know where I'm heading. I follow the current that links me to Maybe. Trail it, bare-footed, through flurries of wind and dust. Run, even as my bones tell me that before the sun sets, I'll have to face the woman I'm fleeing.

I run, knowing that like a lioness tracking prey through savannah, once I return, I'll have to step warily, waiting for exactly the right moment to pounce. With the power within me and the courage of the greatest of my ancestors, Nana Gyata su, I'll fight, if I have to. Didn't happen last time, but now that I'm almost grown, if I'm to live the life I want with Maybe and Gaza as my friends, I've got to stand tall and challenge Ma.

I have to! Even so, pursued by dread, I feel her hand on my shoulder. Ma's stalking me, hoping I'll bend to her will once again.

Little chick. Fainted-hearted. The Queen of Sighs.

I shake my head to clear it, to reason with myself.

Ma won't dip her beak into me a second time. While I have breath and the will to live, Mother Crow will never again take me on her night-travel.

Wind howls, spitting leaves at my face while a blue-black drongo, a sister-bird to crows, glides to a branch of an almond tree. Red eyes fastened on me, it flaps its wings, cawing, as if imploring me to go home. The bird trails me, flitting from bush to bush as, half-running, half-stumbling, I'm pulled by the tide between Maybe and me. It glimmers and swells, sweeping me past the cotton tree and then through the village.

'Isn't that a nightdress you're wearing, girl?' someone sniggers. 'Rich folk like you can't afford to dress properly? On a Sunday too!'

'Look! She's off again,' another on-looker cries. 'Before the sun dips in the sky, before she sets foot in Zongo, Nana Serwah will be on to her!'

'Aba! Without shoes as well! Go home, Sheba,' a woman calls. 'Quick, quick, or you'll disgrace your grandmothers and Nana Gyata su will rise from his grave. Put some shoes on, Princess!'

That's the drawback to living in a village as small

as mine. Tongues wag. Eyes leer. Even the red-eyed drongo seems to join in. 'Go home, girl! Go home!' it squawks, as, darting from tree to stalk and then up again, it ribbons fields of corn and cassava, while wind, nipping at my heels, corrals me to Maybe. I press on, the bond between us towing me close, so close; his scent fills my nostrils, and despite everything I endured the night before, my cheeks dimple in a smile.

He's with Gaza on a stretch of river ideal for fishing. Bent over, hands dangling beside the sunken roots of a mangrove tree, the two of them are up to their knees in water. Serene as statues, if they remain silent, an unsuspecting fish will emerge, and with luck and a flip of the wrist, will join the rest of their catch on the riverbank.

One glance and Maybe smells it, sees it: fear, twitching behind my dimples, throbbing in a vein on my neck. I crumple to the ground.

Stealthy as an eel, he glides out of water. In a single bound, he's up the bank without making a sound. There's no splash to alert fish that hunters are on the prowl. No sign whatsoever that seconds ago he was standing beside Gaza.

'Hey, what is it?' he asks, a hand on my shoulder, his cheek against mine. He pulls away.

My voice still knotted by Ma, I hold my tongue.

'What happened last night, Sheba? I couldn't feel you... you were absent, as if dead somehow.'

I nod, touching his hair.

The lake of kindness in him laps my feet. I close my eyes. Within seconds, I'm calmer, anchored in Maybe. Even if what Grandma Baby said is true and I alone can save myself, if anyone can help me break Ma's spell, it's him.

Yielding to the twist of his curls, our foreheads slump one against the other. Fingers sizzling, I open my mind, creating space for him in a place beyond words. As I begin showing him my journey with Mother Crow last night, memory unfolds in a sequence as vivid as our adventures by the river.

Exhilaration, Terror's sister, sings in my blood as Mother Crow circles the moon. She soars and, feather-light, I soar with her. Yet as soon as I remember my father, my throat tightens. Breath snags while I excise him from my story and try to hide the truth about my mother.

Maybe's breath mingles with mine but before I've finished replaying my journey, he draws back troubled. 'So, you know what she is now.'

Seems he knew long before I did.

'Did she hurt you, Sheba?'

I open my mouth expecting to hear the grating caw of Mother Crow, her chatter knotting my tongue. I pause, then gulp at the sound of my voice. Bruised. Hoarse with shock and grief but my *voice* – not Ma's. *Mine.*

'No,' I say, a hand on my throat.

'Are you sure?'

His question reminds me of Nana's advice to keep my lips sealed when it comes to family matters, to keep our secrets under our roof. I hear Nana. Feel her shame as *my* shame, *my* fault.

Can't shake her hold over me, so I shrug, then look away in case Maybe winkles out the truth.

'I thought we were friends...' he says.

'We are!' I reply. Then mumble, '*Family.* What my mother does, affects all of us. Everyone knows us. Everyone talks.'

Sympathy lightens Maybe's face. '*Everyone* talks. We came south for that reason.' He pauses, takes hold of my trembling hands. Warms them with his breath and says, 'When my brothers and sister died, my mother didn't want to live. But what almost killed her was gossip. People said her babies' deaths were her doing. Even after I was born, they kept on calling her an eater of souls, a mischief-maker.'

Maybe hasn't mentioned this before, but having known him for years, having listened to the silence between his words and heard the rumble of what he's left unsaid, I ask, 'Why has your father never visited you? Don't you belong to his line?'

Maybe nods, then shakes his head, embarrassed.

'Did he listen to gossip about your mother?'

He shrugs. 'I can't explain what I don't know,

Sheba. My mother won't talk about it, so I've no idea what happened between them. What I remember is that one day everything seemed fine and next, Ma woke us up and we were running for our lives.'

'Of course. No one's able to find us unless they're desperate,' I remind him.

'They would have lynched her if we hadn't fled. And if I'd been born a girl, they'd have said I was a soul-eater as well.'

My mouth opens, aghast.

'Family,' he says and turning my right hand over, he strokes the lines on my palm. He holds it to his cheek as Gaza, in the river, stretches, irritated by the clatter of the bird overhead.

It's that red-eyed drongo again. The one's that haunting me, taunting me as it tells me to hurry home.

Gaza looks at the bird, then notices Maybe's hand in mine.

'My mother can't go back now, because if she did, those who accused her of murdering her children will kill her. They saw 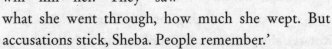 what she went through, how much she wept. But accusations stick, Sheba. People remember.'

I recall something else. 'Didn't you tell me that one day, one day you and Better Life are sure to go back?'

'I was much younger then. I won't go now,' he insists. 'Not without my mother.'

I laugh at the difference between us. 'You won't leave your mother, while I've just run away from mine!'

'Because she hurt you. She harmed Gecko to get at us – to get at you especially.'

I stifle a sob as words scramble up my throat.

Determined to scoop out the truth, Maybe's eyes glitter, while the bird in the mangrove tree clamours: 'Go home, girl! Go home!'

I think of Ma and swallow. Think of Snake, shudder. Nana, my family – all of them: Aunt Clara and Ruby, Grandma Baby. I smother slurs about each of them. Bury them deep. Push them deeper still, in the hope that Ma's utterances will never see the light of day. Seems there's no escaping Nana's training. Her grip is such, I can't wriggle free.

That's what I feel, until Maybe's touch gentles me. Rubbing my hand again to stop my shivering and shaking, he clears a path.

My account of events flows even after Gaza, having caught another fish, guts the catch and builds a fire. Lays three sturdy sticks side by side and using them as a grill, cooks a meal of fish and yam for the three of us.

Gaza works, listening intently. Turns tilapia over. Rotates slices of yam till cooked through; he dishes our food on plantain leaves. 'Enough talking,' he says. 'Eat.'

Then, a hand hiding his mouth, Gaza begins whispering.

My stomach spasms as suspicion, light as a spider on my hand, insinuates that he's talking about me.

The spider scuttles along my arm, across my shoulder, down the back of my neck. What's Gaza saying?

I start eating, eyes moving from Maybe to Gaza, and then back again. The taste of wood-roasted tilapia and yam saturates my tongue as we eat quickly, my ears itching.

They're itching, Nana would say, because I'm eager to hear what may have been said about me.

Grandchild of mine, people with itchy ears are hungry for gossip. Their ears flap like those of an elephant because their appetite for tittle-tattle never ceases. Steer clear of "Have you heard? Did you know?" Stay above the fray, child. Be true to yourself.

Truth is, once my stomach's full, I'm ravenous to find out what Gaza whispered to Maybe, and having disobeyed Nana once, I do so again. 'Were you talking about me just now?'

Gaza snorts, disapproval draining kindness from his eyes. 'You see,' he says to Maybe.

'You see what?' I snap.

'*Women!*' he hisses. 'Trouble. Always trouble.'

Before I can stop myself, before I remember my promise to Gaza's mother to help her 'boy', I reply,

'And your mother? Did she cause trouble as well?'

The scent of neem flowers rubs my nostrils. I sense his mother's presence and so does Gaza, for as his brow furrows, his eyes flash.

'My mother was kind and true, never cruel. You see what I mean?' he says to Maybe, scowling.

'Why would we be talking about *you*, Sheba, when what worries me most is Gecko?'

He retrieves the tail-less lizard from his shirt pocket. 'That mother of yours has no kindness in her. Only someone who has a bad spirit would do what she did.'

Gecko's tail is little more than a stump, making his look of a dejected princeling more tragic than ever.

'I'm sorry, Gaza. Ma shouldn't have hurt him.'

She shouldn't have told me about Aunt Ruby and Gaza's mother, either. For a moment, I wonder if Gaza's aware of rumours that his father murdered his mother. It's hard to tell which of Ma's utterances are true, which are false. After all, she convinced me years ago that my father was a creature of the forest.

I shake my head in an effort to rid it of insinuations and smears Ma bludgeoned into me last night: Nana, my aunts Ruby and Clara. Reputations tarnished.

Eyes downcast, I mumble, 'She shouldn't have hurt Gecko. I'm sorry, Gaza. I'm sorry for what Ma did.'

'Ma?' Gaza rolls the word in his mouth as he would a curse. 'Ma?' he sneers. 'Your mother wants us to call her *Madam*. I shall call her Madam Sasabonsam, Madam *She*-Devil.'

Maybe places a hand on Gaza's thigh. 'Chale, cool it.'

Gaza inhales, his chest heaving as he tries to hold his anger in.

'Gaza, please forgive my mother.'

'You take me for a fool?' Gaza snarls.

'Cool it,' Maybe urges again, a hand reaching to our friend.

Gaza pulls away. Usually hesitant when speaking, today his palaver talk spurts out of his mouth with the speed of machine-gun fire. 'Madam Sasabonsam is wicked and I'm not afraid to say so. Me, afraid? After my father's beatings?' Gaza shakes his head. 'I fear no one.'

The fragrance of neem flowers circles me again. 'No one?' I demand.

'No one!' he replies. 'I may not talk much. I may at

times speak slowly, but that doesn't mean I'm stupid. My mother, God rest her, taught me right from wrong. And Madam Sasabonsam is wicked *paaah*!'

Gaza's hatred punches me in the gut. I lurch back to steady myself. We Asantes are proud people and members of a royal household are prouder than most – that's why Ma's nickname is Madam High and Mighty. I often disagree with her. I know she can be cruel, devious, untrustworthy. Nonetheless, we share the same family, the same roof over our heads, the same ancestors. And whether I like it or not, the woman Gaza loathes is my mother. The tang of lemon floods my mouth, I ball my hands into fists. Anger and shame flay my cheeks as I gnaw my tongue to check a roar that surges in my throat. In that instant, at the very moment that pride overrides shame and soars in rage; just as I'm on the verge of blasting Gaza to the moon and back for daring to bad mouth a member of my family, Ama appears.

'Sheba!' she cries, silencing my rage. She doubles over, panting. 'They're coming for you. Gaza's father and your mother. They're coming to take you home. Run, Sheba! Run!'

I close my eyes. Shake my head and groan. 'I need to return,' I admit.

'But not like that... not with them.' Not with Ma scolding me, all eyes on me, as I stumble home in Grandma Baby's nightdress on a long road of shame.

'Is my father with her, for sure?' asks Gaza.

'Ah! You doubt me? My friend, I saw them fili-fili with my own eyes,' says Ama, pointing her forefingers at her eyes.

The spark of an idea brightens Gaza's face. Galvanised by the possibility of outwitting his father, he bundles Gecko in a pouch and hauls me up.

'Come, Sheba. Let me show you a way out of here.'

Gaza jumps into the river and Maybe and I follow.

14

WE WADE IN Gaza's wake beyond the mangrove tree. He ventures deeper and as he does so, he plucks river reeds, blowing through them until he finds one he can breathe through. Maybe and I do the same. At Gaza's nod, we dip our heads under water and hide.

Minutes later, I hear noises that take a while to decipher. Voices, muffled at first, then loud and booming as they pass through my skull and vibrate in my body. Ma's utterances, along with Gaza's father's, followed by grunts from friends he drinks with – men he calls on to enforce the will of our village elders. Our gutters need cleaning? Gaza's pa, nicknamed Big Man, rouses his mates and together they make sure that at a set time, everyone who can, does their bit. Big Man appears drunk most of the time, but when he's sober, he's as beady-eyed as a hippo calculating how wide he has to open his mouth before he swallows you.

'Small girl, have you seen your friend?' he bellows.

He's talking to Ama. Big mistake calling her a small girl.

Sure enough, Ama replies in a tone hot with indignation: 'Who are you calling *girl*? Me? You call a young woman like me *small girl*? Ah!'

'Ama Smart! Don't play with us,' Ma interrupts. 'Where is she? Where's my daughter? Where's Sheba?'

'Madam Sika, if I knew, I'd tell *you* of all people where my bestie-best is. As it is, I have no idea where to find her.'

'We saw you running,' says Ma, 'so we followed. If you don't know where she is, why did you come here?'

Ama sighs the deepest of sighs; a sigh so heart-felt it makes the waves above me ripple. 'I believed that if anyone could fathom where Sheba is, Gaza and Maybe would. They said they'd be here fishing but, as you can see for yourself, they've gone. If anyone knows where she's hiding, they do.'

'Hiding? Who said anything about her hiding?'

'Madam Sika, if she's not at home and she's not here, she's squeezed herself small-small so no one, not even you, can see her.'

'Foolish girl!'

Ma curses loudly, prompting Big Man to reassure her. 'Madam Sika, those boys can't have gone far. These embers are still warm. Araba – young woman – are you sure you haven't seen them?'

Silence.

I imagine Ama preening herself at being called 'araba'. She preens, searching for an answer that trips off her tongue. 'There was no one here when I arrived,' she claims. 'Perhaps they've gone to Maybe's house.'

'That yama-yama house in Zongo? That hut made of mud?' Ma grumbles.

'We'd better track him down sharp-sharp. Once we find those boys, we'll discover where your daughter is.' From the sound of it, Big Man is clear-headed today.

'Me, step foot in Zongo? *Me?*' Ma cries. 'Never!'

'Madam Sika, if you want to find your daughter that is where we have to go first. Araba, show us the way.'

We remain hidden until the conversation fades and the only sound we hear is the rush of water in our ears. I raise my head first; Maybe follows. When Gaza surfaces, he splutters, clearing his nose. 'If you want, I'll show you a way back where no one will see us,' he says.

'No one?'

'No one,' Gaza assures me.

Dripping wet, hair bejewelled with river droplets, I pad behind him. He retrieves Gecko from his hiding place, opens the pouch, and the lizard scrambles into his pocket. Gaza chuckles, content.

Recognising the path, I tail him, trudging through

wetland over fields of rice. We all know this route, but I let him take the lead, for I don't want to be seen as I am now: shivering and shaking, miserable as a baby with fever. With every step I take, my heart lurches, knowing that before the sun sets, I'll be with Ma again. What's more, unless I'm able to gather my wits and harness whatever courage I have, that glare of hers will pin me to the wall and strip my soul bare.

A red-eyed drongo shrieks.

I pause, half-wondering if it's the same bird that's pursued me all afternoon. It cocks its head, and screaming a second time, clings to a stalk of maize.

While Gaza hurries ahead, Maybe slams into me.

My legs won't lift. Won't move. My heart won't let them.

It flutters, stampeding, stuttering in my ears.

Whether I decide to go back, turn left, right or forge ahead, every path returns me to Ma.

'Nana Gyata su, help me! Help me be as brave as you once were. Help me stand my ground and do what's best when I face Ma tonight. Please!'

'Are you all right, Sheba?' Maybe asks, his hand clasping mine.

A clap of thunder thrashes the afternoon sky, sending rain clouds scudding. Wind whistles, flapping the leaves of banana trees ahead of us. Flurries damp with condensation slap our faces, beading them with sweat as the heavens press down on us.

This is what it's like before the rains come: the earth holds its breath. The world waits, and so do I, as from one moment to the next, relief spreads down my spine as a voice says softly: *'Fear is where courage begins, great-grandchild of mine. Feel it. Seize it, and then use all that's in you to shape it into whatever's right for you and our family.'*

The voice merges with the portrait of the ancestor I carry in my mind; the voice behind the smile I curtsey to every day.

'When the time is right, great-grandchild of mine, the world will hear your roar and tremble!'

Maybe's eyes quiz mine as my heart settles.

'Feel it. Seize it. Shape it,' Maybe murmurs. 'Did you hear him, Sheba?'

I nod.

Gaza turns. 'Are guys coming or not? I don't want to get wet, even if you do.'

Hand in hand, Maybe and I huddle behind Gaza and sprint. To avoid the market, and the embarrassment of being stared at, we scuttle over burrows of yam to a track that runs all the way to the back of our house.

The moment the mansion looms, I'm beset by waves of panic. They circle me, raising me higher and higher; so high an image of Mother Crow appears. Coal-black eyes blinking, she flaps her wings and swoops.

Heeding the advice of my ancestor, I trace tentacles of dread that I've been hiding from all day. Their heft almost overwhelms me, but once I realise what I'm prepared to do to save myself, my vision of Mother Crow fades.

Breathing eases.

Pulse steadies.

By stepping into it, I discover that fear holds me aloft, much as the river did when I was learning how to swim. 'Thank you,' I whisper to my ancestor.

'You don't have to go inside if you don't want to...' Maybe assures me. 'You can stay with us at Zongo until you're ready to face them.'

'I'm ready now,' I reply.

15

THEY'RE WAITING FOR me in the courtyard
when I tiptoe in: Nana in her special chair, Grandma
Baby beside her, and at either end, my aunts Ruby and
Clara, fingers probing hair and cloth. On Ruby's lap
is the gift Ma gave me this morning; on Clara's palm,
strands of hair taken from my comb. She teases a wisp
between her thumb and forefinger, then rubs it against
a cheek, while Ruby, caressing fragments of material
– the skirt of my up and down, allows ribbons of
flowers to tumble over her knees.

To my horror, the garment's been shredded.
Someone has slashed it with a razor. I remember
wanting to rip it apart – it was way too tight anyway –
yet I have no memory of damaging it.

I suspect that Ma must have done it when she found
me gone.

'Where have you been, grandchild of mine?' I'm

struck by the raised vein at the side of Nana's forehead. It pulses when worry festers, inflaming her anger. It's throbbing now.

Nana looks me up and down. Shakes her head as her gaze, peeling away my skin, delves into my soul. She doesn't say a word. Doesn't need to.

Nana knows me better than I do. She saw me enter the world. Held me, inspected my fingers and toes to make sure I was as I should be. She bathed me, stretching my limbs to help me grow; and, at my outdooring, it was Nana who raised me to the sun to feel its cat's lick on my skin.

Imagine her surprise then, when, instead of apologising as I should; instead of explaining my absence and behaving with the humility expected of me, I return her gaze. I demand answers to questions I wouldn't have dared ask before: 'Why didn't you warn me, Nana? Why didn't any of you tell me the truth about Ma? The truth about our family.'

The women in the house do what they always do when caught unawares. Eyes flit from one to the other. Aunt Ruby to Clara, Grandma Baby to Nana. They wriggle and squirm, pretending to be flustered to protect the oldest among us who, for the first time ever, prefers not to look at me.

Nana's fingers fiddle with the loose thread of her midnight-blue robe as she inspects my feet. I wriggle my toes, then say her name loudly.

My voice, bouncing off the walls, accentuates her silence. Moreover, the throne she's sitting on to channel Nana Gyata su's wisdom, isn't doing what it's supposed to today. Nana appears uncomfortable, even as her hands leave her dress to rest on the arms of the chair, her fingers clasping the lion's paws at the end.

'Before Ma comes back, won't *one* of you tell me the truth? Do I have to beg to make you tell me?'

A tear slides down Nana's cheek. Another follows, pooling at the edge of her lips. She brushes them away.

'Que sera sera,' Grandma Baby murmurs, patting Nana's arm. 'Whatever will be, will be.'

Aunt Ruby harrumphs. Then, the rumble of her voice softening to a purr, she says to my grandmother: 'There's no use crying over a decision you made years ago. What's happened has happened. It's over. Sika is a law unto herself. This is who she is, who she's always been.'

'What are you talking about, Aunt Ruby? Someone. Anyone. *Tell* me!'

Noses wrinkling, each of them stares at me as if my exasperation is a putrid smell they can barely tolerate.

I'm about to turn my back on them, head off to Zongo and be done with them once and for all, when the Snake reveals itself. Scales shimmering, it glides beneath Nana Gyata su's chair towards me.

Snakes are deadly here. A single bite can kill a grown man in minutes. Yet it's not the poison in its venom that alarms me. What's terrifying is that once again, no one else can see its emerald eyes fastened on me. No one can see the flick of its tongue. No one can see it at all.

Almost stumbling, I step back, my mind screaming: *Run, Sheba, run!*

I can't.

The snake's eyes hold me transfixed. My spine tingles as I remember Nana Gyata su's advice. *Feel it. Seize it. Shape it.*

Moment by moment, I step into my fear and then concentrating on the snake, stare into its eyes, blinking at their glitter, their silvery shine. The more I eyeball it, the more the snake gradually retreats until, after collapsing in a heap in front of me, it disappears.

Astonished, I glance at my family.

Flickers of shame shadow Nana's face. 'Come closer, Sheba,' she says. 'Let me tell you what I can before your mother returns. Come, grandchild of mine.'

I perch on a stool at her feet; the stool I sit on when she's about to tell me tales of our family's history. Like a warrior getting ready for battle, Nana prepares herself when she has something important to say.

She washes. Powders her face. Tidies her hair. Rubs musk into the folds of her robe, so that when everyone's assembled before her, not only does she smell fragrant, all eyes are on the spectacle she's created. All eyes are on her now. Around her neck is a gift from Nana Gyata su, our family emblem, a gold pendant shaped like a lion, while her fingers on the chair's paws gently stroke its claws.

Black coral skin offset by gold and dark mahogany.

I blink, and in that instant, skin and wood transform into scenes from long ago: Nana holding her father's hand, walking by the river, a lion beside her.

Is that why she can't see me? Why she won't look at me?

'What is it, Nana?' I ask.

'Shush!' Grandma Baby murmurs. 'Our family head will speak when she's ready. Can't you smell it on her?'

'Musk?'

'Try harder, Sheba.'

I sniff, then shrug.

'A day to end all days, grandchild. *Stress*,' Grandma Baby hisses. 'Didn't you hear them? They had the mother of all quarrels.' Then, in case I hadn't understood what she was insinuating, she nudges me, mouthing, '*Your mother.*'

After last night, nothing Ma does surprises me. And yet, when, at last, my grandmother meets my gaze, I begin to appreciate what I didn't earlier. Like the drongo that chased me this afternoon, Nana's eyes are red with sorrow.

I place a hand on her knee.

She smiles, covering my fingers with hers. 'Grandchild of mine,' she says. 'I shall be as truthful as I can, but before I say anything, I want you to remember that depending on how you look at it, depending on where you're standing, the truth has different faces. Be mindful that what I'm going to tell you may bear little resemblance to what your mother reveals later. Remember, grandchild of mine, the truth rarely smiles. It can be harsh. Yet, like a rainstorm in the dry season, it clears the air, sweeping layers of dust away until we're able to see what's right in front of us. The truth is what it is, and your mother will always be your mother.'

I nod, even though I've heard some of this before. Whenever I'm tempted to rebel by questioning my mother's absences; whenever I've grumbled about not knowing my sisters in Accra and not seeing them, or I've asked why Ma has never married, Nana's refrain has been: 'No matter what she does, your mother will always be your mother.'

'Go on, Nana.'

'I've told you before and I'll tell you again, we women of royal blood are gifted.'

'Indeed, we are, sister.' Grandma Baby chuckles. 'Say it! Say it! Speak the truth.'

'Each of us in our different way,' Nana continues, acknowledging Grandma Baby and my aunts, 'has the ability to help those less fortunate than we are. We're blessed with wisdom and a powerful sense of touch and smell. We're able to heal people, Sheba, and give them solace when they most require it. What's more, we keep our families safe by performing rituals that ease us from one season to the next. If the rains fail, it's up to us to hurry them along. We do what we can, and in exchange, our village celebrates us. They trusted Nana Gyata su and now they trust me.'

'Nana, Ma will be home soon.'

'Grandchild of mine, I'm too old to be hurried. You are your mother's daughter. Her blood flows in you, so listen carefully to what I'm about to say.'

Another tear slides down her cheek. I bite my tongue.

'I've told you many things over the years, Sheba. What I've never mentioned, what you don't yet know is that once in a generation someone born into a family such as ours is especially gifted. Indeed, what she accomplishes is above and beyond anything any of us here can do. Isn't that so, sister?'

Grandma Baby pats Nana's thigh. 'Above and beyond anything any of us here can do,' she repeats. 'True, true, my sister. Say it. Say it. Tell the truth.'

Nana presses on. 'My daughter, your mother, is as talented as your great-grandfather, Nana Gyata su, was. Like him, she can transform into a being altogether different to what she is. And yet your mother does what he never did: she binds people with her power. Men who love her are never seen again. She won't marry. She can't marry, because she refuses to abide by rules the rest of us live by. Instead of using her gift to help people, Sika uses it to control them, to destroy them – that's how she is. And from what I can gather, that's what you experienced last night.'

'I wondered if I was dreaming to begin with, Nana. I hoped I was. I could have been, but it's *true*. *It happened.*'

'Hmmmm,' the women around me moan in unison. 'Hmmmm.'

Murmuring the same note again and again, the air in the courtyard hums, vibrating in sympathy as their eyes bore into me: questioning, apologising – Aunt Clara's in particular.

'What we never told you, Sheba,' she says, 'is that we kept you with us on condition Sika took her mischief elsewhere. She promised not to meddle with you, not to harm you in any way. She didn't hurt you last night, did she?'

I'm not sure how to reply. How can I, with hundreds of questions dancing on my tongue, each so eager to jump out that as one elbows the other aside, another stumbles? Questions fuelled by Ma's rant last night and what Nana's just told me about Nana Gyata su. I want to know when Nana realised that Ma was different? When did she realise Ma was bad?

My mouth opens, then closes as my questions pile, one on top of the other, leaving me dumbstruck. Before I can order my thoughts and express them, Aunt Ruby raises a finger.

'Tell us exactly where your mother took you last night,' she says. 'Tell us what happened, Sheba.'

16

SO, I DO.

I tell them everything I remember of my journey with Mother Crow: the ecstasy to begin with – the flash of stars as we soared in the sky, the moon's smile on our descent. Then I tell them about the bats and moths nestled in the cotton tree, the guzzle-nuzzle of antennae and stamens.

The more I talk, the more the memory of bird sensations quickens an itch I need to scratch; an itch just beyond my reach.

Neck cricks, twitching.

Feathers flutter beneath the skin.

Fur bristles, yearning for air.

I rub my shoulders, patting them to soothe a twinge there.

But as I go on to describe what I saw and smelled in the cotton tree, I notice Nana cocking her head the better to hear me; Grandma Baby's rubbing her nose, while Aunt Ruby raises an eyebrow. Aunt Clara, face gleaming, peers at the rise and fall of my halo of hair; the dangle twist of curls that shake and flicker with drops of river as I talk.

They watch me. Then, in a single swoop, the four of them lean in, as if they're seeing me for the first time.

'You're your mother's daughter,' says Nana.

'You seem to have enjoyed it…' Aunt Ruby, as surprised by her observation as I am, mumbles: 'She's Sika's daughter, all right.'

'I didn't enjoy all of it,' I reply. Which is true. And yet, when I recall the throb of heartwood, the thrill of crimson-petalled flowers turning to greet the moon, my blood spins, singing.

There's no denying my exhilaration because four pairs of eyes drill into me once again.

I hurry on. I've been raised not to pass on gossip, not to tell tales, yet in describing the nightmare at the core of my journey, I repeat what Ma said about my father. 'I wanted the truth,' I go on, 'so I travelled to her heart's shrine, the flame of her soul.'

Aunt Clara smiles. 'Good girl,' she says. 'Your mother tried to bind you. Even so, you used what I've taught you to interrogate her.'

Grandma Baby agrees. 'I told you your talent would be the making of you, Sheba. You did well.'

They applaud, mesmerised by the tale I'm telling, while Nana, a hand on her chest, moans. She rubs her heart, easing tension there. When her breathing has steadied, and she's able to talk once again, she asks: 'And what did you see in your mother's shrine, grandchild of mine?'

All of them inch closer, so close their curiosity buzzes like bees over pollen. 'Grandchild of mine,' Nana insists. 'What did you see in your mother's flame?'

'What I saw?'

'Must I ask a third time?'

It takes me a moment to grasp what's going on, and when I do, the answer is in Nana's eyes. They're begging for a crumb of comfort, a drop of honey to sweeten the taste of bile on her tongue. After years of Ma's antics, on a day of sorrow and rage, Nana's still looking for the best in my mother. Anything to make up for the havoc she's caused.

I get it. I see it. I am not an okra mouth, yet I cannot lie to Nana. Not now, not ever. 'Grandmother of mine,' I say to her. 'Ma took my father's life as easily as that!' I click my fingers and the image imprinted on my soul of Ma draining my father's blood flares. I bristle with anger as, once again, I see Ma feeding on him and hear her words: *Better to eat a man than marry him.*

'My mother's a monster, Nana. She's sasabonsam. Not only is she cruel, she'd like to claim the power she believes Nana Gyata su gave you. She called you a hypocrite last night! She said you're the biggest hypocrite of us all.'

Word for word I repeat Ma's rant. 'She said that one day, one day, I should ask you how you got rid of your husband, the grandfather I never met. You bore him three children. Then *whoosh*! The man's gone forever.'

Nana's mouth tightens into a thin line of pain. But having started, having fanned a cauldron of rage at my mother, I'm boiling over. Nothing can stop me now. In fact, Mother Crow's utterances spill out of me in her deep, ragged voice.

'Ask your Nana exactly what your great-grandfather Nana Gyata su possessed that made her cleave to him more than her husband. Even in death, he has power. Power, he's passed on to her.'

'Enough!' Nana moans. 'Enough, Sheba!'

I pause and, in that moment of quiet, Grandma Baby's nostrils flare and my skin prickles warning me that Ma's close by. It's almost dusk. The cotton tree will soon be singing its song again. Moths and bats will begin nestling in its branches and darkness will fall.

I feel that itch, that rub beneath my skin.

Feel it. Seize it. Shape it.

I stand tall, fingers balled in a fist, toes cradled by the strength of the earth beneath me as a gust of wind rushes in.

A crow's feather drops at my feet. The scent of river licks my face.

The door slams shut and there she is, hand on her hip, reeking of liquor, chuckling.

She's been listening to our conversation for a while, I reckon, because when Nana says: 'What was hidden is now revealed. How long have you been standing there, Sika?'

Ma replies: 'Long enough to see that my little chick here has found her voice and started squawking at last.'

She laughs. A belly burst of glee that jiggles the length and breadth of her, from swept-up locks to sandaled feet. Wobbling from side to side, slapping her thighs, Ma shrieks: 'Aba! You people should see the look on your faces!'

She giggles, covering her mouth, before a peel of laughter, luscious as sucking a mango in the sun, circles the yard. A mango with a maggot in it.

The worm wriggles to the surface, for as Ma's delight recedes, contempt glitters in her eyes; contempt for me and those she believes beneath her.

As suddenly as she started, Ma stops sniggering. 'You people were talking about me,' she says, folding her arms. 'Tell me, Your Righteousness,' she adds, addressing Nana. 'What have I done wrong now?'

'What haven't you done, my daughter?'

145

17

FROM THAT MOMENT on, Ma calls us 'you people'.

She claims that we're pitted against her, our granite hearts closed to a hard-working woman; a woman with children to care for who's doing everything she can to make a success of her life.

'Where haven't I travelled to sell your trinkets, Ruby? Where haven't I gone to find the best pomade for your clients, Clara? I've journeyed over savannah to the hinterland of the north to find shea butter for those brides you dress. I've scoured markets to find the best Gonja cloth, the finest woven baskets for their trousseaux. And you, Madam Righteousness! What about all those gifts I've given you, Ma? Gifts for you and your hyena of a sister over there, who – every day, every day – spits splinters in my eyes.'

Grandma Baby kisses her teeth.

Ma purses her lips in reply. 'Not a *pesewa* have I spared in buying rice, soap, oil and flour for this house. And *this* is the thanks I get? You take the word of a teenager over the assurances I gave you this morning? Aba! Have you people lost your minds...'

Ma struts up and down arguing with my elders in such a way that they have no chance to retaliate or back me up. Instead, drowning them in torrents of outrage, she forces them to acknowledge every single pesewa she's spent from when she started travelling, years ago, up to now. Until, bludgeoned into submission, her attention pivots to me.

'As for you...' She glares. Incensed there aren't words powerful enough to slam me against the wall, she points a finger. 'You, my daughter, have a traitor's heart.'

There's no point in reasoning with Ma when she's blasting everyone in sight. No point when she's clearly enjoying herself. I refuse to tremble, refuse to take the bait. I've seen the shape and size of her, felt the twine of her strategy, which is to use abuse and anger to silence everyone else, Nana included. I'm not surprised my elders are too exhausted to confront her, because I'm worn out just watching.

I sigh and looking Ma straight in the eye, imagine

she's Snake and like Snake will eventually fold in a heap in front of me. That's when I say: 'I'm not frightened of you any more, Ma. My heart is my own. And from this day on, I swear on the memory of Nana Gyata su, who watches over me, that I shall never sleep beside you again.'

'Swear? Who are you in that filthy nightdress you're wearing, to *swear* such an oath, child? Didn't I shelter you in my womb for nine uncomfortable months? Didn't I suckle you with these breasts here? My bones made your bones, my blood your blood. No one should say such a thing to her mother!'

I adopt her pose: back straight, a hand on my hip. And on my face a smile every bit as scornful as hers.

She rushes forward, palm itching to strike me. I step aside, extending a foot she tumbles over.

The women of the house gasp.

Nana hisses, 'Sheba!'

Grandma Baby winks.

Hands flap. Heads shake, anticipating an eruption of molten rage as Ma, heaving herself up, looks at me, loathing on her face.

My stomach clenches. 'After I saw what you did to my father, I can spit further than I trust you,' I tell her.

'Saw? What you saw was a dream, Sheba. You slept soundly by my side all night.' Ma begins laughing again. There's no scent of mangoes in her mirth this time, only the lash of a whip she'd like to use on my back.

'You know nothing about your father! Nothing!' she snorts. 'Because if you did, you'd thank me. You would go down on your knees every day and say, 'Thank you, Ma! Thank you!'

She imitates a maid, face glowing in gratitude, curtseying to her 'madam'. 'If I were you, I'd be thankful I have no idea how *hopeless* my father was. A useless, kyenkyema man. A dreamer, like you. Big, black and *ugly*. Head in the sky, mouth full of complicated, book-long words. He'd use ten when two would do! Plenty words but no money in his pocket to feed his belly. Ha! Your precious father couldn't pay for this handkerchief even if he'd wanted to!'

Ma mops her brow. Then, her voice drizzling honey, she sidles closer. 'You want to know more about him, don't you, Sheba? No shame in that. Come now. Come to bed, my daughter.' She extends a hand. 'I'll tell you all I remember about the smell and touch of him. His smile… his lips… lips that remind me of yours, little chick.'

Turning my face to hide the shine of tears in my eyes, I bite the inside of my cheek to hold my anger in. For as surely as my mother will change into a crow tonight if she chooses to, this is what happens each and every time she mentions my father. Talons out, a smirk on her face, she enjoys nothing more than pecking at a wound that won't heal: the place in my heart where my father remains.

'Come, child.'

Before I can swallow, hunger loud as a belch betrays me. 'His name, Ma? What was his name?'

Her smile widens. Like her laugh, there's malice on her lips. Even so, my spirit clings to the hope that this time, having revealed more than ever before, my mother will be truthful and deliver.

'Tell her! Tell her his name, Sika!' Grandma Baby urges; a plea taken up by my aunts and grandmother.

'Tell her! Tell her!' they cry.

'Come, Sheba,' Ma replies. 'Bed.'

I shake my head and raising my arms to fend her off, a door slams in my heart. I'm done with the back and forth of my mother's games; the push and pull of frustration whenever I'm snared in her shadow. Not so long ago, I heard Nana say that what destroys us in life isn't darkness, but people who travel in darkness.

'What sort of person travels at night?' I asked.

Without missing a beat, Grandma Baby replied, 'Your mother.'

I now understand what she meant. I may no longer be Ma's little chick, but to me, she'll always be the crow that peck-peck-pecks at my heart until there's nothing left.

That night I sleep in Nana's bed. My forehead, a whisper away from hers, entices her dreams to creep into mine. But before sleep gathered us in her arms and our dreams merged, I asked my grandmother questions I needed answers to, questions about our family.

'Did you ever see your father turn into a lion, fili-fili, with your own eyes, Nana?'

'Yes.' she replied. 'Once and only once. Just before he died, when his will was ebbing away, he no longer controlled his comings and goings. That's when I saw him in his majesty.'

'Did he know you?'

'Of course he knew me! He put his hand in mine. A hand covered in fur. I held him till he died.'

'And when the family buried him, Nana, did they bury a lion or a man?'

'Grandchild of mine, you ask too many questions!'

Usually such a comment would silence me. Not

that night. Anxious to know more, I changed the subject by asking about Ma. When did Nana realise that my mother was different to her other children? My grandmother filled me in while I plaited her hair.

She'd unpicked it at her dressing table mirror before my return home, unleashing her glory in all its splendour. The natural kink of her braids intact, her mane appeared electrified, a spiky crown of white light underlined by the pendant of gold around her neck.

I massaged Nana's scalp, the gift from my ancestor nestled on her lap. She kept touching it, a finger fondling its eyes, a thumb rubbing its mouth as the weight of her age tickled my fingers. Though luxuriously long and white, I sensed frailty in the lightness of my grandmother's hair, as well as fierce determination to protect everyone in her household, Ma included.

Why share a roof with a murderer, I wondered. A serial killer, most probably. Why bother to protect a daughter who had no place in her heart for anyone but herself?

'Never forget, Sheba, my daughter is your mother. Her roots are under this roof, the same as yours. She has a right to be here.'

I hadn't opened my mouth and yet she read me as clearly as leafing through a book. The gift of touch, I was beginning to realise, when combined with a

talent for wisdom, moves in both
directions.

For instance, Nana's mood
contemplating her father and
my mother laced itself around
my fingers, tugging, insisting
I press harder than usual. I
did, and, bit by bit, as the
tension that had gathered beneath
her scalp eased, she smiled at my
reflection in the mirror.

'You're kind and gentle, grandchild
of mine. I hope that one day soon, you'll be as kind to
your mother as I've tried to be. I'm proud of you as
well. Proud of how you stood up for yourself tonight.
But let me warn you, now Sika's seen your strength,
she'll try to crush you.'

'And yet you want me to be kind to her?' I slid a
comb through Nana's hair, carefully untangling it as if
she were a child and I the adult looking after her.

Soft as a sigh, the sadness in Nana swept over me
while she held my gaze.

My arms jerked.

Fingers flexed, unbidden.

The comb fell.

I stepped away from her. It
was only then that I realised the
expression on her face was one

of pity: not for herself, but for me.

'I shall never be like Ma!' I picked up the comb, wielding it like a weapon. 'Never! How can I be when I hate her?'

'You're more alike than you care to admit, Sheba.'

'No! My mother's a soul-eater. She... she...' My tongue faltered, unable to speak the truth unless it crashed out of me. 'She *murdered* my father, probably did away with the fathers of my sisters as well! You said she was *different*, Nana... you said you knew right from the start she was strange.'

Nana pulled a shawl over her shoulders, tucked a cushion behind her back. At last, she said, 'You're right, your mother wasn't as pliant as you were as a child, Sheba. She was exhausting. She still is, of course. But, compared to Ruby and Solomon, your mother was like a star that dazzles the night before a storm. In truth, Sika is the brightest of my three.'

Her description reminded me of a time when my life revolved around my mother. Before she started travelling, Ma was my sun, my moon, my everything, and to be in her shadow was the comfort I wanted most in the world. Had I changed? Or had she?

'Your mother dazzles,' Nana explained, concerned that I hadn't yet caught on. 'That's how she catches her prey: that lilt in her walk, the glossy sheen on her face. Her light hides her darkness, hides confusion and pain. How else would you describe her behaviour today? Or what she did to you last night?'

Nana's eyes needled mine, demanding answers. 'Why did she call you big, black and ugly just now, when you're beautiful, blessed with skin that glows and is smooth as mother of pearl? Darkness feeds her soul, Sheba. My late husband, who dabbled in such things, recognised it straightaway and turned his back on us.'

By now, the prickling sensation gone, I parted Nana's hair into three sections, ready to cornrow.

As soon as I started plaiting, her memory tugged with such force, I saw in quick succession scenes she'd witnessed.

A child grabs liver from a bowl of entrails.

The greedy chomp of teeth as the child eats it raw.

Then, after ripping a purple cloth, a family heirloom, the girl flees, running though fields of corn, to find her twin. 'Solo! Solo! Look what I've found!'

A razor drops into her palm. Mischief on her face, she slices his thigh before saying, 'Have I been very bad today?'

Nana nodded. 'Even as a child she was trouble. Within four years of Sika's birth, my late husband threw us out. He said your mother made him uncomfortable. As if being a parent is always comfortable, always easy, always a joy. Pa Kwesi sensed her power and saw himself. If it hadn't been for Nana Gyata su's kindness all those years ago, my three would never have had a place to call home.'

'So...'

'So, I didn't get rid of my husband as your mother claims, Sheba. He got rid of us. Your mother's never forgiven him.'

'So, why are you asking me to do something she can't do?'

I'd finished plaiting the second cornrow. Nana placed Nana Gyata su's pendant in her jewellery box at the very moment the noise of the cotton tree changed from faint rustling to a moan, serenaded by the crick-crack-twang of ancient bark.

'It's singing us a lullaby,' said Nana, a foot moving to the lilt of the tree's song. 'After today's wahala it wants us to sleep early and dream long. As for your mother, my dear, you have to learn to be as careful with her as I am, because when I'm gone, Sika's going to be *your* responsibility.'

I shook my head, determined to have nothing more to do with my mother as that curious sensation of being buried alive crept over me again. I closed my eyes, clenched my fists, shook my head a second time to calm the hammering in my heart, the noxious stench of soil in my nostrils.

There's no tenderness, as far as Ma's concerned, no kindness whatsoever. Convinced of my cause, my resolve hardened. When it was as tough as an elephant's tusk, I said through gritted teeth, 'I can't, Nana. You said yourself, Ma will try to crush me now. She destroyed my father and as surely as the cotton tree sings before the rains, Ma is going to come after me. I won't have her near me.'

'Maybe if I were your age, I'd think the same.' Touching my hand, Nana stopped me plaiting. 'Promise me,' she said, a finger curled around my thumb. 'Promise you'll listen to Maanu when we visit her this week and you'll consider her advice?'

I promised.

The final cornrow in place, I smoothed Nana's hairline as her eyes sought mine in the mirror. It's not our custom to thank someone after they've done your hair, so Nana beamed at me instead.

I helped her change into a nightdress and after slipping into bed beside her, our foreheads touching, she smiled as her dreams spilled into mine.

18

NANA'S LAUGHTER RIPPLES through our dream of a girl strolling hand in hand with her father. One moment, Nana Gyata su is striding between us on the riverbank. Next, he's purring, his lion's head on my lap as Nana asks him why he's appeared.

'I need to talk to you both,' he says, 'before the rains arrive, drowning us in danger.'

'Danger?' I reply.

He growls, raising his head. 'Danger of the worst kind. Our village divided will destroy the veil that's kept us hidden for generations. Unless we prepare for the challenges ahead, lives are going to be lost. Will you be the plover that picks meat from the crocodile's teeth?'

'What do you mean?' I ask.

It seems impossible, but even as a lion, he appears to

smile at me. A huge shiver of a smile that warms my heart and shakes my soul.

'Will you meet danger with intelligence?' he demands. 'Will you confront lies with truth?'

Nana nods on my behalf, then explains. 'You behave like a plover with your mother, Sheba. You take what you need but when her mouth snaps shut, you're off like a bird. We need you on our side to face what the future's about to bring.'

Fear flickers over my face.

'You're braver than you realise,' says my ancestor. 'I've watched you over the years and talked about you with your grandmother. What's more,' he adds, 'whenever you've seen me prowling the corridors of our home, whether as a man or a lion, you've never once flinched. You've always welcomed me and that's exceptional.'

I stroke the lion's jowls, but as I'm about to bury my face in his mane, he changes yet again. He is younger now, and Nana is no longer an elder, but a young woman, same as me. We lie either side of him, cradled in his arms. My head on his shoulder, I think – is this what having a father feels like? Is this what I've been missing?

Within a heartbeat he says, 'Our parents stay with us, Sheba, even when we think they're gone. They're never far away, even when they seem to be.'

'Will I ever see my father?' I ask him. 'Will he ever come to me in my dreams like you have now?'

'You'll have to wait and see.' He chuckles, a rumble of a laugh, half-way between a purr and a roar; a laugh that reminds me of Aunt Ruby and Nana when they slap their thighs cackling and, bodies shaking, lungs filling with air, I join in because where they are in that moment is the most glorious place in the world. Grandma Baby hugs herself giggling hysterically, Aunt Clara too. And united, rocking back and forth, clapping each other's palms, we tumble to the ground. So that's where our laughter comes from – Nana Gyata su!

I grin and though his voice remains the same, his face becomes that of a lion again. And it is as a lion that he chooses to enlighten me further.

'You've seen it, haven't you, Sheba? Your dream-snake, a being nobody can see but you.'

'Yes,' I admit as my grandmother looks on.

'It's appeared to you for a reason,' he continues. 'It's what we've hidden in our family; the darkness we've tried to shield you from. If you're able to befriend it and talk to it, not only will your gifts of sight and touch flourish, but you'll also have the courage to do what I asked just now: face danger with intelligence; confront lies with truth. But first, you must talk to it.'

Talk to a snake? Disbelief slinks into my bones. 'I am not as courageous as you...' I murmur.

'And yet you've taken on your mother!' The lion's paw turns into a hand, which Nana Gyata su places over mine. 'Listen, child,' he says. 'Next time you see it, do this.'

He leaps to his feet holding aloft what, at first, I think is a heavy blue rope. As it writhes between his hands and then coils around his neck, I realise that what I'm looking at is a cobalt-coloured snake, a reptile with eyes sharp and radiant as sapphires.

Nana Gyata su towers above us, his creature a necklace that unravels, gliding down the length of his arm. He lifts it again, brandishing it like a warrior would a living, magical sword. Then, in a voice loud as thunder before a storm, he says: 'In the same way that a snake sheds its skin, once in a generation a member of our lineage can take on another form and become much more than what we are in flesh. If you choose to, Sheba, you can safeguard our tradition of being a sanctuary for runaways and outcasts, a place where traders in human flesh are unwelcome. Great-grandchild of mine, you can become a champion of our family and village.'

'A champion?' I repeat.

'You have it in you,' he assures me, sensing my uncertainty. 'But let me warn you child, once you embrace the snake you've seen, there'll be no turning back. Once you acknowledge its power and learn how to work with it, you'll see mysteries and beings beyond the scope of human eyes.'

A streak of lightning illuminates Nana Gyata su's body and straightaway the scent of earth after rain floods my nostrils. He smells of home, our village, our river. 'Do you have the courage to fulfil your destiny, child?'

I can't answer him because as soon as he says those words, he vanishes.

19

DREAM-DRENCHED AFTER MY night in Nana's bed, I'm relieved that Ma's off on her travels again. On her departure this morning, tension – a spring coiled around my heart – eases. I fill my lungs with gulps of air and the moment I sense Maybe on our porch, eager to share my dream with him, I'm out of the house, off to school.

Before I utter a word, Maybe pauses, looks at me and says, 'She's gone.'

'You can tell?'

He chuckles. 'You barely breathe when your mother's around, Sheba. She muzzles your breath. She clouds your shine.'

My eyes dwell on his, and as Maybe takes my right hand and places it on his cheek, the sensation that drew me to him the first day we met, sweeps over me again. I'm his finest, his brightest, his very best. Even in my ugly brown-and-yellow school uniform with hair bunched either side of my head, like stepping

from earth to water, shade
to light, the world shimmers
when he's around. In fact,
as I describe fragments
of my dream last night:
the thrill of Nana
Gyata su's presence;
my uncertainty as
to whether I'm
able to meet his
challenge, there's
no skin between us,
because what I feel, Maybe
does as well.

While I talk and our little
fingers link, the current between
us sizzles. Amber eyes glisten, then
darken, molasses-black, as Maybe's
sweetness seeps into me.

'What are you going to do?' he asks.

I search his face for an answer only I can
give.

'You have to decide,' Maybe urges.

As the clamour of bustling school children grows
ahead of us, we stop beneath a banana tree. The faint
rattle of seed pods in a breeze hums in my ears. The
sound circles Maybe before sparking glimmers of
light on his skin.

He drops my finger, frowning. 'Before you decide, perhaps you should see this.'

He opens his rucksack, tears a sheet from a sketchpad that he takes with him everywhere, and hands me a picture.

It's a drawing of me working on Aunt Ruby's hair, Aunt Clara in the background. Ruby, hair almost done, grins delighted, while my teacher, butterfly light and wistful, flutters behind me. I'm tall, loose-limbed, resplendent in a pair of cut-off jeans and a woven batakari top; everyday 'house' clothes portrayed with a deftness that makes me look elegant.

I should be flattered, I know. But what grabs my attention and draws me in is a necklace Maybe's given me: a necklace of green, overlapping scales which resemble those of a snake. Indeed, the beaded clasp, a smooth delicate triangle, reminds me of the shape of Snake's head. So much so, that on closer inspection she seems coiled around my neck.

I haven't yet mentioned Snake to Maybe. How can I share what I don't have words for – a being that excites but terrifies me at the same time? 'Are you able to see her as well?' I ask.

'No,' he replies. 'But they can.' Maybe's talking about his dead-departed, his siblings. 'They're able to appreciate what can't be seen. The bits I glimpse, they help me piece together.'

Even so, I'm puzzled that he can intuit what no

one else in my family can.

'They talk to me when I'm drawing,' Maybe explains. 'They sense things I can't see. Make suggestions. You may be in danger, Sheba.'

I shrug, unsure what to say. If there's one thing I know it's this: in the same way that our little fingers search for each other and link up, my destiny is coupled to Maybe's. So my heart tells me. It also tells me that even if I were to try to hide from him and keep my family's secrets under our roof as Nana advises, it would be easier to stop the sun shining than to turn away from his face.

'Well?' he insists. 'Are you in danger?'

'Nana knows there is danger present – waiting, but what matters is how I face it. My family's spent most of my life trying to protect me from the queen of mischief-making in our house, my mother.'

'They know what she is as well?'

I nod, then hesitate, remembering what Nana mentioned last night.

The truth has different faces. And it rarely smiles.

I remember what Nana said and add thoughts of my own. 'The women of my house have always known about Ma. Deep down, I have as well. They struck a deal with her. She was supposed to let me be, allow me to grow without dipping her beak in me...'

I shiver, and when that door in my heart slams yet again, and I turn my back a second time on the woman whose bones made my bones, there's a tremor in my voice. 'She's my mother.'

Maybe's jaw hardens. 'You don't have to be like her.'

I want to believe him. I need to, but the most important thing I've learned is to appreciate what I'm up against. A mother's might should never, ever be underestimated.

'If it is left to me, I'll go my own way – no problem,' I admit. 'In fact, tomorrow, I'll find out exactly what Ma has on me...'

Maybe folds my hand in his. 'Has she cursed you? Woven a spell over you?'

'I don't know. Whatever she did happened a long time ago. I'll find out tomorrow when my grandmother takes me to see a friend of hers, a diviner, Maanu.'

Pressing my hand gently, Maybe replies, 'Promise me you'll be careful, Sheba. *Promise*,' he says.

I promise.

20

THAT SAME DAY, a whole day without Ma's talons digging into my back, I'm basking beneath the boughs of the cotton tree after school, Ama and Gaza either side of me. A stone's throw away, behind a blur of legs and sandals, Maybe is selling the last of a tray of boflot to our schoolmates. His mother makes the buns and Maybe sells them, sometimes with the help of Better Life, whose brain is big enough now to endure instruction.

Finishing off his boflot, Gaza murmurs, 'Trouble dey come. They dey cook trouble in big, big pot.'

'Who dey cook?' Ama asks, as Gaza licks grease from his lips, savouring the combination of fried, sugared dough in a stomach that craves food.

Aunt Ruby claims that boys around Gaza and Maybe's age are always hungry. They shoot up as quickly as seedlings in the wet season, she says. And like seedlings, if they're not watered regularly with love and food, they grow into men as stunted as her ex-husband. Or worse, they shrivel up and die from the weight of their hopelessness.

'Aren't girls just as hungry?' I once asked her.

'Of course,' she said. 'But you're stronger and can do without food for longer.'

'Not me,' Ama replied. 'I need to chop quick-quick same as they do.'

'Me too,' I agreed.

Aunt Ruby feeds Gaza at least once a day. Even so, though he isn't what I'd call *stunted*, he isn't like other boys his age. But then neither is Maybe.

'Did you not hear my question?' Ama sits up, wiping dust from her hands. 'Who dey cook mischief in big pot?'

'*Madam*.' Gaza jerks his chin at me. 'Sheba's mother and my pa.'

Gaza called her *Madam*, not *Madam Sasabonsam* as he did yesterday. Intrigued, I roll over and sit up cross-legged.

'How can they be cooking trouble when they're not even friends?' I protest.

Gaza hauls himself into a squat and begins tapping the gnarled roots of the tree. 'Yesterday, after we left you at your house, Maybe and I split up. He went back to the river while I walked to our compound.' Gaza continues, his root music underscoring his words.

'When they couldn't find Sheba anywhere. When they couldn't find Maybe as well, they returned to our house and drank cheek to cheek.'

'Cheek to cheek?' I shake my head in disbelief.

'Impossible,' says Ama. 'Madam High and Mighty with your *pa*? Ah!' She slaps her hands, rubbing them as if dusting gossip from her fingers.

I frown. 'They boozed cheek to cheek while your step-ma was in the house?'

'She's travelled to Kumasi. Funeral wahala.' Gaza's hands switch from playing root music to patting his thighs.

Seconds pass, punctuated by the flutter-slap of his body-beat, before he's able to describe what he claims he saw fili-fili, with his own eyes, on the porch of his home.

'First, they quaff Akuffo beer. Two each. Then four tots of akpeteshie – kill-me-quick liquor. *Hmmmm.*'

Gaza's palms move slowly from his thighs to stomach. Stomach to ribs. Ribs to shoulders. In between, he taps his elbows. *Ba-doom. Ba-doom. Slap-slap. Ba-doom.* 'My eyes see red. My stomach turns over until I'm almost sick. Then, when it settles, I put my ear to the wall to hear them better. Whisper, whisper. All they do is whisper-talk and laugh "He-he-he-he". They're plotting mischief, I know it.'

The scent of neem tree blossoms suddenly fills my nostril and sensing that Gaza's ma is present, I touch his knee.

Gaza gulps, stifles a sob, and then, he bashes his

head with his hand as if trying to erase an image he's seen; a memory that won't let him go. His eyes glare at me with the same sheen of spite as yesterday.

Unlike yesterday, words don't leave his mouth until Gaza picks up a stone and rapping again on the roots of the cotton tree's trunk, settling into its beat, he tells his story.

'Before my mother passed,' he says, the fragrance of neem flowers wafting between us, 'the two of them, Madam and my pa, whisper-talked and drank plenty. They hurt my mother. Hurt her so much, day after day she cry-cry.'

'Stop bawling, woman!' Pa says. 'Stop it! Stop it!'

'Pa! Pa!' I yell. 'Leave her! Leave her!

'I holler loud as can be. Loud as if a crocodile's chasing me, snapping at my feet. So loud, Old Man Yankey runs to our house.

'Old Man can't stop Pa. Fetches Aunt Ruby. But not even Aunt Ruby can break the might of Pa's right arm that day until together they grab him. Then, voice deep as a lion, Aunt Ruby roars. She snarls and curses, calling on the gods of our village and Nana Gyata su to protect us. *Boom!* Pa collapses. His turn to cry now, to say sorry and bawl while Ma crawls to her sleeping mat and leaves me without saying goodbye.'

Gaza's never uttered a word of this before. Ama and I have heard rumours. Aunt Ruby's hinted at it more than once, and yet, to see an undercurrent we've lived with gush into the open as it tumbles out of Gaza's mouth is shocking.

Ant-bite tongue paralysed, Ama stares into the branches of the cotton tree, embarrassed. I should be embarrassed as well. After all, it's my mother and aunt Gaza's talking about. His pain hurts my heart as shame turns to grief for Gaza and his mother.

Ma didn't say goodbye this morning. She always bids me farewell, even when she's going to be gone for a few days. Always. After Gaza's revelation, I can only wonder what I'd feel if she disappeared without a word? Would I be happy? Or as upset as Gaza is today?

Mindful that I've got more in common with him than I thought possible, and that like him, I've lost a parent as well, I reach out. 'Chale,' I say. 'Mek I plait your hair?'

Gaza nods. 'What style you dey mek um?'

'Mek I twist um into locks to mek a true Ragga boy from downtown Accra.'

'For sure!' says Gaza. Then, his smile lightening his eyes as Gecko clambers from his pocket on to his shoulder, he adds: 'Inside, me a Ragga boy through and through!'

Every once in a while, when Big Man claps eyes on his son, he likes nothing better than to sit Gaza down and shave off his curls.

Takes a razor, lathers up soap and, before Gaza has time to name the gods of our village, Big Man has made him as ugly as a naked mole-rat. No hair whatsoever! Just a scalp with nicks where the blade has nipped.

'An ugly tree can still give sweet sap,' said Aunt Clara the first time she saw Gaza's razed scalp. What she meant was that despite Big Man's behaviour and shouts of 'Sakora! Sakora!' – Bald head! Bald head! – that greet Gaza as soon as he steps out of his yard, what's inside Gaza, what he chooses to give to the world could still be amazing.

Luckily for me, at the moment, Gaza's hair is between cuts. Too short to plait doesn't mean I can't style it somehow. First, I dip my fingers in a special concoction created by Aunt Clara for her brides – baobab oil – a healing oil guaranteed to soothe hesitant brides-to-be; those whose hearts are as melancholy as hers.

Then, I dribble beads of oil between shafts of Gaza's hair. Slowly, slowly I massage it on to a scalp that's so parched it's crying with hunger. I soothe its craving, feeding famished hair follicles and skin. As I work my fingers over Gaza's head, I'm sensitive to subtle shifts within him: an easing of threads tangled around his heart. As one dissolves, so does another until Gaza's chest swells contented.

'This be good-o! Mek you tickle my head plenty, Sheba,' he says. 'Mek you tickle um today and tomorrow forever.'

In that moment of satisfaction Gaza relaxes and pictures slide from him to me. Gaza and his mother. She smells, as she always does, of neem tree flowers: light as a breeze, fragrant and sweet. More images emerge: snapshots of family life from a time before Aunt Ruby returned to our village, her heart broken, her marriage over. Yet here she is, alive in Gaza's mind, pounding maize with his mother.

The two of them sing, wooden pestles slamming a mortar, thumping, grinding, hips jiggling, legs moving, one in front of the other, in a sister-dance of friendship. Sweat drenches faces bright with laughter as Gaza, laughing with them, claps his hands to the beat of their song.

Suddenly, the expression on his face changes. He's looking at something he doesn't want to; something that's hurting him so much he's cowering under a table. Shivering, hands covering his ears, his soul's flame flutters towards mine.

I try to make out what's terrified him. Delve, peer, but I can't see a thing.

I close my eyes, and as I do so, I sense shadows

hovering between Gaza and I as the aroma of neem flowers rubs my nose once again.

I rub the soft ridge between Gaza's hair and temple. I rub and *whoosh*! A nightmare of rage fills my vision. Rage on Big Man's face as he shoves his wife aside to get to his child.

The closer his hand, the more Gaza retreats, until, back against the wall with no place left to hide, his tears fall.

Within the hour, I'm almost done. Not quite, because while I'm working, creating a new Ragga boy look for Gaza, while I'm straightening strands of his hair with the tooth of a comb and then twizzling them into tiny, tight twists with hair gel, I'm thinking of my conversation with Nana Gyata su last night. Whether I decide to follow my great-grandfather's example or not, there's one thing I know for sure. I shall never follow in Ma's footsteps and become a soul-eater. I'd rather do anything than be like her. I'd rather be doing this – weaving magic with my fingers.

With every twist in Gaza's hair, sparks sizzle from my fingers, fanning his soul's flame. I'm bigging him up, making his beauty shine as much as his mother did. The moment his thoughts turn to her, turn to the last time she combed his hair and said: 'My boy. My handsome boy,' the scent of neem flowers trails about him.

Her shade hovers, drawn to his memory of her. Gaza smells her fragrance as clearly as I do. She doesn't try to touch him this time. No, already on her way to the village where her ancestors dwell, she pauses to smile at her son one last time.

And Gaza's hair is done.

21

BEFORE THE RAINS come, when the little rains have been and gone and seedlings of maize and cassava are sprouting, the sky grumbles with clouds. Thunder rolls, lightning flashes, but not a drop of rain falls to satisfy earth's craving for water. This is our in-between season, a time of waiting when the river recedes. This is the season the cotton tree sings.

The tree's song echoes in my ears next day as Nana, Aunt Clara and I begin our journey to the forest. It hums as we glide in a dugout canoe – Nana and my aunt at one end, me on a plank opposite them, Boat Man at the stern. He guides us upriver to where Nana's arranged to meet Maanu at the river goddess's shrine. Deep in the forest, it was built by Maanu's husband, a priest, Okomfo Granpa – so-called because the power of his wisdom is way beyond his years. The shrine is an hour and a half away.

We set off before dawn, the river dark as night; velvet dark, ripples streaming beneath us. The motor at the stern chugs and splutters, a restless dog snapping at everyone. As the day brightens, fog on the river clears, revealing banks overflowing with plants. Behind them, gigantic hardwood trees reach for the sky, unfurling ribbons of birdsong. Monkeys leap from tree to tree. Doves fly overhead, pigeons serenade us, while higher up, hidden by trees and clouds, kites whistle.

Suddenly a murder of crows appears. They swoop on us, cawing and then banking as if determined to drive us back.

Nana shrugs, shakes her head. *Don't worry*, her eyes tell me. *I'm with you.*

Out loud she says, 'Boat Man is used to the ways of our river. He'll make sure we reach the shrine safely.'

Nana rummages in Aunt Clara's basket, gives me a piece of bread, a banana, then opens a packet of biscuits. She offers them to everyone before she starts nibbling one herself.

Above us the cacophony of crows continues to dive and caw as the river churns, splashing the canoe, jolting it back and forth.

This is Ma's doing. Ma and her brethren. Ma trying to stop me from seeing Maanu the diviner.

Convinced this is about me, I try to get up. As I do so, the canoe lurches sideways and I fall on to Boat Man.

He steadies me, eases me back to my seat, as the sky swarms with a cloud of crows and ravens.

'Boat Man, what's happening?' asks Aunt Clara. 'You dey make me sick plenty.'

'River spirits,' Boat Man replies. 'They fit make the river tremble in this section. I beg you, Madam Clara, wait small, small. Soon the river be smooth and calm.'

The canoe rocks. As the river roils, the crows retreat into the branches of a gigantic wawa tree where, perching in rows, they watch us sail by.

We arrive at the shrine when the sun's heat is still mellow. I help Nana and Aunt Clara out of the canoe. Boat Man stays with it while we trail behind Maanu and her granddaughter, the shrine girl, to the river goddess's sanctuary.

Hidden in a grove of fruit and hardwood trees, there's no altar to speak of, just a circular space surrounded by the lush foliage of banana, guava and lemon trees. Beyond them, at the shrine's outer rim, concealing it from intruders, are taller, older trees – rosewood and mahogany. A breeze rustles leaves, swishing them back and forth like the murmurs of our ancestors. Nana Gyata su! I think of him and straightaway the murmurs dissolve in the purr of a satisfied lion.

Once Nana has introduced me to Maanu, the diviner pours libation, inviting those who walked before us to honour us with their presence, while the shrine girl plays music from a bamboo flute. She plays the same note again and again until we're settled on raffia mats in the shade of a guava tree.

That's when Nana describes my situation to Maanu. She tells her of my gift of touch and how I'm wary of Ma even though, at times, I've cleaved to her shadow. Nana goes on to inform the diviner of the sensation I described of being buried alive and what our ancestor revealed in our dream the other night: our village is in danger.

Maanu's nutmeg-brown face radiates kindness. She listens, nodding, coal-black eyes twinkling, and when Nana finishes by saying: 'Help us understand the unseen hand that's driving these events. Help me protect my grandchild,' the diviner touches Nana's hand in a gesture of support.

'Is this the daughter of your baby-last, the daughter you wanted advice about?'

'Yes,' says Nana. 'She's Sika's daughter.'

'How are her other children?'

'They're with their uncle in Accra as you suggested.'

'Good,' says Maanu. 'And Sika?'

Nana sighs, shaking her head. 'Whatever's in her grows as she advances in years. If I could, I would stop her. I'm too tired to now.'

Though younger and smaller than Nana, their conversation tells me that my grandmother's been consulting Maanu for years – long enough for them to respect and have grown fond of each other. Maanu chuckles and, turning to me, her eyes closed, she opens a hand in front of my face. Her fingers tremble. Her hand judders until she removes it and one after the other, cracks her finger joints.

'Your granddaughter sees,' says Maanu. 'She sees what most of us can't. Your mother's watching you, girl, and you know it.'

'Yes,' I reply.

'Have you seen your dream-snake yet?'

'I have,' I tell her.

'Even better. You're going to need her to face what lies ahead.'

The diviner retrieves a clay pot from the base of the guava tree, which her granddaughter fills with river water. When the pot is full to the brim, Maanu places seven pebbles in a basket and passes it to me.

'Choose three,' she says. 'One will show us the face of whoever's bound you and stolen your destiny. The second will indicate how to undo the spell, while the third will reveal your future.'

The stones, polished clean by the river, gleam in the morning sunshine. Flecked by light shining through the leaves of the tree sheltering us, the pebbles seem to pulse with life. The first I choose is dark as granite.

The second is a moist reddish brown, the colour of earth after rain. The third pebble, bright as a gemstone, flashes green and yellow – its green the emerald of Snake's eyes, the yellow the tawny gold of our family emblem.

'Put the first one in the pot,' Maanu instructs.

I feel the warmth of the pebble on my palm as the shrine girl behind us begins an incantation to the river goddess, asking for her guidance to untangle deeds hidden from human eyes.

The girl chants.

The pebble drops.

River water whirls, and all at once, what seemed murky clears into shapes and shadows which reveal themselves in a flurry of scenes.

22

IT TAKES TIME for my eyes to adjust, for like stepping from sunlight to shade, what unfolds occurs on a night so dark it's velvet black.

A woman slips into a garden, a baby on her back. The whites of her eyes flicker. Clutching a bag, she slopes through shadows to hide beneath the boughs of a frangipani tree.

The tree sighs as she hunkers beneath it. It sighs again when the woman removes a trowel from her robe and starts digging. Down, down she digs, past knots of roots to the tree's main arteries.

She opens the bag, pulls out a mud-cloth pouch and slides the sleeping baby on to her lap.

'*Blood of my blood,*' *she says,*
'*In this pouch I place the cord that binds a child to its mother,*
The cord that bound you to me!
To it I add:
Clippings from my nails,
Hair from your comb and
Spittle laced with bile for my brother's wife.'

The woman mutters her spell, and fear clutches my throat so I can scarcely breathe. I may not be able to glimpse her face, but I know that voice better than the skin on the palm of my hand. It's Ma. Ma talking to me – the baby on her lap – as she channels malice towards my uncle's wife. Why, in the name of all that's good and true in our family, in the name of the gods of our village, why is she using me and my body parts to cast her spell?

I must have asked the question out loud because Maanu replies, 'She's binding you to achieve her goal. She's taking what's yours, and yours alone to harm her rival.'

Ma drops her nail clippings and a whisper of my baby hair in the pouch. For good measure she adds a curl from the crown of my head. Then she spits in the pouch three times, and twirling it into a ball, buries it in the hole, crooning as if singing me a lullaby that I'm hearing now, years after the event.

'*Bone of my bone,*
  May your soul burn the woman who sleeps by my
brother!
  May you steal her fate when
  With teeth steeped in venom
  You bite her.'

The tree shudders and as the hatred blazing in Ma's heart blisters mine, I gasp, rubbing my chest.

What has my uncle's wife done to her, I wonder. What could have happened between them for her to be the target of Ma's spite? Questions scurry through me while the bark and branches of the tree creak, gifting the scent of frangipani to the plants around it.

Tainted by what Ma's said, the perfume curdles over a column of lilies and drifts to a mango tree. A mango drops, and rolling through a grove of guavas, settles at the foot of a palm tree.

I watch appalled as Ma's hatred coils up the palm's trunk, and tumbling over fronds, latches on to windows. Slowly, silently, the house absorbs Ma's prayer. Walls whisper it along corridors, across marbled floors, until every brick in every room bristles, and malevolence snakes through the mansion.

I watch memories curled in crannies stir. Mahogany bookcases screech. Memories pressed between the pages of books surface, and quickening into ghosts, float upstairs.

There, they gather in a room where the mistress of the house, tossing and turning, sleeps. She opens her eyes. Sees a shape forming above her. A knife. Blinks. Sits up. Looks again.

On the knife's blade she makes out a face, a girl's face.

Aunt Lila screams.

The moment she shrieks, I do as well.

It may be years later.

I may be in the safety of the river goddess's shrine, seeing what Aunt Lila saw, but I can't help my shriek and sob, because the face on the blade is mine.

'Hush, Sheba,' Nana says. 'Hush.'

I'm too distraught to hide my distress, too terrified to pretend otherwise. Ma intends to use me to destroy someone I haven't even met. How's she going to do it? What can I do to stop her?

'Calm yourself,' orders Maanu. 'This is a time to think and plan. The time for wailing is long gone. Be the woman you're about to be, Sheba, and compose yourself.'

I close my eyes, stem my tears, and even as every fibre in my being trembles with shame and horror now that Ma's plan has been revealed, I seize the moment.

Focus, Sheba, focus, I tell myself.

My mind quietens. I listen to the shrine girl's music. Her prayer over, she's weaving a song to the river goddess on a bamboo flute. She teases out the same three notes again and again, in such a way that the air seems to vibrate, bathing the shrine in the luminous light of early morning. The more I listen, the more the shrine speaks to me, easing my soul.

'Now,' says Maanu, 'put the second and third stones in, one after the other.'

I do as I'm told.

This time the water takes on the reddish-brown hue of wet earth. A few seconds later another change occurs, for as the second pebble pulses, the liquid froths. Heat exudes from the pot as if its contents are simmering. Slowly the water darkens, becoming black as pitch before it glows red in a cauldron of blood.

Nana places her hand over mine. Aunt Clara strokes my fingers, while Maanu, observing the signs and wonders in her pot, moans. I'm almost certain she's seen what I glimpsed in my dreams of crows circling the roof of our house. Pupils dilating, Maanu glances at Nana, who nods.

The boiling subsides. The water clears, and our family emblem ripples to the surface. Only now, coiled around the lion's neck, her scales shimmering, is Snake. Her eyes open and as they fix on me, a snarl of fur crawls beneath my skin. Fingers and feet whorl with claws and in that instant, I see a she-lion racing through savannah in the midday sun. She turns mid-stride, catches sight of me and a spark of recognition kindles. That's when the lion in our family emblem roars. It roars so loudly that its call reverberates around the shrine until a surge of feline power rushes through my heart and I can't help but reply. Heart and soul awake to the wild, I howl, a lioness on her way home.

23

ON MAANU'S ADVICE, Aunt Clara travels before the sun rises to Accra, to dig up and retrieve what's mine. That same morning, I meet Maybe in Zongo and, hand in hand, we stroll to the river. It's not the first time we've played truant, but by my reckoning, it's likely to be the last. Events are moving faster than I can grasp. So fast, in fact, that the one thing I'm able to think about is how to stop Ma once and for all.

'Maanu and Nana say I should claim my power,' I tell Maybe. 'Only then will I have a chance of defeating her.'

He shrugs.

'What else can I do?'

He now stares at me as if somehow, I'm lacking. His eyes search mine, revealing more with their questions than a year of words would: I'm a girl from a house of plenty; a princess in a mansion; the girl who never goes hungry and yet somehow, somehow, this girl hasn't the wit to look beyond her cocoon?

'We could leave this place… go elsewhere,' Maybe explains.

That's what he says, though we both know he's not in a position to leave Salmata and Better Life behind. 'In time I can come back for them…'

'My mother will find us, follow us…'

'And so? Where I come from, we believe that the only way to deal with soul-eaters is to destroy them. If we don't lynch them, we send them to live with others of their kind in camps.'

I drop Maybe's hand. 'You want me to murder my mother when you wouldn't let people who pursued Salmata harm a hair of her head?'

'My mother isn't a witch.'

'You think a daughter can kill her mother?' I clench my fists, repelled. Shaking my hair loose, I bunch it into a topknot and ask: 'Could you butcher your mother?'

'My mother doesn't eat souls,' Maybe replies, his gaze holding mine until, shrugging, once again he allows his dead-departed to flit over his face to take the measure of me.

They whisper, giggling, infected by the boldness of my stride, the skip and bounce in my body.

The spirits of the dead are not dissimilar to those of the living, I realise. Curiosity kindles interest and Maybe's shadows seem to appreciate that sometimes, hoping for the best, focusing on it to push dread to one side, can make all the difference when getting ready to confront a mother such as mine. Focus on fear and you've lost the battle before it begins. Either that, or you'll end up dead like my father, your light snuffed out completely.

This morning, Grandma Baby caught a whiff of danger on the breeze. Ma's on her way home. 'If my nostrils are to be trusted, your mother's returning with barrels of trouble strapped either side of her,' she said. 'And when I say trouble, Sheba, I mean trouble tall as a giraffe walking hand in hand with Sister Strife.'

'Strife? How much strife?' I'd asked.

'Double trouble. Trouble venomous as a wife wielding a knife,' quipped Grandma Baby. 'Believe me, Sheba, this house will not sleep easy when your mother returns.'

'Show some courage, sister!' Nana mopped beads of sweat off her brow. 'Courage is the fruit of a decision of the heart. Sheba and I have made our decision; so have Ruby and Clara. We've plucked the fruit and are eating it a bite at a time.'

Nana winked at me, savouring a slice of mango as its flavour melted on her tongue. I grinned while Grandma Baby snapped: 'Who's been telling you for years that the mischief-maker in our midst should be dealt with? Who's been saying that daughter of yours is going to be the end of life as we know it, if we're not careful? Yet your solution is to take this child to a diviner – as if Maanu has an answer to the mess we're in. Take her to Accra, sister. Let Solomon look after her until we sort Sika out once and for all.'

'Solomon is doing everything he can already... trust me...'

Surprised at the tussle between my grandmothers, I looked from one to the other.

'I trust my nose,' Grandma Baby snorted, tapping the menace-sniffing bump on her face. 'It tells me that I should be more concerned about *you*, sister, than this child here.'

'I am not a child!'

My grandmothers gave me one of their 'You'll always be our baby' looks. A look of tenderness that burrows beneath the skin to unearth the truth of my soul.

They gazed at me and then Nana, touching my shoulder, said: 'Thank you for listening to Maanu yesterday, Sheba. Now that you've heard her advice, do you understand what to do?'

I nodded. 'What about you?'

'Grandchild of mine, do whatever's required to protect our family's honour. Don't worry about me. I'm ready for what's coming...' She fluttered her fan, exhausted by our trip upriver yesterday and the weather today.

It was stifling inside and out. Hot and humid, so that breathing was like trying to suck air through a sponge. It was the time of year when everyone can sniff the promise of rain and believes that as soon as it arrives the air will clear.

I collected leftovers from our breakfast of mangoes and pineapple for a picnic with Maybe. I wrapped portions of kenkey and fish. Scooped freshly ground pepper and tomatoes into a carton. Then parcelled them up in a rucksack, added a flask of water, and headed to Zongo.

My plan? To wallow in the calm before the storm in the certain knowledge that what Grandma Baby's nose had ferreted out was true. Determined to break me, Ma was conjuring up a storm of magic. I felt it my bones. But until her return, I intended to spend my time with my forever friend.

'Wallow' is what Maybe and I do when we visit our haven on a bend of the river. Hidden by reeds and mangrove trees, it's where he taught me how to swim, how to gut and grill fish. It's the place we drift to share stories; the haven we go to whenever we need to talk.

Today there are two little egrets fishing on the far side of the river. Their elegance unruffled by our presence, they ignore us as I strip out of my clothes and dive in. Maybe follows.

The water's cool, velvety. I fill my lungs and

plunging deeper still, circle Maybe's legs until he joins me underwater. I surface, flip on to my back and eyes closed, float wherever the current takes me.

An egret trills. Another, quick as a dragonfly, catches a fish and gulps it down.

I'm filled with yearning for Maybe as he swims towards me. The closer he comes, the more I want him. *More*, my heart urges. *More*.

The current between us surges and soft as a dream, Maybe's on to me. That yearning call must be in him as well, for he kisses my cheeks, my lips. We dive underwater, surface, and any trace of our talk of killing and leaving this place is gone. Cleansed by the river, we're holding hands. Maybe leads me to the riverbank, we clamber up, and collapse in a heap on a raffia mat.

I stroke the curve of his cheeks and lips. His hand caresses my shoulder, the back of my neck. Pulls me closer and any softness in me gives way to feelings so urgent, they threaten to tip me over.

I pause. Search the gleam in his eyes, touch his hair and as I taste the lake of kindness in him, I press my lips against his, savouring skin, fingers, breath, every bit of him.

Tongues curl and glide in a dance of joy: then, teeth clashing, I nip his lip and taste blood. I shiver, for in that instant, my heart capsizes, and I see the lioness again. Neck outstretched, she's lapping at a pool of water. At a lick of blood, she raises her head and growls.

I pull away as Mother Crow's words return to me. *Better to eat a man than marry him.*

'What if… what if…' I stutter.

Before I'm able to drag my thoughts into the open, Maybe catches them. 'You are not your mother,' he assures me. 'You're nothing like her…'

'Are you sure?'

He pulls me into his arms. My heart soars with his, his breath merges with mine and I'm reminded of what I discovered the first day I met him: we belong.

After we've eaten our picnic and gorged ourselves on kisses, we play a new game.

'What do my lips taste of?' asks Maybe.

'You taste of guava,' I tell him. 'And mine?'

'After you've eaten pepper and fish? Or before?'

I pinch his cheek. 'Before!'

'Ah, your lips are like the inside of a watermelon, cool and lush.'

'Eeeei! Boyfriend, your romance-talk be fine-oh!

And my tongue?'

'Bitter-sweet, like sour-sop. And mine?'

'The same, only I tasted star apples.'

Maybe laughs, and so do I, until the scrape and squawk of a crow reminds me that Ma will soon be home. I tug the lobe of his ear. 'You have to go now. Ma's coming and I need time to get ready.'

'Get ready for another tongue-lashing? Is it worth it, Sheba?' He sits up and taking hold of my hands, gentles my fingers as he says: 'Come home with me. Forget this craziness. Let it be.'

'I can't! Nana and I must face her. There's no other way to defeat her. It'll be worth it. You'll see.'

Maybe doesn't agree. A shutter rolls over his features, sucking any trace of emotion from his eyes. Switches off. Click! In less time than it takes to welcome a stranger to our village and say: 'Akwaaba,' he makes it clear as the day is bright that he wants no part in my 'craziness'.

He hauls a clump of driftwood on to his lap, tracking the groove of its contours with a forefinger. Lifts it up. Turns it upside down, and seeing a shape within it, he pulls out a penknife and begins hacking.

Aunt Ruby bought him that knife. She pays for his sketchpads and has been dropping hints recently that she'd like to help Maybe develop his craft when he's finished school.

Last time we came to our haven, I told him that he

reminds my aunt of one of the sons she left behind; the son she aches for. And yet my friend wants no part in our *craziness*. Huh!

My thoughts flow and catching their drift, because there is no skin between us when it matters, Maybe pauses. Breathes in, out. Breathes heavily, mightily, blowing fragments of wood shavings away from him.

A glint of pride lightens his face. 'My mother may be poor,' he says, 'but she is not a witch. She is not.'

'While I am?'

'Believe me, Sheba, what you're doing is dangerous, deadly. Don't go any deeper than you have already.'

He places the palm of his right hand on top of his left, imploring me to think again. 'I beg you, Sheba.'

Mind made up, I shake my head.

'Isn't what you weave with your hands enough?' he asks. 'Any more and a time will come when people may accuse not just your mother, but you too.'

I shrug, unsure where the path I'm on is taking me. It's pulling me away from Maybe while binding me closer – if not to Ma – to my family. Nana needs me in her corner. Nana Gyata su claims that the village does as well. This I know. But there's something else, something gnawing at my heart that Maybe doesn't understand. He didn't see what I did at Maanu's – that river of blood churning in her pot. I have to protect my grandmother, and the mystery that keeps our village hidden, from what lies ahead.

'Maybe, you have to go *now*.'

The shutter down again,
he continues whittling.

'I'm not going
anywhere,' he tells
me. 'I'm here to
watch your back,
make sure you're
OK, even if you think
you don't need me.'

'I have to be alone to do this.'

'Sheba.' He whispers my name,
closing his eyes as if I'm a source
of sorrow. Whispers: 'Sheba,'
again, as if I'm someone who's
lost to him. 'You have no idea
what you're messing with. Your
family won't have told you, so
I will. You dabble in these things at
your peril. Once you're in it, there's always a price to
pay. I'm going nowhere.'

I fold my arms. 'Same here.'

I'm going to sit this out, going to wait long enough
for Maybe to grow tired and leave. I have to, because
by my reckoning, this is the only place on our stretch
of the river that's completely secluded. Nana Gyata
su's instructions were clear: to claim my power, I have
to be by the river, far from prying eyes.

The sun, still warm, is beginning to dip. If I'm lucky, there's at least an hour and a half of light before dusk. Once dusk settles, night falls quickly, shrouding everything. I know myself well enough to realise that I don't have the courage to do what I've agreed to do in darkness.

I glare at Maybe. He may not be as proud as I am at times, but he's fiercely protective. Has to be, otherwise Aunt Ruby wouldn't have asked him to keep an eye on me after we met. The way he's sitting there working on his carving, when I need space and time to myself, is almost more than I can bear.

'You're as cruel as red pepper on a cut,' I snarl. 'Meaner than Gaza at his worst. Meaner than Big Man. You're kobi mean, mean as spit.'

He doesn't look up – just twitches his mouth in a half-smile that says: *You're going to have to try a lot harder than that, Sheba, if you want to shift me.*

I pack my rucksack, pretend I'm about to stomp off.

Pays no attention. Keeps whittling and whistling, happy as an over-fed cockerel in a coop of hens.

I hold my nerve. Hold on to my anger, honing it razor-sharp and bright. When it's about to slice me unless I leap on Maybe and tear him apart limb by limb, he turns to me, surprised that I'm contemplating such a thing.

Turns, and as soon as I feel the kiss of his eyes on

me, the ebb and flow between us drags us together, and I change tack.

'I don't think I can do this if I have to fight you as well. Help me, Maybe. We're alike, you and me. You see your dead-departed, while I was born with magic in my blood. What I'm about to do is not crazy at all. It's family lore passed from one generation to the next. Please, go. But remember, even when you're away, you're here.' I tap my head. 'Forever and always.'

He pulls me towards him and as our foreheads touch, I sense his frustration and feel the sting of hurt pride.

'Here.' He drops his latest offering on my lap. 'Tomorrow,' he says.

'Tomorrow,' I reply.

Maybe's gift is a rough carving of the head of a snake. The head is large and triangular, its mouth open, revealing jagged fangs. Disappearing between them, a smudge in the wood, is the dark shape of a girl.

I don't need a soothsayer to explain the danger Maybe thinks I'm in. He's told me already. But seeing my predicament through his eyes, helps me understand it as he does, and unnerves me. I shiver, I feel a spark of flint in my soul. It's the spark of my ancestor who tells me that having come this far, it's better to face danger with courage, than to live frozen by fear.

24

I WAIT UNTIL Maybe has gone before following Nana Gyata su's instructions.

To begin, I recall the shrine girl's music, the strange mood she created of quivering air and leaves. Once I've captured it, everything around me hums with life and I imagine myself playing the same notes of the girl's flute. I play them again and again to relax mind and body.

Heartbeat slows to a crawl. I breathe slow as a snail sipping morning dew. I breathe and bit by bit, like a flower turning towards the sun, my soul opens to the goddess.

At this time of day her river realm of water and foliage dazzles. The tangled roots of mangrove trees, fanned by flurries of leaves overhead, serenade her. The swish of palm fronds dance to the rhythm of her waves. I listen, and glide into a state of reverie.

'Now,' Nana Gyata su tells me. 'Summon your dream-snake.'

From the depth of my being words surface, and half-singing, half-pleading, I call her.

'Through stardust and desert
Dream-snake come to me.
In drought and in harvest
Dream-snake be with me,
In savannah, in forest,
Light and darkness,
Stay with me dream-snake
Forever.'

I summon her at the golden hour of dusk, and as I do so, a grey-headed sparrow chirps, digging its beak into the ground.

I appeal to my dream-snake a second time.

Swifts dive into the branches of a palm tree beyond, while along the river, a blue-breasted kingfisher flashes its chest.

'Focus, Sheba. Focus.' Nana Gyata su's voice fuses with mine.

I inhale. Whispers of wind tickle my fingers and toes. Wind kisses the lobes of my ears and cheeks, anointing my skin in a scent of musk: the scent of the river goddess. Her breath fills me as I summon my dream-snake a third time.

In the hush that follows, I hear her before I see her. A crackle creeps over parched grass. She hisses, slithering over wilting ferns and reeds.

I wait. Wait until the setting sun glazes me and eyes and skin aflame, my haven glows. I wait and softly, softly the hissing comes closer, revealing Snake in rippling scales of green and gold. Emerald eyes fixed on me, she slides closer.

I don't look at her. Not yet. Eyelids lowered, I murmur the final words of the summoning.

'Dream-snake, dream-snake,
Be my spirit guide
Dream-snake, dream-snake,
Be my sister-bride
My touchstone and pride,
Now and always.'

As soon as she's close enough, I meet her gaze, and quick as a cat stand up and raise her to the darkening sky. Legs astride, hands trembling, inviting her once again to be my guide, she writhes, sending waves of energy through me. She twists and turns and with every twirl of her tail, every shimmer of her scales, she fills me with surges of power so tremendous they swell into a tornado.

Her embrace loosens my hair and lashing it skyward, she binds me to earth, sky and water. The more she loops and hoops, the more her strength enters my bones and sinews. Blood pumps. Muscles stretch. Heart on fire; I can lift mountains now! Leap over rivers. Run through savannah and desert. I'm sprinting and jumping, a queen of the forest, wild as the whirlwind encircling me.

In the storm and fury of that moment, the snarl of fur and paws surges and Snake coils around my neck. The wind's embrace enfolds me, pummelling my limbs until I tumble on hands and knees.

Bones crack and creak, shifting shape.

Skull slopes leonine.

Claws spread.

Whiskers twitch, while nose and cheeks fur tawny pelt.

Faster than the swish of a tail, the wild breaks free, and girl yields to lioness. I prance in the fading light of day in praise of the river goddess. The moon's scythe in the sky glistens, gambolling with me. We dance and leap. Indeed, we're still dancing when a leaf twitches in the undergrowth.

I sniff, pad closer.

Hidden behind a brushwood thicket, a pair of dark molasses eyes marvel.

I see him, remember the taste of his blood in my mouth, and as my mother's words return, her rage pierces my heart.

25

MA'S HOME WHEN I get back.

She sees me and wrinkles her nose. 'You smell of Zongo,' she says. 'You've been with that Fulani boy again. His scent is all over you. *Kai!*' She pinches her nostrils in a gesture that insults me as it pushes me away.

No hugs and kisses from her today.

No nuzzling of noses or a pat on the arm.

'*Don't mind her*,' Grandma Baby mouths.

I don't need anyone's advice on that score. After years of living in Ma's shadow, I'm as nimble as an egret foraging between the legs of cattle when it comes to dicing and dancing with Sasabonsam. I shrug, ignoring Ma's jibe. What matters is that with every breath I take, I'm getting to where I need to be to hobble her.

The thought zips through me, and as if sensing a scorpion at her feet, Ma scuttles upstairs.

'I told you she'd bring trouble with her and she has.'

My junior grandmother sucks in air. Head tipped sideways, she says: 'Cat. You smell of cat, Sheba.'

She lifts my arm, sniffing the aroma at my elbow. 'Earth, water and sky. But there's something else.'

Grandma Baby takes me in, probing the glow on my river-kissed face. She notes the amber sheen in my eyes. On the little finger of my left hand is a green ring.

She can't see it, but sensing it, Grandma Baby appreciates what I have to keep hidden from Ma and everyone else: my sister-bride disguised as a band, a circle, which when I rub, transforms into Snake.

My junior grandmother hugs me. 'You've found your dream-snake, your living talisman, at last,' she says, naming the change in me. 'Don't let anyone take it away from you, baby girl. Keep it close to your heart at all times. Keep it well hidden.'

Within an hour, Ma's presence has cast a pall over the house. What was light and carefree when she was away has gone. The air is flecked with dust. Walls hiss, chairs creak, and when Ma drags a rattan chair to the veranda outside, it screeches in protest.

First chairs, then a keg of palm wine are hauled out of doors. Finally, a table, a set of calabashes to drink from, and it's clear to anyone who dares look the direction Ma's evening is about to take.

She opens the keg. Fills a calabash with palm wine and drinks. Once the wine is in her stomach, she burps, before moaning, as if the weight of the world is on her shoulders. She's half-way through her second drink, when Big Man and his friends appear carrying bottles of akpeteshie.

'Sika is being Sika,' Aunt Ruby sighs.

Panic glimmers over Aunt Clara's face like the reflection of flames in the eyes of an antelope. Weary after a daytrip to Accra, her mission accomplished, she can feel our evening teetering as well as I can. Doesn't take much to hear trouble inching closer, to feel her crackle at the back of the neck before she burns you. Ma's dousing our house in petrol before she sets it alight.

'Someone, anyone,' Nana yells. 'Tell my daughter to stop laughing like a hyena.'

Eyes swivel. Auntie Ruby gapes at Grandma Baby. Grandma Baby at Aunt Clara who, doe eyes filling with tears, turns to me.

I shake my head. 'She's your sister,' I tell Aunt Ruby.

In a heartbeat she replies: 'And you, araba, are the youngest at our table.' Her hand grazes my shoulder, patting the sleeve of a woven batakari dress I'm wearing. She gathers the folds in her fingers, then looks at me askance.

A frown griddles my forehead because in our house, it's always the youngest who runs errands. Always me.

I get up. Aunt Ruby beckons me back but before she can stop me, I close the dining room door.

Instead of going on to the veranda to speak to Ma and her friends, I make my way to her bedroom. If I'm going to stop her wreaking havoc on Nana and me; if I'm to stop her burning our house down and our village as well, I need to track down her talisman: the enchantment she uses to hunt her prey and become Mother Crow. Mine is Snake. With Snake's help, I intend to find the source of Ma's power.

I tiptoe upstairs and slink down the corridor avoiding every floorboard that squeaks. Ma's bedroom, beside Nana's, is usually left unlocked when she's home. I loiter outside trying to imagine the most likely hiding place for Ma's charm.

I turn the door handle.

'Go inside now,' says Snake.

I push the door open and we're in.

After a few breaths to take stock, for eyes to adjust to the darkness within, I rub my ring. Snake glides free and weaving in and out of my thoughts, she coils around my arm. She slithers down my legs and over my feet. Wriggling up again, she dangles from my neck as I open and close drawers.

'Does your mother have a piece of jewellery she often wears? A pair of earrings, a bangle, a necklace?' she asks.

I remember a gold locket Ma once threatened to imprison me in. If I didn't behave, Ma said, she would cast a spell to make me shrink before sealing me inside. Her words come back to me at the same time as the tap-tap-tap motion of her finger on the locket.

Panic creeps up my spine.

I won't let you out, Ma had warned me. *Not until you've learned how to behave properly and do what I say. Only then will I let you out for occasional gulps of air.*

I'd run to my grandmother terrified. Ma claimed later that she'd been joking. Even so, from that day on, I didn't dare disobey her.

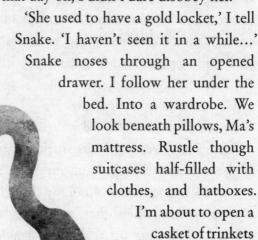

'She used to have a gold locket,' I tell Snake. 'I haven't seen it in a while...'

Snake noses through an opened drawer. I follow her under the bed. Into a wardrobe. We look beneath pillows, Ma's mattress. Rustle though suitcases half-filled with clothes, and hatboxes. I'm about to open a casket of trinkets hidden at the back of another chest of drawers, when Aunt Ruby calls: 'Sheba! Sheba! Maybe's mother's here.'

Snake glides back to me. When she's settled, a green band around my finger, I slip out of the room.

Salmata's in the courtyard, Better Life at her side. Gaza's with them as well, and Ama. Everybody's trying to calm Salmata, trying to talk her down from a pinnacle she's marooned on. Anxiety has her in its grasp. Too agitated to look anyone in the eye, she can't keep still.

'My boy,' Salmata trills, her voice shrill as an ox-pecker's cry. 'Where's my boy?'

A tear trickles down Better Life's cheek. He's not used to seeing his mother this distraught. She's clutching her arms as if only by embracing herself can she hold her innards in place. If she doesn't, mind, body and soul will fly away. Salmata rocks back and forth, stamping her feet on the ground, while she calls for her son.

The moment I reach her, I grab her wrists and as her eyes fix on mine searching for a trace of Maybe, she asks: 'Have you seen him?'

'Just over an hour ago. Perhaps an hour and a half…'

'Where?' Aunt Ruby touches my dress, fumbling for clues.

'We went to the river.'

'Take us…' Aunt Ruby pauses, sensing my body

stiffening as I try to remember exactly what happened when I saw Maybe in the undergrowth.

Nana Gyata su's instructions were clear. I had to be alone the first time I summoned Snake. Alone, because initiating a partnership with a spirit guide can be perilous. Moreover, memory plays tricks when someone first dances with their talisman and transforms into something else. Not only is the encounter charged with intent, it's also infused with the ferocity of the river goddess. It's thanks to her that the ritual is possible.

Unless... I try to swat the idea dead, but it buzzes, zigzagging here and there. Unless... I couldn't have. I refuse to think of it.

Aunt Ruby turns to Salmata, who's now surrounded by Nana, Grandma Baby and Aunt Clara.

Aunt Clara removes Salmata's hand from mine. Strokes it, tells her to sit down. Asks her if she'd like a cup of Milo – hot chocolate, Ghana-style. 'Milo always soothes me,' Aunt Clara purrs. 'Have you eaten yet?'

Salmata shakes her head. By my reckoning, given the state she's in, she won't be able to eat for some time.

Even so, Aunt Ruby's mind is made up. 'Stay and eat,' she says to Salmata. 'Sheba knows where your son is. We'll find him and bring him back to you.'

To Better Life, she adds: 'Eat with your mother, son. Look after her. She needs you here. The rest of you, come!'

Grandma Baby hands me a lighted kerosene lamp. I hold it aloft, and jostling past Ma's friends on the terrace, manoeuvre a path through them to leave the compound. Aunt Ruby follows with Ama and Gaza.

'Son?' Big Man sticks out his foot, hoping to trip up his boy. 'Who said you could be out tonight?'

Gaza ignores his father. No surprise there. Ignores Ma as well. I try to follow his example, especially when she yells: 'I told you to stay away from that Fulani boy, but you wouldn't listen, would you, Sheba? See what you've gone and done now?'

Her words sting. Having been stung time and time again, I bundle my hatred into a ball of grit, which I fling at Ma. Never used my eyes as a sling before. One second. Two seconds to think, *Murderer! You took my father from me. You will not take Maybe as well.* Three seconds is all the time I need for her to read my eye-talk and sit up, but by then, I'm gone.

I run ahead, eager to return to where I last saw Maybe. I run as if my life depends on seeing him alive once again. Run so fast, Aunt Ruby bends over and catching her breath tells me to ease up. 'You're going to kill me if you don't slow down, Sheba.'

The crescent moon bright in the sky, I pause, and then close my eyes the better to locate Maybe's whereabouts. He hasn't moved far from where I last saw him, I'm sure of it. But there's something wrong; something I can't quite pinpoint that disturbs me as much as the idea buzzing in the air: the possibility that I may have hurt him when I became more than I am.

I set off again, running through a grove of bananas and oranges.

The earth, starved of rain, throws up clouds of dust. Fleet of foot, I scramble through fields of shrivelled corn. More dust. Huge wafts of it lobbed by the stamp of my feet. The air quivers as the thump-thump of heart and feet vibrates up the trunks of trees into the leaves of African almonds that sprinkle me in grimy confetti.

In the distance, Aunt Ruby coughs.

'Wait for us,' Ama cries, while Gaza taps my shoulder.

'Is Maybe OK?' he asks.

'I'm not sure. He may be hurt. How badly, I can't say.'

I forge ahead, Gaza behind me. Swerve towards the river and then slowing down, I feel the familiar tug of the current between Maybe and I reeling me in. He's less than a stone's throw away.

I call his name. Call a second time.

'Sheba!' he whimpers.

I follow his voice, stumbling through undergrowth until I find him huddled in a ball.

'Sheba,' he says again, raising his head from his knees.

I crouch, touch his hair and jolted by what it tells me, I close my eyes trying to decipher what on earth has happened. 'No!' I moan.

'I'm sorry, Sheba. I stayed behind, but then…'

I put a finger to his lips and fondling the curls at the back of his head, his tears scorch my cheek. For Maybe to sob in my arms is almost more than I can bear. My world tilts and turns upside down as my heart breaks, knowing that day will now be night, and in that never-ending darkness, the sun will no longer shine.

I hold Maybe, folding his body into mine while my hand prickles with images gleaned from his curls of a bolt of light directed at him.

Snake's presence in my mind nudges me to an answer before I have time to ask: *Why?*

No one apart from those involved should witness a summoning, she tells me. *This is punishment from the river goddess. A penalty he's paying.*

I wave a hand in front of Maybe's face. He feels a whisper of wind and that's it. Molasses eyes no longer blink. Lashes don't flicker.

He finds my fingers and gathers them in his. 'I

knew if I waited, you'd find me,' he says. 'I knew you'd come, Sheba.'

'Of course!'

Gaza, too stunned to even try to speak, takes his cue from me. Together we pull Maybe up. Once he's upright and steady on his feet, I turn him in the direction we've come from.

The moon's scythe is behind us now, and ahead of us, half-shuffling, half-running, gasping for breath, is Aunt Ruby, escorted by Ama.

I hold the lantern in such a way that even from a distance they see us moving towards them. They see Maybe stumbling over stones a few hours earlier he'd have stepped over, his tread light and agile. He moves with the trepidation of an old man now: hesitant, trundling.

Aunt Ruby pauses. 'You've found him,' she cries and clapping her hands, sashays in jubilation. Not for long though. The closer we get, the less her hands clap until they fall slack at her sides.

Ama shoves her wrist in her mouth. Far better to bite than scream on a moonlit night such as this.

Aunt Ruby trembles. 'Sheba's friend,' she calls Maybe. 'A boy with magic at his fingertips.' 'How possible?' she wails when we reach her. 'What's happened to you, son?'

'One moment I could see everything,' Maybe replies, waving his hand in a gesture that embraces the world: the crackle swish of parched corn; the croak of tree frogs thirsty for water; the sky up above, the ground we're standing on. 'I saw, then a flash of light dashed me to the ground. I only came to half an hour ago. Auntie Ruby, I can't see anything now.'

Aunt Ruby and Ama, stirred by the same horror that Gaza and I felt on seeing Maybe, begin clapping. They clap again and again, and as they clap Aunt Ruby's lament grows wings and soars in a song of sorrow.

Ama claps on the half-beat while Aunt Ruby leads.

'*Our boy with magic in his fingers is blind,*' they sing.

'*Our friend Maybe can no longer see.*

A flash of light stole his sight and hurled him to the ground.

What will he do with the magic in his fingers now?

What will become of our friend who no longer sees?

Gaza and I join in. Maybe, whose hand I'm holding, weeps tears to fill a river. His tears mingle with mine, for as it dawns on me that his snake's head carving may be his last, I'm able to understand what I didn't before: that dark smudge disappearing between the fangs of the snake's mouth wasn't me after all, but him. Who else could it have been, when the boy I once followed is now compelled to follow me?

26

THAT NIGHT NANA Gyata su enters my dream, a coil of blue aggrey beads around his neck. Dressed in the regalia of a chief, he's alone apart from the noise of an invisible retinue behind him.

'*All hail to our chief!*' voices sing.

'*All hail to a king who's saved us from our enemies!*

Enemies who would crush us like an elephant pulps a mouse

Enemies greedier than mosquitoes sucking blood

Who would sell us for gold if they could.

All hail to the memory of our chief, Nana Gyata su!

A king with the courage of a lion!'

The voices fade and my ancestor settles on the wooden stool at the heart of my dream. His beads glint and writhe. 'Have you found it?' he asks. 'Have you found your mother's charm? Are you ready to do what you have to?'

'Not yet.' In truth, my mind is too full of Maybe to have space for much else. All I can think about is whether he'll be able to see again and what I should do to help him.

As soon as my grandmother heard us wailing outside and Ma's cry of: 'I told you! I told you!' rang through the house, Nana hurried downstairs.

Wahala! Come and see! Children and elders united in tears. Wahala big time!

'I tried to warn you, Sheba,' Ma kept saying. 'But you wouldn't listen. You think you're different but we're the same, you and I.' She held out her arms.

I pushed her away, snubbing her with the sling in my eyes. 'You're drunk, Ma,' I said. 'Boozed. Drunk as tilapia in a barrel of palm wine.'

'You think you're the first to fall in love?' she snapped back. 'You think I've always been like this?'

Nana hustled Ma away, urging her to go to bed. But after shaking herself free, Ma murmured: 'You're in deeper than you realise, Sheba. Be careful.'

I don't often agree with Ma. Of late, everything that comes out of her mouth riles me, which made what she said all the more remarkable. It touched me, hitting a place of truth where heart meets soul. Thanks to her, I was in over my head, pulled in such different directions that when I remembered revelations Maanu, the diviner, had shown me, I shook with trepidation. My mother was the thief who'd stolen my destiny; the murderer who intended to use me to exact revenge on a woman I barely knew.

'I shall defeat you! I shall be a guardian of our village!' I said to myself. 'I am nothing like you.'

As if sensing my unease, Nana patted my back. 'Did Clara bring back what you need?' she asked. 'Better now?'

I was. Aunt Clara had indeed fulfilled her task. Nana smiled, a smile that gave way to an intake of breath as her attention turned to Maybe. She took a step back, placing a hand on her heart, unnerved by his unblinking gaze and the golden specks where the brown of his eyes had been. 'Krachi, what's the matter with you?'

His silence was just as disturbing. Maybe swayed, eyes shimmering as Nana's expression changed. Her body shrank, horrified at the state of my friend.

'You'll stay with us tonight,' she said. 'Sheba, once you've prepared a room, take our friends to their quarters. Tomorrow, Ruby will escort you and your son to the clinic,' she assured Salmata. 'The eye doctor will examine him and find out what's damaged his eyes.'

Nana looked from Maybe to me and then back again trying to

winkle out the truth. Grandma Baby did the same.

She touched Maybe's cheek and after stroking his arms and inhaling his scent, she shook her head. 'What did you see?' she asked him.

He couldn't remember. So he claimed. But whether he was saying he had no recall of events to protect me or not, I wasn't sure. When eyes no longer see and are covered in flecks of gold, it's impossible to read them.

'I thought… I thought…' Maybe mumbled. 'But it can't be…'

'He's in shock,' said my junior grandmother. 'Let's hear what they say at the clinic tomorrow, then we'll know what to do next.'

While Gaza stayed close to Maybe, wheezing on his harmonica to distract him, Ama and I prepared a room for our guests. We swept and dusted. Made up a bed, rolled sleeping mats on the floor. Ama opened shuttered windows to let in air, and all the while, Ma and her friends drank tots of kill-me-quick on the terrace.

Whenever I passed the door that opens out to the veranda, whenever Ama and I dashed back and forth fetching towels and buckets of water for our guests, Ma yelled: 'I told you. I warned you, Sheba. We're the same you and I!'

'Not true!' said Ama, whirling a finger around her head to show that, in her opinion, Ma was as mad as a rabid hyena.

'I am nothing like you, Ma,' I muttered. 'You're a thief, a murderer. Not a wisp nor a whisker of me is anything like you!'

Ma, lassoing my thoughts, replied, 'Oh, but you are, my daughter! Admit it! Admit it!'

As I escorted Salmata and her boys to their quarters, Ma, once again, reproached me.

I paused, the taste of bile flooding my mouth.

Salmata slipped an arm through mine, pulling me along. 'I don't know what's the matter with my son, Sheba,' she said. 'But if what my heart tells me is true, with Allah's help, we'll get through this, just as we have other obstacles. Thank you for finding him.'

'*We shall* get through this,' I said, handing her a key to their room. 'Maybe will get better. He *has* to.'

The evening's events had taken a toll on each of us, Salmata most of all. Her features drooped, adding years to her age. Moreover, eyes that usually sparkled when she spoke had dimmed to pools of despair.

I led Maybe in behind her, and after squeezing his hand, placed his palm on Better Life's shoulder. 'You look out for him, you hear? Be his eyes until he's able to see again.'

The boy, dismayed by the change in his brother, perked up. 'I'll take care of you, bro,' he said, smiling. 'I'll be with you night and day. I'll be your shadow-walker.'

Maybe laughed for the first time since I'd found him.

'Tomorrow,' I said, touching his cheek.

His eyes blinked as he turned towards the sound of my voice. The gold in them glinted, and for a moment, I hoped when his forehead touched mine, as suddenly as blindness had struck him, it would go, disappear for ever, and he'd see me. I hoped, even as the blankness of his stare hollowed me out as thoroughly as it had his mother.

'You're going to be fine, you hear?' I said. 'Just fine.'

Maybe pulled away. The instant his forehead moved, I heard loneliness, loud as a stone dropped in a well. I heard it, but on feeling the swell of its echo, I realised that Maybe's fear of unending darkness ran as deeply as mine.

'Will he ever see again?' I ask my great-grandfather.

'I am not a seer,' he replies. 'You've already visited a seer. What did she tell you?'

'She said our house is in peril. She said that if our

house falls, so too will our village and those who need it most.'

'And yet what concerns you is your friend?'

'Yes, Nana Gyata su. Tell me! Will he see again?'

'Great-grandchild of mine,' my ancestor replies, 'such decisions are not up to us. Has your dream-snake explained what happened?'

I nod.

'Good,' he says. 'So, you already know what the problem is.'

I nod again, but as I struggle to keep my eyes dry of tears, a sob escapes me. I ball my courage into my fists and cover my face. 'I told Maybe to leave, to go away when I did the summoning. I thought he'd gone, but he *stayed*.'

'Ah, the river goddess's punishment. The goddess and her spirits don't take kindly to disobedience. Moreover, their rage is powerful because their element is in every tear we shed. It's the water we drink. It's in the blood in our veins. So, when they disapprove of our actions, the repercussions are severe.'

In the silence that follows, Nana Gyata su's sympathy flows through my dream, warming my heart, until the rest of me flames like an ember catching fire. My ancestor's breath is on me, his kindness swaddles me; I close my eyes and begin to relax. Truth is, I've been knotted with anxiety since Maybe lost his sight.

A moment in a dream can feel like eternity, for when

LIONHEART GIRL

I next look at my great-grandfather, he's changed
into a lion. He growls and before I understand
what's happening, I'm a lioness, whiskers bristling,
gambolling beside him at the river.

'Has your grandmother told you how
our village was settled?' he
asks.

I remember a few
of Nana's stories,
stories she used to
tell my friends and
I long ago. I recall
us pausing in play and
listening as Nana's voice
streams through me.

'Story! Story!' she calls.

I close my eyes and I'm back with
my gang, delighted at my grandmother's
summons. We huddle, winching our bottoms
to wherever she's sitting.

Nana on her favourite chair towers above
us. She pats a stool – my story stool – and
I clamber on to it, catching a whiff of the
musk on her clothes.

'Story, story,' she says again, and
her tale, light as a strip of adire cloth
from Yoruba-land, unfolds.

'We are special,' she begins. 'We are

protected and blessed because long, long ago, those who came before us, those who still guide us created rituals that conceal our village behind a veil no one can penetrate.'

'No one?' asks Ama. 'How possible?'

'No one,' Nana insists. 'Apart from us, the only people here are those we invite to work with us and those who've come for their safety.'

'Like my mother?' asks Maybe.

'Indeed!'

Even though she's told us this story many times before, my grandmother insists on repeating it again and again.

'Why did our ancestors have to hide?'

That's me asking a question. Me, enveloped in the warmth and smell of my grandmother.

'Long, long ago,' Nana begins, 'we arrived here in a time of war and made friends with our neighbours. We traded with them as well as merchants who came from far away in search of gold and ivory. They gave us salt in exchange for kola nuts, but it was gold they really wanted; gold to make jewellery and coin; gold for the faces of their gods, gold to adorn their kings and queens.

'We traded with them,' Nana continues. 'But when their love of gold became a passion for dealing in human flesh, our ancestors pulled away. The ancients understood what our neighbours did not: if you dare sell someone's body and soul, one day, one day, you too will be sold. So, they cast a veil around us to make sure that prisoners of war about to be sold as slaves, or women and children accused of witchcraft, could find their way here. They cast a veil which those looking for runaways could not see beyond.

'Story! Story! Are you children listening?' Nana sings.

'We're listening! We're listening!' we reply.

'Then come closer.'

I lean on her lap, while my friends form a knot around her feet.

'To begin with, those who escaped arrived in a trickle, a faint drizzle of runaways every once in a while. Then, many years later, after lakes and valleys above us had turned into desert; after forts were built along the Guinea coast and our neighbours pillaged to trade in human flesh – that trickle turned into a flood of people – and our ancestors decided to intervene.'

'How so?' asks Maybe.

'Listen and learn,' Nana replies. She pauses, and eyes widening, she inspects our faces. With bated breath we return her stare, our gaze mirroring hers.

'Our chief at the time called a meeting between the living and the dead. He poured libation and summoned the greatest of our ancestors to advise us. When the spirits were gathered with our elders, they discussed not only how best to protect our community and the strangers who came to us, they also talked about how to scupper the plans of those who, having captured prisoners, pursued them if they escaped.'

Nana's voice dims and I pause, unsure what to say next.

'Didn't your grandmother tell you the whole story?' asks Nana Gyata su.

In a blink of an eye, he's pulled me into the present. I'm now a cub he's carrying between his jaws. A cub he drops on the ground.

We're in the forest, in a grove of hardwood trees littered with leaves. I sniff their scent, running in circles as I catch whiffs of grass cutters and mice, perfect for a cub's first kill.

Nana Gyata su taps me on the head and I fall flat on my face, legs and paws splayed. 'What happened next, Sheba? Focus, child. Focus.'

I vaguely remember that in Nana's tale another of our ancestors, the noble woman my grandmother is named after, recalls a fable her mother once told her. A fable, which reveals an affinity between humans and animals, a bond that can be re-ignited with the help of a special kind of snake.

I furrow the pelt of my brow because like so many of Nana's stories, this one is laden with proverbs; complications and nuances unappealing to a girl raised on the Kung-fu movies of Video Man's van.

'Well?'

'From what I remember, great-grandfather, snakes help us change from one species to another. The rest – protecting runaways from those who would rather kill them than let them go free – we learned how to do ourselves.'

'Correct. Now, let me show you.'

How he does it, I don't know. But with a bound we pass through a loop in time to the past, a shadowland where I catch sight of Maybe and Salmata. They're running, stumbling over clumps of earth as they flee for their lives.

Salmata, knee-high in lemongrass, pauses, catching her breath. Better Life, a toddler asleep in a swathe of cloth on her back, is weighing her down.

Ahead of her, Maybe whispers: 'Hurry, Ma, hurry!'

It's dusk, the air clear of mosquitoes repelled by the fragrance of lemon underfoot.

Night approaches.

Shadows blur. Then, a whistle.

Lion's tongue curled, my ancestor whistles again – a single, high-pitched note that only felines hear.

Salmata rushes to her son. Before she reaches him, she turns, sensitive to the thud-thump of pounding hooves in the distance.

She feels their vibration and as she scans the horizon, looking for a baobab tree or an acacia, any tree large enough to hide in, dismay gathers on her face.

'May the gods of the village with no name protect me,' she pleads. 'May they have mercy on me and my sons. And should I perish, may Allah avenge my death and save my boys from their father!'

As far as the eye can see, there's nowhere to hide on this stretch of savannah. Nowhere at all. Apart from thorn bushes and saplings between sprinklings of grassland, her family is dangerously exposed.

My ancestor whistles again and one after the other, prides of spectral lionesses appear in the undergrowth. At another signal, they form a protective ring around the runaways. They prowl, circling them, looking outwards, ready for their prey.

Four men appear on horses, silhouetted against the setting sun. Men whooping and yelling. Horses, legs stretched, gallop, their thundering hooves releasing whorls of dust.

'Grab my eldest child and then kill my wife the moment we catch her,' says their leader. 'It's my eldest I want. He speaks to spirits and possesses power that can make me chief.'

The man giving orders resembles Maybe but is older; much older. Wiry, in late middle age; he must be his father.

His horse, sensitive to the whiff of predators,

bridles, almost tipping him over. Whip in hand, the rider lashes his steed. The mare won't budge. Pawing the ground, eyes rolling, she neighs, tossing her head.

The man hits her again, tightening the reins.

Horse bucks and rears.

The rider falls and my ancestor roars – a roar that, ripping the veil between the quick and the dead, compresses time into an eternal quiver of dread.

Sweat gleams on the man's face. He's shaking, even as his friends lift him to his feet. Shaking, as they corral his horse and heave him astride. And when we lions, following a signal from Nana Gyata su, bound forward, and with one voice roar in such a way that the air shivers with the intensity of our rage, the posse turns tail and gallops away.

'You see how we do it?' says my ancestor.

'Fear,' I reply, the wild-eyed frenzy of men and horses etched on my soul. 'They heard the beast in our roar and fled.'

'Indeed, child,' says my great-grandfather. 'When fear claws you and shakes you about, before it devours you, you feel and see nothing else – unless you've learned to control

it. Those men took fright and forgot their prey. This is what we do, child. This is how we succeed. Come closer.'

I do what he asks and between one step and the next, I'm a girl again. Around me an army of lionesses sniff my hands and feet, inhaling my scent to remember me. Palms damp with inquisitive noses, a sea of amber eyes mirrors mine, mesmerised, as my fingers graze flanks and necks, tickling heads and ears.

I touch, and pictures light as pollen flicker through me. Pictures of zebras and antelopes pursued by lions over savannah. A lioness jumps on a gazelle's back. Massive jaws muzzle breath. Seconds later, the gazelle falls. Then, as she rips open its throat, I taste blood and flesh. Above us, vultures circle, waiting to partake of the feast.

I marvel at the throng of lionesses and as they spray me with their scent and make me their own, their odour nuzzles my nostrils.

'Now whistle,' says my ancestor.

I repeat his signal and, in a breath, each and every one of us disappears.

27

I WAKE UP to Nana shaking me. "You're raving,' she cries. 'You're snarling and snapping like a wild animal. What's the matter with you, Sheba?'

I open my eyes, questions buzzing in my mind: questions I need to ask Maybe, alongside doubts I'd like to raise with my ancestor. For instance, how was Nana Gyata su able to register Salmata's cry for help? How was he able to be in the right place at the right time? Moreover, when I'm ready to be a champion of our village and follow in his footsteps, if someone calls out to me, how will I fare?'

I am not a seer, Sheba, I hear him reply.

I sit up. 'I was with Nana Gyata su,' I say to Nana. 'Learning his signals, recognising the scent of the lionesses who walk with him.'

'Is that what your friend saw? Your transformation?'

I nod again.

'How could a grandchild of mine be so foolish? Didn't you know he would suffer if he saw what no one else should see? Sheba, when will you realise that what we're doing isn't a game for children?'

It's not often my grandmother lambasts me. She does it so rarely, I reel. I'm aflame with guilt already. I don't need anyone, Nana especially, sprinkling kerosene on it.

'I told him to stay away. I warned him, begged him...'

'Beg? A noble woman should never beg, Sheba. In my day, we commanded. Ordered. Instructed. If he wouldn't go, you should have found somewhere else by the river to do what you had to.'

'I know, Nana. I know...'

Yet no matter how much I try to explain myself, Nana is incandescent.

Least she could do is congratulate me on following my ancestor's example. Pat me on back maybe. Or prepare a meal of Eto – yam mashed in palm oil eaten with hard-boiled eggs – to celebrate. If I had my way, Nana would smile at me and say: 'Grandchild of mine, I'm proud of you!'

Instead, in a tone that reminds me of Ma, she goes on and on, saying the same thing in different ways which all add up to: '*See what you've done!*'

'What if Maybe sight doesn't return?' she asks. 'What will he do then? What if taking him to the clinic doesn't help in the slightest, because what's at stake is *spiritual* in nature, not physical?'

'Grandma Baby and I will have to perform rituals to placate the river goddess,' she continues, thinking out loud. 'You can never tell with her. She's impulsive, defiant when her authority has been challenged.'

'But Maybe didn't challenge her! He challenged me!'

Nana shakes her head, exasperated. 'You are aligned to the goddess now! Her power is your power. You are more than just yourself. You are no longer a child!'

Again, I hear my mother in Nana's complaints, and as I dwell on the resemblance between the two of them and wonder why I've never noticed it before, an image flashes before me. Of course! Why didn't I think of it? Ma's toma. Her love-beads: beads she wears to accentuate the curves of her hips, the dip in her waist. They're so much a part of her, a second skin, in fact, that I forgot that she almost never takes them off. So that's where she hides her charm! Of course!

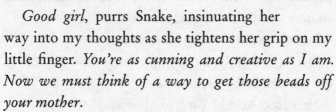

Good girl, purrs Snake, insinuating her way into my thoughts as she tightens her grip on my little finger. *You're as cunning and creative as I am. Now we must think of a way to get those beads off your mother.*

My heart blushes at Snake's praise. My cheeks

dimple while Nana continues lashing me with her tongue.

'Oh! You think I'm funny, do you? You think this is a joke? Aba! Young people today…'

'No, Nana. I hear you! I hear you!' I insist, communicating with Snake at the same time. *We'll get her toma tomorrow*, I tell Snake. *By then we'll have a plan.*

By my reckoning, from all the carousing and laughter on the veranda last night, Ma didn't go to bed till early this morning. While she's still asleep, Aunt Ruby and I take Maybe and Salmata to the clinic we share with our neighbouring villages.

My aunt guides Maybe through a series of tests with an eye doctor, who, shining bright lights on the gold specks in his eyes, examines his irises and pupils thoroughly.

'This is odd,' the doctor remarks. 'Very odd.'

Undeterred, determined to make sense of how trauma to such a crucial part of Maybe's anatomy could have left him blind, the doctor asks questions while peering under Maybe's eyelids; probing his retinas; shining eye-lights up and down, until perplexed and defeated, he puts his instruments away.

'He says there's nothing *physically* wrong with his eyes,' Aunt Ruby explains later.

'In that case, why can't my boy see?'

Aunt Ruby sighs as concerned for her protégé as

Salmata is. 'He may have gone somewhere he shouldn't have. He may even have seen events not meant for human eyes.' My aunt pauses, taking the measure of the woman opposite her. 'I suspect,' she continues, 'that his problem isn't one that can be solved by a doctor.'

'You mean my boy is bewitched? Are you telling me that someone has charmed him and, in doing so, blinded him?'

Aunt Ruby opens her hands in a gesture of helplessness. 'Who can say?'

We're back in the courtyard at home. While our elders chat in an alcove, I'm trying to persuade Maybe to let me dress his hair. Having already unplaited it, it amazes me how soft it is, and how fondling his curls always returns me to the sensation of water lapping at my feet.

Of late, Maybe's been wearing his hair long. I've been braiding his crown while Aunt Clara shaves the sides of his head. More often than not, he's eager to let me in and, when I enter, and he opens up to me, I revel in his locks. Like a bee sipping nectar, I flit from flower to flower as the pictures within him sweeten my tongue.

Not today. In the same way

that Salmata has had to persuade him to do just about anything since I found him: get out of bed, wash and dress, eat breakfast and then see the doctor, I have to coax Maybe to submit to my touch.

'What's the point,' he says, 'when I won't be able to see what you do?'

'Other people will see. They'll look at you and shower you with love. Wait and see.'

'There, you've said it yourself. Why wait *ahhhhh*, when I *can't see*?'

'Are you going to stop eating? Stop breathing?'

'No, because you're going to stop treating me like a doll you play with...'

'You'll feel better, much better,' I insist.

Maybe kisses his teeth. He wants to be left alone, I know. I can't leave him, even if I'm tempted to. Grandma Baby gave me strict instructions to stick to him like a limpet.

'That boy's depressed,' she said earlier. 'His skin smells of mould. Stay with him, Sheba. Keep an eye on him. Stop him doing anything stupid.'

'Maybe, you need my help,' I whisper. 'To help you see again, I need to get an idea of the last thing you saw.'

At this, he explodes. 'How many times do I have to tell you? I don't remember. There's the carving I gave you... then nothing. Nothing at all.'

'Do you remember us swimming?'

He fumbles for my hands. When he finds them, he clutches my wrist, dragging me down to sit beside him and Gaza.

The melancholy whine of Gaza's harmonica underlines a cloud of gloom hovering over all of us. There's wind and rain in the cloud, flashes of lightning and claps of thunder that rumble in my bones. Unintentionally, I've unleashed events as maddening as the season we're in – the season of suffocating humidity when everyone craves rain.

What I realise as I try to cajole Maybe into doing my bidding; what becomes clear as he brushes me aside with lip-talk followed by the loud kissing of teeth, is that Maybe is more impatient now than ever. No longer able to do what he wants as soon as he pleases, he has to wait for others to take him from A to B. I can only imagine his frustration, and yet determined to use my gift to help him, he finally consents to let me do his hair.

The minute I begin combing it, he howls.

'My hands!' Maybe jumps up, itching his palms, the tips of his fingers. Shakes them out, trying to rid them of surges of restless energy.

Aunt Ruby rushes to his aid. Rubs his fingers. Fills her lungs and blows on them. 'It's the magic in them,' Aunt Ruby explains. 'If magic can't find expression, it hurts. Come, Gaza! Hurry!'

Aunt Ruby sends our friend to the market. While

we wait, I wash Maybe's hair, and after drying and massaging his scalp with Aunt Clara's healing oils, I part his head in sections. I give him a middle parting, and I'm off.

Straightaway my fingertips sizzle as I connect with the flame of Maybe's soul. Before I realise what's happening, the hands of his dead-departed grasp mine, plunging me into the world they share with their brother.

This has never happened before. They're usually jealous, secretive, and keep out of my way when I'm dressing Maybe's hair. Today, they reach out to me. There's desperation in their touch, a scorching heat to their grip that puzzles me, tinged as it is with the aching loneliness I heard in Maybe last night. I hear it again: a rock dropped in the deepest of wells; a cry for help that I answer by allowing them to seize me, transporting me to wherever they are.

I feel a paddling motion of a river crossing, a rocking from side to side until their presence envelops me: Musa, Jebril and Moona. The three of them, inseparable on an island of moon-lanced shadows, mist and wind.

'What's happening?' Moona wails. Her voice, pitched higher than the wind circling us, is raw with grief. 'What's wrong with our brother? Why isn't he talking to us?'

She howls and for a moment I'm not sure if it's the

wind speaking or if I'm listening to the unravelling of a ghost. 'What's going on?'

'Hasn't he told you?' I reply.

'He hasn't spoken to us for hours and hours. He only talks to *you*.'

Moona, the youngest of the siblings, appears to speak on behalf of the three of them. What she says, her brothers punctuate with sighs and whispers that give the impression that they're talking with one voice. A voice which tunnels through the wind before it echoes in my fingers braiding Maybe's hair.

Moona begins a sentence; her brothers complete it, their cries sharp as blades piercing bone.

'Told us what? What?' they scream.

'Your brother can't see. He's blind.'

'Blind? That shouldn't stop him talking to us. What he can't see, we'll show him.'

Their voices vibrate through my hands, but as the departed-dead tighten their grip on me, my fingers grow numb.

I pause. Swallow my panic. Gently, I try to release myself. But in their land of shadows, they grasp me even tighter. Hanging on to my wrists, their anguish persuades me that without a human anchor they'll scatter, insubstantial as dust in the wind.

'Stay! Stay!' they scream.

I blow on the spot where – if I could see them – their hands should be. My breath warms them, I can tell. They murmur, and as they do so, the scent of cloves fills the air. Reassured by the tenderness of my breath, Moona and her brothers tell me more.

'We tried to warn him but all he could think of was you. You. All he thinks about is *you*.'

Moona's voice quivers and quails as a tornado of air almost tears us apart. The louder it blows, the more she cleaves to me. And yet the harder she clings, the lighter she becomes as if bit by bit she's disappearing, a wisp in the wind.

'We spoke to him,' says Moona, while her voice still reaches me. 'Told him to move from that place, and when he didn't, when he refused to listen, he cast us into darkness. Now he won't talk to us. Without him, we're nothing. Nothing, I tell you. Oh, my sister, you know how he is...'

'You know how he is,' Maybe's brothers repeat. 'You know. You know.'

I flex my fingers. They're still stiff. Nonetheless, I continue braiding Maybe's hair to soothe the distress of his siblings.

Yes, I know how their brother is. And I know from experience how galling it is to make a mistake and be told: 'I told you. I told you,' again and again. It's worse than falling in an ant's nest. Worse than being tongue-whipped over breakfast by Nana, Grandma Baby joining in.

'Sister?' Moona cries.

'Sister,' her brothers rustle, as they too begin to melt into air.

They haven't called me this before. I'm considering what Maybe's silence to his dead departed means, when Gaza returns with a packet of plasticine.

Maybe pounces on it like a ravenous beast on meat. Breaks it into pieces, squeezing fragments between his palms. Moulding and kneading, twisting, stretching. And while he works, I continue doing his hair, aware of a prickling sensation along the length and breadth of my fingers. A prickling like the scrape of a kitten's tongue.

The wind drops in their shadowland. The mist clears and as the sun emerges, what was about to disintegrate like sand in a storm, gathers, coming into focus. I glimpse the shape of faces. The curve of lips and then, *whoosh*, a sudden rush of laughter as, from one moment to the next, Maybe talks to his dead-departed with his hands. It's as if he's caressing them while they help him shape figurines he can't see. Moulding them in colours that no longer register in his mind, a purple cockerel appears. Then, a red hen, followed by two green chicks.

One after the other, fowls are nudged into being by the bond between Maybe's hands and his dead-departed.

The cloud hovering over my friend lifts. A smile cracks open his lips and as the scent of cloves wafts over us, his face brightens. Musa, Jebril and Moona are back where they belong and there they remain as Maybe begins crafting another bird.

We're all working together now, for while he plays with the plasticine, I untangle a knot in Maybe's hair and sliding down a thread of memory, a face bursts through a haze of dust. A man on horseback with menace in his eyes. It's Maybe's father. His anger jabbing at my fingers, he hollers: 'I want my boy back! I want what's in him. Give him back to me!'

I'm tempted to find out more.

'Haven't you finished yet?' Maybe wriggles, stretching his back and shoulders while Gaza's harmonica grizzles and gripes in our ears like swarming locusts.

'Patience,' I reply. 'I'm almost done.'

I've plaited his locks into sheaves of cornrow that dangle either side of his head. I've knotted each one with gold and black beads that match the flecks in the irises of his eyes. Gathering strands of hair in a final plait, I'm thinking of probing deeper to find out why the man is so desperate to have his son back, when Maybe shakes his head.

'Patience…' I say again.

The ring on my finger digs into me, a warning from Snake. 'Don't venture there without permission,' she tells me. 'You're here to help, not pry.'

I hold my breath and as the urge to delve rises and

fades, I weave the memory thread into the last braid. Once it's adorned with gold beads, I pat Maybe's head and stroke his cheek. 'There! All done!'

'Here,' he says.

Sitting beside me, his shoulder slumped against mine, Maybe nudges my arm. 'Take it.' He places a plasticine bird in my palm.

A pink bird; beak, head, body and wings, every inch of it the pale, mottled wash of obroni skin – the shade of foreigners and uncooked chickens.

I turn the bird around, inspecting the size of its head, the length and breadth of its wings. It could be a crow by the look of it. A crow plucked of its feathers, unable to fly – as Ma will be, when I find her charm.

28

TOWARDS THE END of the day, as the sun begins slipping away, a colony of bats swoops into the cotton tree. Their high-pitched chirrups harmonise with the tree's song: the creak and crackle of bark, the flutter-slap of leaves that coincide with Ma getting up. Until now, apart from brief excursions to Aunt Clara's kitchen to forage for food, she's been cocooned in her room. Eating sweets and browsing through magazines, I reckon. As dusk approaches, she's wide awake. Washed and refreshed, she's getting ready to party again.

'You people had better get used to having me around,' she grumbles. 'This is my home and I'm here to stay.'

From the look of it, from the number of chairs she's dragging on to the veranda, tonight's party is going to be larger than the one last night.

Grandma Baby sniffs. Tight-lipped, a smoky cloud of disdain in her eyes, she's smouldering, while Nana is exhausted. What with me snapping and snarling in my dream last night, and the uproar that comes with a free flow of liquor, Nana didn't sleep well. She's tugging the sleeves of a kaftan she's wearing, one of her favourites, in red. A dress with a white adinkra symbol woven in the fabric, Gye Nyame – *through God all things are possible*.

In case her gods are listening, Nana shakes her head, covering her face with her hands, while I glare at Ma.

I don't understand my mother. What puzzles and irritates me to the point of fury is why she's chosen today, of all days, to provoke our elders? At a time when the weight of Maybe's blindness is heavy on our hearts, she's behaving like the shoe that doesn't fit. Too tight, it's pinching our toes making it impossible to walk or sit comfortably.

I think the thought, and straightaway I hear Nana saying what she always does when I'm considering ditching Ma.

'Be kind to her,' Nana says. 'Remember, she brought you into this world, so you must do your best to treat her with kindness and patience.'

Nana urges forgiveness, while Grandma Baby believes that the only way to thrive in life, is to 'fight fire with fire'.

My pool of mother-love trickling away, Ma hurries to and fro, tugging and pulling, a chewing stick dangling from her mouth. *Kapa. Kapa. Kapa.* The clip-clop of her mules follows her to the terrace.

I watch bemused, until a smidgen of a smile nudges her lips. Of course! Like a prize fighter preparing for a bout, she's limbering up. When she's ready, when the rumble eventually erupts, it is going to be *huge*, I tell you! Bigger than the whole of our village and the souls within it. Her intent tunnels into my bones, a warning of what is to come.

'You people...' Ma repeats her new refrain, including me in the sweep of her gaze. 'You think you're better than everyone else, don't you? You believe all the gods are on your side, and yet you can't see what's right in front of you!'

She glowers at me.

The hairs at the back of my neck prickle. Before I understand what's happening, I'm staring at the dark, pebbled eyes of Mother Crow: all-seeing, all-knowing, terrifying.

Does she realise what I'm up to, I wonder.

That's the thing with Ma. She's able to spin a web of uneasiness with a scowl that blisters the gut.

My stomach clenches. I'd like to lion-up and pounce on her. Instead, I mirror her pose, shoulders back, hand on hips. I'm about to ask her what she's hinting at when Snake squeezes my finger.

'If we're going to remove her waist-beads and use them against her,' she reasons, 'we have to be as cunning as she is.'

So I slap a smile on my face and, dribbling puddles

of kindness and patience around her, I give Ma a hand.

We lug a teak recliner to the terrace. Then, as I'm helping her place it in a semi-circle with the rest of the chairs, I imagine her draped over the recliner as her friends arrive. I see her swigging palm wine late into the night, so that when I check on her tomorrow morning – as a dutiful daughter should – sodden with alcohol, she'll be dead to the world. That's when I'll take what's hers.

I visualise tomorrow's scene and then ask politely: 'What is it we can't see right in front of us, Ma?'

She gives me that Mother Crow look again. 'They can't see you, little chick. I can. I see a daughter who will soon be as ruthless as I am.'

'Are you sure, Ma?'

'Sheba,' she replies, 'You have no idea how well I understand you. I've watched you and that boy together. You're the cause of his blindness. *You* and you alone.'

A smile butters my lips. 'You're wrong, Ma. Maybe's responsible for what's happened to him. If I were to blame, why would Nana and Grandma Baby go to the river to plead on his behalf?'

'They did?'

'They talked to the river goddess for hours. Poured libation to her. They even sacrificed a chicken and got down on their knees to ask her to forgive him.'

'They did that for a boy from Zongo?'

'He's my forever friend, Ma.'

'You're still such a child, Sheba! Even so…'

Refusing to be deflected, I press on. 'They did what they could, but when they returned home…' I lower my voice, enticing Ma to lean in. 'His condition was worse. Have you seen Maybe's eyes?'

She shakes her head as I describe how, between my grandmothers' trip to the river and their return home, the flecks on Maybe's irises expanded, covering his eyes in a luminous golden sheen. 'He now has the eyes of an eagle, Ma.'

'What?'

Sidling even closer, I murmur in her ear: 'Salmata doesn't know what to do. Nana says that until Maybe is able to see again, he can stay with Gaza in Nana Gyata su's room.'

'Lawato! You're lying!'

'True, true, Ma. Grandma Baby thinks that Nana Gyata su's spirit may help him. It may shock him into seeing again.'

'Aba! That old crone gets crazier by the day, but this time she's gone too far.'

I'm tempted to say: 'That's exactly how I feel about you, Ma.' But I don't. I'm being kind and patient, aren't I? Arms folded, I watch her trundle, *kapa*, *kapa*, *kapa*, to where my grandmothers are sipping fresh coconut milk in the courtyard.

Ma comes to a stop. Stretches to her full height. My mother is tall, I tell you! Tall as a woman warrior. Amazon tall. Tall as in 'Don't-mess-with-me-or-I'll-smack-you-down' tall. Tall enough to make you shrink, as I used to in her presence. Ma stretches and then launches herself. 'You people! Have you gone mad? You're worse than a pair of bats dangling in the dungeon of Elmina Castle. Is it true? Have you put that boy in my grandfather's room?'

Nana puts down the coconut gourd with a sigh, one of her special sighs: a heaving moan that rattles the bones of everyone close by. 'Sika, I am not going to answer a question from someone who calls us, "you people". I am the head of this household. I can invite Sheba's friends to stay in any room I choose.'

'But Ma! That boy isn't even a relative. That room should be Solomon's room...'

'Is Solomon here? When was the last time your twin brother and his wife came to visit us? Ask yourself, Sika, why won't they set foot in this house? Is it something you did? Are they frightened of you? Should we follow their example and keep out of your way?'

Ma pooh-poohs Nana's comment and, as usual, gets away with it. Too many questions are left unanswered in my family. Too many wriggle, like worms in sand, searching for a way out. While Ma jabbers on about my friend being an inconsequential boy from the north somewhere, a useless, kyenkyema boy from Zongo, Nana replies saying that instead of ridiculing him, Ma should have the grace to say his name; Ma should say it and stop her nonsense.

'Say it! Say it!' Grandma Baby heckles.

My innards squirming in sympathy with unspoken secrets, I wonder what Ma's done to incur the wrath of her brother. What did Aunt Lila do to her? Why does Ma hate her so much that she's prepared to use me to wage war? Is that why she named me Sheba, to steal my uncle from his wife? I want to ask, but as surely as dusk heralds night, I'll be told as I have been again and again: '*You ask too many questions, child!*'

The worms writhe and for a moment, I'm convinced they're about to nose into the open, but as my mother hisses and blusters, refusing to let Maybe's name stain her lips, they recoil, afraid of the light.

Ma would rather have her tongue cut off, I reckon, than say Maybe's name out loud. She'd rather drink poison or raze her long, thick hair to stubble than share me with anyone else.

Lips compressed in fury, she wags a finger at my grandmothers while Grandma Baby grins, delighted that her suggestion has inflamed her blood rival. The moment Nana splutters, rubbing her chest in pain, the grin disappears and jumping to her feet, Grandma Baby on tiptoe, goes nose to nose with Ma.

My junior grandmother is much smaller than I am now, but when she's seething, what she lacks in height is rewarded by sucker punches of ferocity. 'Sika,' she hisses. 'A visitation from Nana Gyata su may be just what the boy needs.'

'What is wrong with the two of you?' Ma cries. 'Can't you see you're being played by this minx of a daughter of mine? Anyone would think that consorting with wayside characters is what we Prempehs do. We're better than that. We live in a palace. We're royals!'

At which point Nana, in spite of the ache in her chest, collapses laughing. Not a gentle snicker of ladylike twittering, but laughter loud as a dog's bark. A never-ending bark in Nana's case, punctuated by screams of: *'Adjei! Adjei!*

Sika, you're killing me!'

An outburst so extreme that my aunts Ruby and Clara rush into the courtyard. As usual, Nana's glee infects all of us and within seconds we're grunting and cackling, fist-pumping and backslapping. I tumble to the floor. Writhing in their chairs, my grandmothers shriek, supported by my aunts perched on their armrests. All of us are rolling about laughing; all of us except for Ma.

Her lips scarcely moving, she says to Nana: 'You've never liked me, have you? You always favoured Solomon. You petted him, made much of him, while me… You've never had time for me. Even now, you're more preoccupied with a boy from Zongo than *me*, a Prempeh, your baby-last.'

Nana sits up. 'Yes, Sika, we hail from a royal family and our pedigree is a long and honourable one. Most of us here were born under this roof. By right we each have a part to play in what our ancestors created. So, tell me, my daughter, why are you determined to turn my father's palace into a drinking den for you and your friends?'

There's no way Ma can answer that! Caught in a clinch she can't twist out of, Ma does the next best thing. She turns her back on Nana and sends me on an errand instead.

29

MY MOTHER WANTS more palm wine. A lot more. Handed a wodge of notes, I saunter off: first to Ama's house to enlist her help, and then to the kiosk of a woman who sells palm wine.

On our way home again, carrying water-coolers stacked with booze on our heads, our little fingers loop in friendship as Ama practises her list of insults on everyone we pass: son-of-a-toad (our headmaster); daughter-of-a-vulture (a new girl in our class); daughter-of-the-worst-witch-in-the-world (our head-master's daughter); devil's spawn (Gaza's uncle). She flashes a smile at each of them before muttering abuse under her breath. For some reason or other, Ama's in a foul mood. So much so, we're almost home before she catches my eye and I ask: 'Bestie-best, what happened?'

'I dey tear head and talk plenty,' she replies. Face tight with fury, Ama lip-talks disgust. Spits. Lip-talks some more. 'Our classroom be full of rumour-mongers, They say, they say… rumours *paaah*.' Spits again.

'What dey say?'

'Dey say Maybe walk wi too much swagger, so your mother blind him to save you.'

'Ma? She had nothing to do with it.'

Ama shrugs. 'For sure! And you?' In a heartbeat, she answers her own question. 'Mother trouble! What's Queen Sasabonsam done now?'

It's not easy having a chat with a heavy load on your head.

'Mek we stop proper. Mr Owusu,' I call to a passer-by. 'I beg you, help us.'

Water-coolers safely on the ground, Ama and I sit side by side on top of them.

I tell her about Maybe's visit to the clinic this morning. I describe the blooming of his eagle-eyes and how he's now staying in Nana Gyata su's old room with Gaza.

Once she's heard me out, Ama gives me a blow-by-blow account of the gossip at school spread by a senior – 'a bush boy, a rat in a rat hole', she calls him.

'That boy is big,' Ama concedes. 'But his brain?' Her forefinger almost touches her thumb. 'A pea brain at best. His lights may be on, but inside that skull of his, I swear, there is *nothing*!'

She grumbles, mumbling to herself until I pluck up the nerve to ask a question that's been bothering me. It's one of those questions which wriggles between us once in a while; a question no one in my family is willing to answer – another secret that bugs me. By now dusk has arrived, and the sun almost gone, bathes us in shadow light.

'Bestie-best, do you know why our mothers stopped being friends?' From my calculations, the friendship ended around the time that my Uncle Solomon's visits to our village ceased. I must have been about three years old when I last saw him.

Ama looks at me strangely. She's used to me shunning gossip by keeping family palaver sealed under our roof. 'You don't know?'

I shake my head.

Ama frowns, chewing her bottom lip as she considers how much to tell me.

'Everyone knows the story,' she says. '*Everyone.*'

'*Then tell me.*'

'Fine, let me be the one to boss you.' Ama quickly reveals the bare bones of a skeleton that's been dangling in our family cupboard for years. I've heard it jangling in the frostiness between Ma and Aunt Esi, next door, but before today, had no idea of its shape or size.

'My mother says that your ma's the sort of friend who steals husbands from their wives, like she stole Big Man from Gaza's ma. Auntie Sika tried the same trick with my father,' Ama declares. 'She failed.'

I pretend not to wince. 'Ah,' I say, while thinking, *Of course. No wonder Ma has no women friends. No wonder women scorn her.*

We stagger home, the drinks on our heads. Sure enough, just as I'd imagined, the first thing we see on our return is Ma lounging on the recliner.

Arrayed in an up and down – a diaphanous flowing gown in lime green with matching trousers – she's glamoured herself in such a way that the gossamer-thin sheda of her outfit shimmers when she moves, revealing three rows of love-beads around her waist. If the river goddess were to take on a human form, I swear, she would look like Ma. Ma glistens, as luminously molten as the element she's named after – Sika. Gold. Bedazzled, even someone like me, someone who doesn't like her much, can't take their eyes off her. Neither can Ama. We're enthralled, drawn to the warmth of Ma's inner glow as we arrange calabashes for her guests on a table.

A question sparks in Ama's eyes, scalding truth off her tongue. 'Auntie Sika, how do you do it? How do you get to look the way you do?'

'Ama Smart, if your mother hasn't taught you how to use bottom-power yet, watch me and learn. Don't pay attention to my little chick here. She's embarrassed when I flaunt what I have. I am woman.' Ma sways her hips. 'And I *revel* in it.'

'We're women too,' Ama replies, thrusting an arm through mine.

'So are my grandmothers and aunts,' I protest, 'as well as Auntie Esi, next door.'

Ma eyes lock with ours. 'Young ladies, you can't compare eating hunks of breadfruit to the pleasure of sucking a ripe mango dry.' Ma smacks her lips in a kiss. 'Take it from me, girls, breadfruit and mangoes may both be fruit, but the sweetness of one is a gift from the gods. I am the mango to those breadfruit women you've mentioned. Watch me and learn.'

Taking Ma's advice to heart, Ama and I stay on the sidelines, watching, as, for the second night running, Ma's guests saunter into our yard and carouse in her company. Among them, to Ama's distress, is her father, Allotey.

Is this how it was for *my* father, I wonder. Did his heart quicken in Ma's presence? Was he dazzled by her shine? Was her charm his undoing?

This is how Ma preys on her victims. This is how my father was murdered.

But what if what happened between them was an accident?

'Do not underestimate your mother,' Snake replies as Grandma Baby calls me inside.

In her hand is a small bottle identical to the ones

in which she stores essential oil. 'Take this,' my junior grandmother tells me. 'Put two drops, at least, in your mother's calabash as soon as you can. It'll knock her out and put her to sleep. Your senior grandmother needs to have a good rest tonight.'

'Will two drops be enough?'

'No more than two, Sheba. Take it from me, murder, even by accident, gnaws at the heart forever.'

I put the bottle in my pocket of the house-dress I'm wearing – a hand-me-down kanga from Grandma Baby's glory days in East Africa. Tonight, of all nights, I'm going to make sure, if nothing else, that Nana has some peace.

'Sheba! Sheba! A glass of water.'

I answer Ma's summons.

Fetch a glass. Fill it with water. Add Grandma Baby's sleeping drops to it.

One. Two. I stop at two.

But then, before I can change my mind, I double the dosage.

Just in case, I tell myself.

In case Ma spills the drink.

Four drops to ensure that Nana sleeps well.

I'm doing this, I tell myself, to keep Mother Crow off the roof of our house; doing this to ease death's talons from my family, Nana especially.

Fighting fire with fire, I return to the terrace and hand the glass to Ma.

She glugs the water down.

I wait for every dribble to slip down her gullet before, stepping aside, I say goodnight.

30

'AH-AH! THERE SHE goes again! Not in a nightdress today, thank God, but shirt and jeans, hair all over the place!'

'Where're you off to this time, Sheba? I've never known a child run away as often as you do!'

'Go home, girl! There's no one to save you now your boyfriend's blind. Go back to Nana Serwah or you'll break her heart.'

I'm running again, onlookers heckling as I leap ditches, a basket on my arm.

Fast as a gazelle chased by a leopard, I zig-zag, heading first to the cotton tree and then away from it. Predator is now prey, for overhead a pair of crows, hot in pursuit, plough through currents of air.

'Stop! Stop!' They caw. 'Give it back! Give it back!'

That's what I imagine they're saying. There's fury in their squawks and, feeling the burn of their eyes on my back, I race past the market, through cornfields dry as dust, towards the river.

I pause, panting for breath.

Those crows have been after me since I left home.

'How, in the name of the gods of our village, do they know what I've got? How *can* they know, when Ma's still asleep and has no inkling what I've done?'

Such things are beyond my comprehension as well, Snake replies, her thoughts flowing into mine in never-ending conversation. *Remember this: one thing leads to another. We've acted. They're reacting. Now, finish what we've started.*

The birds overhead are joined by another twosome. In the distance, six or seven more crows are closing in.

Crouching, making as little noise as possible, I skirt the edge of a banana grove. Then, darting inside, I whisper:

'*Banana tree! Banana tree! Watch over me!*

Use your stem and leaves to protect and disguise me!'

I hide beneath the
largest tree in the grove,
one with wide, abundant leaves
from which I can see without being seen.

The birds scream, and as the murder of crows gathers, they hover, looping in an ever-widening circle to track me down.

Suddenly, there's movement in the cornfield. A girl, the same shape and size as I am, bustles down the track with a basket on her arm, heading in the direction I was.

The crows swoop as one in a tsunami of feathers, attacking her with claws and beaks.

'Stay put,' Snake hisses, anticipating my urge to break cover.

The girl shields her face with an arm; while swinging the basket in the air she yelps in pain.

'Stay!' Snake again.

Nerves jangling, I obey, even as talons tangle in the girl's hair and draw blood on her face.

Not a moment too soon, a labourer and a peanut

seller appear. The woman drops her produce and as the peanuts scatter, shoves the wounded girl to the ground. Covering her with her ample frame, she bellows: 'Do something, man! Kill them! Kill them!'

The labourer, wielding a cutlass, bashes the birds, slashing feathers and wings.

A crow tumbles to the ground. Two, then three are downed, leaving twenty or more whirling above the woman, the girl beneath her. They peck and tear while the man, twisting and turning, lunges at them.

Eight. Nine. As soon as the tenth crow is beheaded, its wings scythed, the others wheel in a flurry of motion, flying higher and higher, until they surge in the direction of the cotton tree.

I never imagined, when my eyes opened to the dream-washed light of early morning, that by midday, crows on the far horizon would try to kill me. No, after a good night's sleep, I surfaced with Maanu's advice resonating in my heart.

As we were leaving the forest shrine, the diviner had said: *This may sound strange to you now, Sheba, but remember – go to the centre of every danger that lies ahead of you. Only there will you find safety.*

Last night, I'd taken another step towards the menace hanging over us.

Now I was about to venture to its heart.

My dreams while I slept hadn't disturbed my grandmother. I hadn't purred or roared. Instead, my body close to hers, an arm over a shoulder, I'd held her, our breath rising and falling in rhythm.

The hinges of a door creaked. I sat up.

Wide awake, Nana was at the far end of the room going through her wardrobe. On a chair, she had laid out her favourite kente cloth in blue and yellow; a woven cloth her parents had given her at her coming of age.

'What are you doing, Nana?'

She turned. Struck by how haggard she looked, skin stretched over gaunt cheeks, I asked: 'Are you all right?'

She didn't answer. She didn't need to. Her face appeared thinner, more fragile than before and around her eyes, plumes of pain fluttered, quivering about her frame as she got up and placed a string of waist-beads on top of the folded kente cloth.

Her discomfort reminded me of the scrabbling of talons on our roof, for on Nana's face, I saw the deathly haze of Ma's shadow.

Unbidden, tears salted my eyes. 'What's the matter, Nana? Where does it hurt?'

'At my age, just about every bit of me aches from time to time.'

'It didn't used to.'

'Remember to say that to yourself when you're over eighty. Come here, child.'

I clambered out of bed.

She handed me the kente cloth, the beads on top of it. 'When I die,' Nana said, 'I want to be buried in this...'

Beside the beads was a note written in her spidery scrawl: For my last journey.

'Nana,' I cried. 'You're not going to die. I'm going to make sure Ma leaves us in peace. I'm going to take care of you...'

A jumble of words tumbled from my mouth. Truth is, I shall never be ready for my grandmother's passing. She's the queen of our household; the queen mother of our village. My teacher. The star I get my bearings from at the start of a new day. What's more, it's thanks to Nana that I'm half-way normal, given my mother's cravings.

Panicked, my tongue gabbling faster than I could reason, I begged her not to leave me. She took my hand and raising it to her cheek, I felt the heat of the fever within her.

'I want you to have this.' My hand in hers, Nana led me to her dressing-table, and retrieving the necklace Nana Gyata su had given her, the pendant of our family crest in gold, she gave it to me. 'This is yours now, Sheba. Wear it with pride and remember me.'

'Nana, you're going *nowhere*,' I insisted. 'Maanu the diviner said... she said...'

In a flash, I realised that Maanu had spent most of our time together talking to me. At the end of the consultation, just as we were about to step into the dugout canoe, she'd said goodbye to my grandmother in a way that had stayed in my mind. Maanu had hugged her, stroking Nana's back tenderly. And when Nana broke away, they both had tears in their eyes.

They're good friends, I'd thought at the time. *Very good friends.*

Now, it dawned on me that their parting had had a deeper significance. 'Did Maanu tell you, Nana? Did she tell you when and how?'

'I don't need anyone to tell me what I know already.'

'Do my aunts know? Does Grandma Baby?'

'Of course,' said Nana.

My throat thick with emotion, I returned the necklace to its usual place. I tried to thank her for it, but even a simple combination of words refused to settle on my tongue. The words hid while, chest heaving, I stifled my tears as Nana showed me where she kept her papers: her will, her records of every land dispute she'd resolved in our village, and disputes still pending.

'Your junior grandmother will take my place,' Nana confirmed. 'Remind her where I keep these, because she's likely to forget.'

'She won't, Nana.'

She sniffed and then scrutinising me in a deep-dive stare that grazed my soul, she said: 'Did Baby ask you to put something in Sika's drink last night, Sheba?'

I returned her gimlet gaze with one of my own: that of a grass-cutter frozen by the eyes of a python.

'I thought as much. Your mother collapsed last night. She was in such a state your aunts had to put her to bed. Let this be a warning to you: Baby's potions can be lethal.'

I nodded as Nana added, a purr in her voice: 'Don't worry about your boyfriend, you hear? I'm working on him.'

'Thank you,' I managed at last. But then, tears coursing down my face, I placed my forehead against my grandmother's and caressing her hair, fingertips sliding down the shafts of her waves, I savoured, once again, the wonder of her love.

'There,' Nana said, releasing me. 'Hurry along now.'

Washed and dressed within half an hour, I stood outside the room I once shared with my mother; the room I was born in. I gripped the doorknob, turned it, and stepped inside.

As I watched my mother sleeping, my heart thobbed in anger and relief. What if I'd put more of the sleeping draught in her water? I trembled at the thought and yet here she was – the woman who wore my grandmother down as surely as waves hammer stones at the river's edge. Her arms hugging a pillow to her chest, her forehead beaded with perspiration, Ma's breath rose and fell as she snored.

I counted the gap between her snores. Counting, I felt their rhythm, the length of the pauses before she snuffled, turning to face me.

'Careful,' said Snake. 'Step softly. Step lightly. Closer, ever closer.'

Barefooted, I crept towards my mother.

Her eyelids quivered from the depths of a dream.

I waited, held my breath. Sure enough, before I exhaled, Ma turned again. Her back to me, her cover cloth slipped, revealing a hip as curved as the hill outside our village. It loomed, while, snuggled in the dip of her midriff, partly hidden by a roll of fat, were three rows of beads: a white one between two that were dark green.

I inched forward, took a pair of scissors from my pocket, and when the trembling in my fingers ceased, snipped the thread of her toma. The beads quickened, and dribbling away from her, pooled in globules that glided towards the edge of the bed. There, I placed a cinnamon bark box into which what had once been beads trickled.

They rippled, coiling, then recoiling. Moving and pulsing like water bedding into a cave, their motion warmed the box. I quickly closed the lid.

'Now burn it,' said Snake.

'But it's alive!'

'Of course it's alive. It's magic. Her magic. Burn it, Sheba.'

My sister-bride and I were down in the courtyard by now. It would have been easy to dash into Aunt Clara's kitchen and fling the box on to the charcoal-fired stove. It would have been easy to watch it burn until all that was left was a sprinkling of ashes and the lingering scent of cinnamon bark. Unlike my mother, though I've been tempted, it is not in my nature to kill unless I'm going to eat what's killed. Even when Nana and Grandma Baby perform rituals at the cotton tree and river, at the moment they're about to slit the throats of chicken or goats, I look away. I don't relish watching life drain from any creature.

'Aba! You're a lioness,' Snake hissed.

'I know, I know, I replied. 'But if my gut says "no" as it's doing now, I go with my gut.'

Snake cackled. I swear, she laughed at me before she gave in; and even though those crows were on to me as soon as I stepped outside the house, she never once said, *You see*! *I warned you*!

Hidden beneath
the banana tree,
I wait for the
girl, cheeks drip-
ping blood, to be
led away. Once the dust of
her screams have settled, I set off again to the haven I
discovered with Maybe.

The river's receded since we were last here, but
compared to the withered fields approaching it, the
foliage on this side of the waterway is still lush. Broad-
leaved shrubs tickled by a breeze sway in a dance to
water and sky. On the opposite bank are a pair of
egrets, beaks gliding against the current. One flips a
fish, and then, positioning its catch, gobbles it down.

I step in the river. The birds fly away while the
strengthening breeze stirs the leaves of mangrove
trees opposite. Waves splash roots, and then, sucking
at my toes, slap my shins.

I pause, listening to the cadence of the
river goddess's call swept by flurries of
air. I listen to her lilt and flow, and
when her melody is deep within
me and I begin to feel her
presence, only then
do I speak.

'Goddess of the river hear my prayer.
Save me from my mother.
Deliver us!
Help us work with one another.
Goddess of the river,
Hear my plea!
Heal my friend Maybe
Let him see again.
Goddess of rivers and streams
Take my mother's power and
Help me defeat her!'

I open the lid of the box. What's inside has congealed into a vibrating, glutinous mass. I fling it in the water. The moment it lands, the wind drops while the river swirls, churning as if a float of crocodiles is about to emerge.

Water splashes my legs. I scramble up the bank, for beneath the roiling and frothing, there's a growl. Low at first, it erupts in a roar as the river spins, creating a tunnel through which it spews feathers.

Hundreds of them.

Black feathers.

Crows' feathers.

Wing and tail feathers alongside plumes that are soft and downy. They surface, and in one ghastly movement they begin twitching, each of them fluttering as they transform into fledglings.

I look on, aghast, for as their wings flap and they begin to soar, the river heaves once again, and the noisy shriek of waves pierces the noon-day calm. The waves swish and swirl, rising higher and higher as, with the same grace and poise as egrets, they devour the birds. The river gulps them down, even as a dark cloud of fledglings escapes.

Screeching in chorus, wheeling in the sky, they fly in the direction of the cotton tree.

31

'EACH BEAD MUST have been a charm,' I say to Maybe, describing the spectacle at the river. 'She's powerful. Worse than Sasabonsam. Worse than I imagined.'

In truth, what I witnessed has filled me with dread. So much so, that I can't say her name out loud. How did my mother acquire such a storm of magic? If Snake is my talisman, as my elders call her, how has she managed to collect a sack full of them?

Questions zip through me and within seconds, Maybe replies in the matter-of-fact manner only he possesses. 'Could those beads be markers of her victims? Were those feathers their souls?'

I don't know. It's the not-knowing that perplexes me, forcing my mind to flex and dwell on questions I can't answer. Questions such as: if those feathers were indeed Ma's victims, are the fledglings that escaped still in thrall to her? Are they still bound to her? Even worse, what if one of them is my father? Or the fathers of my sisters? Waves of despair course through my body. My stomach cramps in revulsion, Maybe caresses my arm.

We're alone in my great-grandfather's bedroom, lying side by side on his double bed while Gaza's gone home for a change of clothes. In a corner is a shrine to my ancestor adorned with a framed photograph of him. Beside it are a bottle of water and a half-filled glass ready to replenish him in the realm of spirits.

'Do you remember how we used to creep in here and drink at the great chief's shrine?' says Maybe.

In spite of everything, I laugh. 'Has he come to you yet?'

Removing a pair of Aunt Ruby's sunglasses, Maybe's eyes open, unseeing. The gold in them, highlighting the beads I put in his hair, gleams, making him seem more attuned to the spirit world than everyday living.

Maybe gathers my fingers, gently kissing their tips. 'He's never far away,' he says. 'He's on the edges somewhere, in an in-between place like this.'

I wonder at Maybe's sensitivity; his understanding of soul-eaters and magic. How does he *know* things which take others a lifetime to understand? From what I've gathered, from what I've gleaned through his hair and that loop in time Nana Gyata su revealed, Maybe's gift is unusual.

I brush my cheek against his. When he smiles, I fondle a few stray hairs by his time bone, the soft ridge above his ear, where grey hair will eventually grow. I rub it gently.

Straightaway, a blast of heat singes my fingers. It's *him* again. Maybe's father, his face threatening as he drills into my mind. Such is the intensity of his rage that as his energy grazes mine, my soul recoils.

'What is it?' Maybe asks.

I dwell on sensations that buzz around us like a nest of hornets. Behind the face is a man with a heart so hard, the pain of others means nothing to him. A man who would walk through fire to get whoever and whatever he wants.

I think before I speak, tiptoeing to tease out the truth. 'Have you ever wondered,' I ask, 'if the reason your mother came here was not to protect herself but…'

Maybe bristles, sits up, and retrieving a clump of plasticine from the bedside table begins thumping it. 'My mother is not a witch,' he mumbles. 'She's not a witch.'

He starts moulding, stretching and kneading before rolling the plasticine into a ball.

'Have you asked her why she left your father?'

'There's no need to. I know what happened. I was there, Sheba.'

'But you were just a boy.'

He mimics my voice, giving it the frivolous tone of a princess in a house of plenty. '*Just a boy*! *Just a boy*!'

The tang of lemon sours my mouth. I bite my tongue, seething.

'Of course, I was young, but I remember what they said about my mother. What they were saying about–'

He slams the ball on his thigh, his face lively with the presence of his dead-departed. They flit over his nose and cheeks, down the side of his neck while his eagle eyes glisten.

More than ever, I want Maybe back to how he was. Back to when he could see me, and our eyes would share kisses.

Flinging the plasticine from one hand to the other, he nods. 'Yes. Rumours spread about me too. I was the first of four to survive, so they said I was…' He sighs, searching for a word that escapes him.

'Weird?' I suggest.

He half-nods before shaking his head.

'A spirit child?'

'Perhaps. They claimed I would bring bad luck to our family, but when Better Life was born…' His eyes unblinking, he turns his face towards mine. 'What did you see just now, Sheba?'

I quickly describe the face that thrust itself in front of mine; the face that resembles Maybe's. 'He came after *you*, not your mother. I think he wanted to speak to those you speak to. He wanted what you have.'

'He must have heard me talking to them…'

'Did he want to use you? Use your power?'

Forced to reconsider his past in a new light, Maybe closes his eyes. When he opens them again, the luminous shine in them makes him look more vulnerable than ever.

'My father wanted to be chief. Where I come from, to lead, you have to know how to walk and talk with spirits… how to use magic.'

He pauses, and for what feels like forever, my friend is silent, unreachable, until surfacing once again, his voice breaks, reminding me of how we used to be. 'Sheba, I need to talk to my mother. Will you take me to her?'

'Will you come back?'

'Would you like me to?'

I think of those feathers on the river, the fledglings in the cotton tree. I think of Mother Crow, her wings cruel as the grave, hovering over us, and say: 'Yes.'

If I'd hoped that stealing Ma's love-beads and throwing them in the river would change her behaviour, I soon discover I'm wrong. When she wakes, she follows a routine she's refined over the past two days. On this, the third day of her progress, she dresses in sheda once again; an up and down in a glorious turquoise blue; a blue guaranteed to warm the heart, if you haven't seen the look on Nana's face first.

My grandmother's wearing her Queen Mother death stare. Eyes dark with curses, her face is a mask of disapproval. In days gone by that look would terrify me: neck and jaws stiff, head held high and those eyes! Not today. Like my aunts and Grandma Baby, I'm doing my best to shield Nana from Ma's noisy glamour as the terrace starts filling with her friends.

The house, sensitive to my grandmother's mood, quails. Timbers creak; steel girders squeal, stretching and expanding in a swell of humidity. Our home, as agitated as we are, gasps, thirsty for an end to the dry season. Walls grumble, while ceilings, weighed down by emotion, sag. And when Nana closes her eyes, trying to shut out the din outside, the air hums with anger.

'Sheba,' Nana says. 'Go and see what your mother's up to. Don't linger. Report back to me.'

Under normal circumstances, I'd do what she asks: be her eyes and ears; spy on Ma. No problem! But today is not a normal day. How can it be when Nana's told everyone present that she's getting ready to die? And after what I witnessed fili-fili with my own eyes this morning, I can't help but wonder at my family, my grandmother especially. Her daughter, my mother, may have murdered many people. I saw what remained of them fly to the cotton tree. And now that her daughter, my mother, is making mischief outside, instead of asking me to lion-up and tear her apart,

Nana wants me to spy
and report back?
Makes no sense
whatsoever.

'Nana,' I cry.
'Why don't you just tell
Ma to stop? If you disapprove
of what she's up to, why don't
you *do* something?'

My aunts, enjoying a light
supper of hot chocolate and cake,
snigger. Sniggers turn to laughter,
strengthened by snorts from
Nana and Grandma Baby.

Snake tells me to cool it, go
with the flow, but after all I've seen and heard today,
being laughed at is more than I can bear. The quills of
my hair, sheaved in cotton, onigi style, quiver in fury.
Lemon drenches my tongue and I glare at them using
the sling in my eyes to say: *Be careful, ladies. Be very
careful indeed.*

Aunt Clara, wiping her face of smiles, says:
'Haven't you realised, Sheba? If you ask your mother
to stop doing something, she doubles down and does
it a thousand times over. The best way to get around
her is to ignore her.'

I shake my head recalling the insults Ma's heaped
on my aunt since forever. *Useless. A sleeping mat no*

one wants to sleep on. Barren. An empty calabash, no pickney dey inside.

The memory of Ma's abuse echoes between us and I shake my head again. 'Ignore her and she'll hurt you whenever she feels like it.'

The truth of my words stings. A tear drops down Aunt Clara's cheek and as I squeeze her hand, the party outside shifts gear. There's more laughter, more clapping and back-slapping, before the first dribble of a song.

'We can't just sit here doing nothing!'

Four pairs of eyes impale me. I'm the youngest, I know. My elders are my teachers, but that doesn't make me a fool! We have to do something, anything, before our house collapses and our village is destroyed. 'Can't you feel it?' I ask.

One after the other, they nod.

'There's a stench of sulphur in the air,' Grandma Baby admits.

Aunt Ruby smooths the unruly ruffles of her blouse. 'I feel the thrill of glamour on my clothes.'

'When Sika's like this,' Aunt Clara confesses, 'I'm reminded of my time in Nigeria, and wish I could have a swig of whatever she's on.'

Nana sighs. Tries to speak, but as the clamour on the veranda grows, she kneads her forehead. 'God is in control,' she murmurs. 'Kwame, the creator of all things is at the helm of this house.'

'Nana, we have to take control
ourselves...'

Nana's eyes snap open and there
it is again: her Queen Mother
death stare, only this time,
directed at me. 'Grandchild
of mine,' she begins, and then,
weighing her words with
such tenderness that her
love trickles into me, filling
me from head to toe. 'You're
too young to understand what my heart
knows to be true. Your mother is a part of us.
Her shadow is in each of us, you especially. You
can't see it now, but you soon will.' Nana places
a hand on her chest, rubbing it as if to ease her pain.
'Now, do what I've asked. Go outside and be my eyes.
And when your ears are full, before I go to bed tonight,
tell me what you've seen.'

Outside, the crowd around my mother is bigger
than ever. Swaying to the music of their adulation she
fills their calabashes with a swing of the hips, a giggle
on her lips. Like everyone else, I'm transfixed by her
presence. I can't look away. Even when Ama joins
me, her chin on my shoulder, my eyes are on Ma. A
flick of her fingers and my feet start to tap. A turn of
her head and I can't help but smile until I notice that
beneath the glow of turquoise that adorns her, the

glow that flows as smoothly as the river on a cloudless day, are two rows of love-beads around her waist. I cringe.

Tempted to look closer, I stay hidden in the shadows wondering if those beads are yet more of her charms. Are they the souls of even more of her victims? Is she ever satisfied? Bewitching her prey is probably what thrills her most. I watch, riveted, while Ma, in her element, conjures her magic, mixing her allure with laughter and song.

Delight hovers in the air like a moth flustered by my mother's scent: the smell of earth after rain. At the end of a long, dry season, there's nothing more irresistible than the first hint of a storm. I breathe my mother in and for a moment, I wish I were a toddler again and could run into her arms without knowing what I do.

Snake crushes my finger and straightaway I recall what my ancestor foresaw. Unless I act quickly, unless I act soon, we shall drown in danger of the worst kind. Our time of greatest peril is right *now,* just before the rains come.

A sheet of lightning flashes, turning night to day. Thunder rolls overhead, and as the night sky sizzles, a group of women barge into our yard. There are twelve of them in the black-and-red robes of deep mourning, red bandanas in their hands. Led by

Auntie Esi, Ama's mother, they're the most important women of our village: farmers, our baker, dressmaker, the queen mother of our market. Important women who happen to be the wives, daughters, sisters and mothers of some of Ma's assembled friends. Slowly, carefully, faces grim as death, they tie the bandanas around their heads, a sign they're on a war footing.

Ma roars with laughter. Her drinking buddies do the same. They laugh until it dawns on them that perhaps the matter at hand should not be made fun of after all.

Hilarity draining into a pit of doubt, only Ma remains firm. A smile lacing her lips, she says: 'Ladies, why don't you join us?'

Cover cloths rustle, flapping in a wave of red and black as the women open and then tighten the cloths around their waists.

Not a word is said.

Ma tries again. 'Esi, old friend, long time. Come and join your husband, Allotey, here. Come.'

Silence reigns. Poisonous, vengeful.

Feet shuffle in a semi-circle, then, Auntie Esi steps forward.

Ma's eyes spark, and tinder stored in the depths of Auntie Esi's heart flames. The whites of her eyes red with rage, she can scarcely speak for her trembling.

'Esi, what happened between us, happened a long time ago… it's over, forgotten,' says Ma.

Still quaking, our next-door neighbour raises her hand, and pointing an accusing finger at Ma, her voice crackles fire, '*You.* You use what's in you to bewitch and belittle. We don't want you here.'

The women clap, grunting approval. They clap and then spit in Ma's direction.

Once they've finished, once they've told Ma to stop whatever she's up to, contempt wrinkles my mother's brow, and hands on hips, she eyeballs them.

If you know her as well as I do, you'll understand why I step into the gloom to hide my shame. I step back, tread on Ama's foot, the sky flashes white, and Ma's insults begin.

'Look at that face of yours, Esi! Pimpled, dark as midnight. Who'd want to wake up to a face as pock-marked as yours? No wonder Allotey is here.'

'Dinah, smell yourself, woman! You should wash at least once a day. Once, *peh*! Next time you step foot here, my sister, I beg you, take time and wash…'

On and on she goes, naming them before shaming them with the blade at the tip of her tongue. Their faces, hair, skin, legs, bodies are as nothing compared to hers. She even points to the leader of the market women, Auntie Vida, someone I've learned to steer clear of.

'Vida!' Ma cries. 'Is that you? Have your ears grown

even larger with age? Aba! They're like the wings of a bat now!'

Aghast, Ama and I look at each, shrinking into the shadows.

Delving into the past, Ma hurls daggers at the heart of each of the women ranged against her: family scandals that hint at murder, theft, broken marriages, disputes. If it happened, Ma lobs it at them, revelling in their pain. She's not laughing now. There's no need to touch her locks to feel the burn of her tongue. No need to stroke her skin to suffer the furnace blast of her spirit. Every word is loaded with dynamite, every sentence saturated with such venom that as my mother rages, her hatred scorches my ears.

At last, a feather floats to her feet, and instead of locks piled on her head, there's a ruffle of plumes. Mother Crow is speaking now in a voice wild as the wind, her resentment unending. Her voice thunders while the sky above flashes with lightning once again. The ground I'm standing on shifts, and bit by bit, our house seems to rise as the roof tilts from one side to the other.

I steady myself by clutching Ama's arm. There's no stopping Ma now. Incandescent, she lacerates her rivals with the noxious fury of Mother Crow, and as she does so, the beads around her waist glitter.

Moving, twitching. Alive.

Magnificent and deadly, her rage soars and the beads squirm, thriving on malice.

Nobody sees them but me.

Not a single person breaks ranks.

Ma's wrath holds them spellbound. Not one of them moves. So it is, that the women, humiliated, slope away, while Ma towers over them, triumphant.

Half in thrall to her, half-ashamed, I say to Ama, 'My mother has no respect. She's more of a child than we are. I bet you, by tomorrow, every woman who hears what happened tonight will hate her.'

'Bestie-best,' Ama replies, 'don't you know? They hate her already.'

32

OF COURSE, THEY do! At times, I do as well, and yet to hear the truth from a friend hurts. It's as if Ama's squeezed a bruise that won't heal. Even though I'm aware of what Ma's capable of, to be told that women loathe her wrenches my guts.

Heavy-hearted, I wander upstairs to check if Maybe's back. He isn't. Surprised by how much I miss him and need to talk to him, I knock on my grandmother's door. Already at her dressing-table, she's preparing for bed. I finish plaiting her hair, savouring its texture along with the floral scent of baobab-seed oil that she uses to moisturise it.

All I do is touch Nana and a stream of sadness swirls around me, drawing us closer. She's as unhappy as I am. Even more so, once I've filled her ears with what I saw and heard outside: Ma's battle with the most powerful women of our village while their menfolk stood by and marvelled.

Nana's shoulders slump. 'In that case,' she says.

'They'll send a delegation to see me first thing tomorrow. Take out my white-and-black adinkra bou-bou, Sheba. The one with the Akofena symbol on it; the sword of war. They came to our house in battle dress. I shall meet them with courage.'

I open her wardrobe looking for the garment she wants: a white dress stamped with black clashing swords. It's the dress she wears when she wants to become the leader our ancestor was – fearless and valiant. I hang the bou-bou on the wardrobe door. Then, I tell her about Ma's toma, those waist beads that turned to feathers this morning and the love-beads she's wearing right now.

'A house divided cannot stand,' my grandmother moans. 'How can our village survive if Sika pits men against women? For what? Her own glory? Shame on her!'

Nana begins pacing the floor, half-walking, half-shuffling back and forth as thunder groans outside. Thunder without rain is agonising, especially when the seasons are in flux and the air is unbearably hot and sultry as it is today.

Nana pauses, and then facing me, asks: 'When the time comes, Sheba, do you have everything you need to set yourself free?'

I don't want to reply. If I do, her going away inches closer.

Nana's eyes search mine. 'Answer me, Sheba.'

'I do, Nana. Aunt Clara returned what belongs to me.'

Thanks to my aunt I have the pouch my mother buried a few months after my birth. The day after our consultation with Maanu, Aunt Clara had visited my Uncle Solomon's house. There, with his permission, she dug beneath the frangipani tree and found the package Ma had planted to sow her spell. Inside a soiled plastic bag was the tattered mud-cloth pouch that held fragments of the cord that once attached me to Ma.

Remembering the strange lullaby she sang, the incantation she conjured over Aunt Lila and me, I hurry to bed. Clutching a pillow to smother an ache in my chest, I ask a question I've raised again and again; a question no one has answered to my satisfaction. 'Why does Ma hate Aunt Lila?'

'You should ask your mother that.'

See what I mean about my family? 'I no longer talk to her, Nana. How can I after what she's done?'

Silence speaks louder than words. I reckon my grandmother must be giving up on Ma as well.

'Thank you for taking me to see Maanu,' I reassure her. 'If you hadn't, I'd be out on the terrace instead of here with you now.'

Nana smiles. 'At least I've done one thing right. Remember, Sheba, it's not over yet. You are the key to what happens next.'

'I'll remember.'

YABA BADOE

Her smile widens, giving way to a bone-rattle sigh, the sigh that gathers me in. Weighing her words carefully, testing them first on the tip of her tongue, she says, 'About your mother and Lila. Let me put it this way, grandchild of mine. What if your Uncle Solomon is the only man your mother's truly loved? What if Lila is nothing like your mother?'

'Like Grandma Baby and Ma?'

'Worse,' says Nana. 'Baby and your mother are blood rivals. The rivalry between in-laws is much worse. Think of a colour.'

'Yellow.'

'Then Lila's purple. And if she's turquoise blue like a clear sky at noon, Sika is blood red like the water in Maanu's pot.'

'But why does Ma hate her, Nana? Why?'

Nana starts pacing the room again. But this time, walking up and down, she rolls up the sleeves of her robe and then shakes them out violently. 'Jealousy can change a woman into a leopard, Sheba. Your mother can't forgive Lila for marrying her twin. Can't forgive her for raising her daughters, for turning them into fine city girls with no taste for people like us. City folk say that people like us come from the *bush*. Now, go to sleep, grandchild.'

294

I close my eyes,
but sleep won't come.
How can it in a house
under siege, in a house
on edge and as jittery as I am?
I hug my pillow, pull my cover
cloth over my head. However,
the rooms and corridors of
our home, even the courtyard
downstairs, are too thick with
emotion for sleep to creep in.

Too overwrought to settle, my mind flits like a flea
from Maybe to Ma, Ma to Uncle Solo and Aunt Lila
in Accra, and then Salmata and Nana. My skin on fire,
Snake hisses, the sing-song of her voice beneath mine,
until eventually the way clears and truth beckons.
Tomorrow, when Nana acts, so must I.

This is what I tell myself as my grandmother pads
the floor. I count her strides, her pauses. Count the
steps of her shuffles before she sits down. Then, as she
paces again, I imagine the worst that can happen. To
guard against it, I plan, setting events in sequence the
better to see them.

'Calm down,' Snake advises, wriggling alongside me.
'We need to sleep now. We have to gather our strength
for tomorrow and the day after. Sleep,' she hisses.
'Better still, think of what we'll do afterwards. Think of
Maybe and the river. Think of Ama and Gaza.'

'What about Nana?'

Snake won't answer. Ignoring her silence, I imagine the future I'd like instead. Above all, we'll be *safe*. Maybe will be able to see again and everyone will be as we were before Ma returned. This is my hope, even as the elements that flash and rumble outside remind me that the worst is yet to come.

By morning the wind is up, slamming and opening doors, shaking the shutters as it strips leaves off the mango tree in the back yard. Aunt Clara, mindful of the guests who'll be arriving later, tells me to sweep and dust our sitting room; the upstairs room in which a portrait of Nana Gyata su looks over us while disputes are settled.

I follow her instructions, but as I fling the shutters open, I gasp. Arrayed on the cotton tree like the black sails of a windswept galleon, are hundreds of crows. Yesterday's fledglings are now enormous birds; birds massed with others of their kind, as well as ravens and red-eyed drongos. Every branch of the tree is heaving. Every twig winged and feathered.

Illuminated by streaks of lightning, their eyes open and close, a monster from a realm beyond the grave, watching me. Their size and number is unnatural. But what unnerves me most, is that on opening the shutter, each and every one of the birds turns, and their gaze on me, blink as one.

Snake tells me not to be afraid.

I back away. Dust the next shutter and the next while murmuring a prayer to the portrait of Nana Gyata su on the wall behind me. Then, flinging the shutters open, I pretend that everything is as it should be. I do it in spite of the creature observing my every move; in spite of claps of thunder and flashes of light in a sky heavy with rain, I behave as if all is well.

The wind howls, a gust blows the front gate open, and in they come. There are only five women this time.

'Ago!'

'Amie! Come in!' I hear Aunt Ruby cry. 'Welcome!'

I scramble downstairs in time to see them taking off their sandals before Aunt Ruby escorts them up to the sitting room. Then, I do what's expected of the youngest in the house. I assemble glasses, fill them with water and after carefully placing them on a tray, carry them upstairs.

My grandmother, her back to the cotton tree, is wearing the adinkra bou-bou, her sword of war dress, a clash of black blades against white.

Head lowered, I offer our guests water. They look at me askance, peering at me as Ma's shadow steps between us.

Picking up a glass, Auntie Esi says: 'Thank you,' in such a way that it wouldn't take much for her to damn me in the next breath. Auntie Vida follows her example, while the rest of them purse their lips as if to say: 'What? Sip water from a glass offered by Sika's daughter? A snake bite would be better!'

Hah! You don't have to be a seer to hear Ma's shadow cackling behind me; Ma scoffing as she says: *Think you're different, do you? Think again, little chick. You and I are alike.*

Grandma Baby, catching my eye, winks, while Nana, beside her, relieves me of a glass, as do Clara and Ruby. I'm about to leave (as befits a dutiful daughter of the house), when to everyone's surprise, Nana calls me back.

'Sheba,' she says, her voice quiet but calm, 'I want you to hear what we're going to discuss. It concerns your mother.'

'Nana Serwah, is that wise?' asks Vida, tugging her ear in consternation. 'This is woman palaver. Your granddaughter's a slip of thing.'

'Sheba has a mind of her own, and if she doesn't hear what we discuss, she'll get wind of it from Ama Smart next door. Am I right, Esi?'

Auntie Esi agrees.

Folding her hands on her lap, Nana's features rearrange themselves. There's a subtle shift. Same eyes, same forehead, mouth and nose, but if you look closely at the framed photograph of my great-grandfather opposite and place it over Nana's face, it's as if the two are merging; as if somehow, after dipping into her soul, she's drawing on our ancestor and channelling him.

Nana lifts her head. She begins as custom demands. 'Vida, what is your mission here today?' She may not be sitting in our ancestor's brass-studded chair, but the power radiating from her sends shivers through each of us.

I hover, listening to complaints about my mother: what she's doing to our village, how she's pitting husbands against wives, creating conflict between and within families.

'Big Man is so smitten by her,' Vida exclaims, 'that he threatened Akosua when he got home. Said she'd shamed him and if she dared pull such a stunt again…'

Auntie Esi nods. 'That's exactly what Allotey said. Sika's a stain I can't remove from our marriage. Nana, what am I to do?'

'Did Allotey harm you? Did Big Man hurt Akosua?'

Ama's ma shakes her head, but as Nana and Auntie Vida exchange glances, the air between them sizzles.

Vida's chin drops. 'We should have rid ourselves of him years ago.'

'We had Gaza to think of,' Nana reminds her.

'He's rough with him as well,' Vida replies. 'And now Sika's rekindled the past. Her anger is too much, even for us, Nana. We women arrived here afraid. If we hadn't left our homes, we'd have been lynched. Yet our anger is nothing compared to your daughter's.'

At this, the women start talking over each other, their voices a chorus of grievances.

'We can hardly breathe,' one says. 'The air in our village has changed since Sika's return.'

'The rains haven't come,' says another. 'And yet since our visit here last night, one, two, *boom!* Thunder! One, two, *zoom!* Lightning! Night and day. It met us here, now it won't stop.'

'This is Sika's doing,' someone mumbles.

Voices tumble over each other. 'Have you seen the crows on the cotton tree, Nana? The eyes of Sasabonsam are on us. Tell your daughter to go!'

'Whatever's happening to us, Nana, arrived with your daughter!'

'She has to go before matters slip out of our hands and bones are broken.'

'Banish her, Nana, before wahala slaps our faces and we're too ugly to care if there's blood on our hands.'

Nana's back stiffens. As her eyes glaze over, freezing any trace of warmth from her countenance, her Queen Mother death stare silences everyone. 'Thank you for coming to see me,' she declares. 'Thank you for expressing your complaints.' She takes a sip of water. 'I promise you, I shall deal with Sika. Tell your men, and those who follow them, that if they wish to remain in our village, they should steer clear of my daughter.'

33

BY MIDDAY NANA'S at it again. Turning in circles, she tugs at loose threads of her battle dress, muttering to herself.

Grandma Baby tries to stop her. 'Serwah, rest,' she insists. 'Stop this pacing and rest, sister.'

'I'm thinking,' Nana shoots back. 'Go away!'

Half an hour later, it's Aunt Ruby's turn. 'You must be hungry, Ma. Come down for a snack.'

'I prefer to think on an empty stomach.'

'But Ma, you haven't been well.'

'If I'm well enough to toss my daughter out, I can go without food.'

'Is that what you're going to do, Ma?'

'*What*?' says Nana.

'Ask Sika to leave?'

'I'm *thinking*.'

'Fine,' Aunt Ruby replies.

Fine, I think. *Fine*? No way can Nana's discomfort be described as 'fine'.

Catching my drift, Aunt Ruby beckons.

Nana raises a hand. 'I've told her to stay here. Sheba's going nowhere.'

'Fine. Fine.'

Nothing, absolutely *nothing* in our house at the moment is fine. Our leader's pacing is making her ill, crows are massing in the cotton tree, and my innards are churning. *Fine*? Don't think so.

Next in is Aunt Clara, who attempts to lure Nana out of her bedchamber with the promise of tea and achumo, Nana's favourite biscuits.

Nana's reply? She sends me downstairs to fetch a tray of snacks.

Even when Maybe returns, chaperoned by Gaza, I stay by my grandmother's side, watching as the turbulence in her heart speaks through her feet: frustration, anger, love, despair. I hear them all in her footfall, and when she wrenches her sleeve, ripping a seam, I see unhappiness on her face.

At last, at one o'clock, a door slams. Ma's door.

'Now!' Nana says. 'Go and give your mother my message.'

I do exactly what she asks, repeating instructions

she's made me memorise. 'Ma, Ma,' I cry, following her succulent mango bottom as it rolls down the corridor to the stairs. 'Ma, Nana Serwah wants to see you at three o'clock. She has work for you to do.'

'What sort of work?'

'I don't know, Ma.'

'You don't know? You two are like a bad drummer and drum these days. All talk, no rhythm, no fun. More fool you.'

I feel her eyes on me. Feel them searing my skin, the hint of a hiss in her voice as the ring on my finger tightens.

'A mother and daughter should work together, Sheba. Work with me, not against me. For goodness' sake, girl! Look at me!'

I gaze into eyes dark as night. Eyes that would gulp me down in a second if I let them. I cringe, even as I force a smile to my lips. A smile that reassures me that I'm as nimble as a plover picking the teeth of a crocodile.

'Did you think I wouldn't notice what you stole from me the other day? You little fool. We are so much stronger than you are. Come home to me, Sheba. Join us!'

Before I can say 'no' she's already changed the subject. 'Have those fat breadfruit women sent a delegation to the High Priestess of Righteousness yet? Do I even care?'

'They came this morning, Ma. Nana sent them away.'

'Is that why she wants to see me?'

'I've told you, Ma. I don't know.'

'As if I care,' she mumbles.

By three o'clock the weather outside matches the commotion in our home. What makes it worse is that the only ones thinking and talking about it are Snake and me. While Maybe describes his visit home and what Salmata has told him about his father, I'm in silent conversation with her.

Sensitive to Ma's presence, the banging of pots in the kitchen, the doors she slams on her way upstairs and then into her room, I'm trying to pay attention, while Maybe confirms what I gleaned when last I touched his hair. The moment she feared for Maybe's life, Salmata fled to protect him from a father whose ambition was greater than his love for their son.

'Did he become a chief?' I ask.

Maybe shrugs. 'What matters is she believed he was prepared to kill me to possess what's mine.' Aunt Ruby's sunglasses hiding the golden glaze in his eyes, he cocks his head. 'Sheba, what's the matter? Your mind's elsewhere.'

I'm about to mumble an excuse, anything to fob

him off, when the crows
in the cotton tree, silent
till now, begin cawing.
Terrifying, ear-splitting
shrieks, which in concert
with whoops of wind
shredding trees of leaves, tighten
my throat. I rub it, remembering when the
only noise I could make was the chirrup of a
chick as Ma's voice tangled my tongue.

Beneath the squawking of crows, the
wind seems to scream: '*Run*! *Run*!'

'Are those the crows Gaza
mentioned?'

'Yes,' I murmur.

'Your mother's crows?'

'Of course.'

'Then go, Sheba. I don't mind being on my own
here. Go, it's started.'

Exactly what it is, I'm not sure. It's in the air we're
breathing, the shiver of excitement on the skin, the
scent of river in our noses, the assault of crows on our
eardrums. It's in the rush of wind as I open the door
and it slams behind me. The creak of stairs as I run
down to join Nana waiting for Ma. While in my ear
Snake hisses what she believes is true.

'That racket is your mother talking to the crows in
the cotton tree,' she insists. 'Why else would they be

making such a din? Today's the day they strike.'

'Not if Nana can help it.'

Snake doesn't reply.

I feel a tickle in my throat as if the cotton tree's trying to talk through me or tell me something. The bricks of our house, plastered white every year, seem to crackle, while the roof rustles with the scrape of talons landing on it. *Boom*! *Boom*! *Boom*!

Ma's birds are assembling. What's coming is here, and with the mud-cloth pouch in my pocket, I'm ready.

This is what I tell myself as Ma waltzes downstairs smiling, a song and dance in her hips. Anyone would think it was another of her party days, the way she's dressed. White Nigerian lace. Sparkling wedding lace cut Senegalese style into a kaftan that ripples over her body.

'Your Righteousness,' she teases. 'What can I do for you this afternoon, dearest Ma?'

My grandmother, seated in the brass-studded chair, fondles the carved paws at the end of its arms. She flexes her fingers, lifts her chin. 'I want you to leave our home, Sika, and stay away from our village. For all our sakes and for the sake of our ancestors who created a place of refuge for runaways, you have to go.'

'You want me to leave my home? *Why?*'

'Sika!' Grandma Baby cries. 'My sister tells you to leave, you leave!'

Nana closes her eyes. When she opens them again,

there's no denying her exhaustion. 'Sika, I don't have the strength to explain myself. Do as I say!'

Ma bounds forward. Elbowing Ruby and Clara aside, she barrels past Grandma Baby and is about to pounce on Nana when I step in front of the brass-studded chair.

'She told you to go, Ma. Please go.'

That's when she lets rip. A few days ago, I believed she was limbering up for the mother of all battles with Nana. Seems she had both of us in mind, for she lashes me with her tongue, railing.

I'm scum, she says. Worse than my father.

A traitor. A viper. A snake under concrete.

A monster, black as night and twice as ugly.

On and on she rants, scorching me with venom until my grandmother, hauling herself up, puts an arm around me. 'Sika, go! Go before I use the powers vested in me to rain curses on your head!'

Eyeball to eyeball, Ma's rage bludgeons Nana as they exchange words that are best left unspoken between mother and daughter.

Words such as slut, whore, murderer.

Words spliced with lies inflamed by anger.

Words of hate and malice.

Words stored in an unforgiving heart that, once unleashed, are never forgotten.

Words of heartache and pain that, stifling love, drain the soul of light.

Words that smother breath.

A lionheart girl, I put an arm around my grandmother's waist, and supporting her, steadfastly hold her upright.

At last, her patience spent, Nana pushes me aside and, in a voice that quells the din of wind and crows outside, she raises an arm. 'In the name of Nana Gyata su who built this house. In the name of the first lion of our line, I erase you from our family. From now on you may call yourself whatever you want. I banish you. This is no longer your home. Be gone.'

There's silence while Ma draws breath. For five precious seconds she turns from Nana to me, her face livid. 'Sheba, go upstairs. Pack my bags and we'll go. I won't leave this house without you.'

'No, Ma. I'm staying,' I tell her. 'This is my home.'

Her eyes fillet me, stripping me to the bone. 'You're mine. Mine alone.'

I shake my head, more determined than ever. 'I belong here with Nana. She filled the hole you left in me when you murdered my father. I shall never follow you, never.'

'Never?' She sniffs. 'Never?' She laughs. 'Don't count on it, little chick. I swear on your grandmother's soul that before the sun sets, you'll be with me again, a feather on my wing.'

34

AS SOON AS Ma flounces out of our door, I'm wrenched in two. A part of me trails her, clinging to her shadow, at the same time as Nana collapses in my arms. I lower her gently into her chair, crying: 'Nana! Nana!' Believing that wrung dry, she's fainted.

'Look! See what your mother's up to,' Snake hisses, revealing a world beyond mine in which my aunts have taken charge of my grandmother. Patting her cheeks, stroking her skin, they're trying to revive her while Snake, my extra eyes and ears, lays bare Ma's progress.

Once she's stepped out, crows dive from our roof and swarm around her. Black grooms to her bride, she shimmers in lace, flaunting her secrets. Half-dancing, she appears to float on air, her arms a glittering shawl of wings.

Ma sweeps along, jet feathers in her hair, on her shoulders. Feathers caressing her cheek, wings at her feet. Black and white in motion, cawing and laughing,

Ma, accompanied by crows, sings a song.

> '*Sika! Gold!*
> *My name is on everyone's lips.*
> *Sika! Gold!*
> *My face is the mirror they pick!*
> *Sika! Gold!*
> *The mirror they see themselves in!*
> *The glass they drink from,*
> *The mango to their breadfruit!*
> *Sika! Gold! Sika! Gold! Sika Gold!*'

Ma sings while Grandma Baby, waving a phial of eucalyptus beneath Nana's nose, cries: 'Sister! Sister!'

'Ma! Nana! Sister!' We're all calling her now, trying to lure her back to where we are. Back to our courtyard, her throne our ancestor's chair.

I warm Nana's hands, kiss her cheek. Aunt Ruby sits her up and fingering her dress, straightens it, shaking her head.

Undeterred, Grandma Baby waves the bottle of eucalyptus like a wand. 'Sister! Sister,' she pleads.

I touch Nana's hair. Breath, light as a butterfly's wing, dusts my fingers.

'She's gone,' says Aunt Clara.

'No,' I reply. 'She's still with us. Gather round.'

For once, the women of our house do as the youngest suggests. Holding hands, forming a circle of love around my grandmother, I call her name. Our breath mingling with her last, we warm her and draw her back.

Her eyes open. Finding my face, Nana smiles. 'My eyes will be his now, Sheba. Your friend will see again. Do what you have to, to set yourself free.' And with that, she leaves.

There's no time for tears. No time for grief. A still, small voice that I recognise as my own, insists that I listen. Faint as a heartbeat, I hear a drum. A talking drum. Muffled to begin with, it grows louder and louder as Snake reveals a scene unfolding in the market.

It's Ma.

Ma, revelling in her power, curses the market women from the depth of her soul. Next, she begins conjuring magic over one of her admirers.

My pulse racing, the drum declares that war has come to our village, and in the tumult a child is begging for help.

'Help me! Help!' I hear her cry as Gaza and Ama race into our house.

'They've surrounded her,' says Gaza. 'They're going to kill her. Come, Sheba.'

'The market women and my mother. They want Auntie Sika gone. She's got my father,' Ama adds. 'Come, Sheba! Run!'

I move quickly. 'Aunt Clara, stay with Nana. Gaza, fetch Maybe. The rest of you wait.'

I race up the stairs in Gaza's footsteps and dart into Nana's room. There, in her jewellery box, is the pendant she bequeathed me. I place it around my neck and after rubbing it to reassure myself that Nana will always be nearby, I'm off.

'Grandma Baby, Aunt Ruby, follow me,' I command.

I've often wondered how the guardians of our village know what to do when they hear a plea for help. Always wondered how they're able to register it and respond. Now I know.

I'm running, Ama behind me. A gale whips our feet and, nipping our heels, almost trips us. The faster we sprint, the harder it blasts us, so that for an instant it's as if we're trapped. We're hardly inching forward, until, as we pass the cotton tree, branches bereft of birds, sigh, blowing gusts to propel us on. With a final push, rain clouds rolling in the sky release sprinklings of drizzle.

Nana Gyata su warned me of this moment. He advised me to finish my task before the rains come; finish before our village is destroyed, and our haven disappears. I run even faster.

At the market, I stumble on Ma, her birds, and most of the men of our village on one side, while on the other are market women and Ama's mother. The women are picking up stones, edging closer, when, as

312

Maybe and Gaza join us, Ama points at her father.

He's changing, shrinking before our eyes. His head already feathered, his torso and legs disappear, replaced by wings and taloned feet. Ma chuckles as he hops on to her outstretched arm.

In the commotion that follows, the screams of 'Witch! Witch!' from women once accused of the same crime, Gaza jostles to his father's side. Unperturbed by the clamour of crows above them, Big Man and his men stand shoulder to shoulder, protecting Ma from the advancing crowd. I scramble after Gaza.

I can only guess what he's saying from his gestures and the contortions on his face. 'Madam Sasabonsam! Monster!' Terror ignites anger. He shakes his father, then lunges at Ma who, repelling him with a glare, grins as the bird who was once a man, nestles in her hair.

Where's the child, I wonder. The child whose call brought me here. As I try to track her down, Big Man struggles with his son. He's shoving Gaza back, when a hurled stone hits Ma. Blood gushes from her forehead and again, I hear the wail of the child.

Auntie Esi picks up another stone.

Before she throws it, before the rest of the women charge forward, my tongue, long as a lioness's, curls, and lips pursed, I make the sound Nana Gyata su taught me.

I whistle. Grandma Baby and Aunt Ruby appear either side of me with Maybe at my back.

Whistle again.

In a flick of a tail, they arrive in droves. Pride after pride of spectral lionesses surge forward, and as they surround us, they roar. Their thunder seeps through skin and veins until the wild, seizing my soul, opens my heart, and I roar as well.

Time freezes and everyone, except for me, is motionless, fear fixed on their faces. In that moment, Maybe's back to mine, I feel Nana's presence between us as a lioness prowls about my feet. She slides in and out of my legs and when she looks up, around the amber glow of her irises are circles of blue. It could be Nana gazing at me, Nana, marvelling.

She lopes ahead, slipping between Big Man and Gaza to my mother.

The lioness growls, baring razor-sharp canines.

Was it Ma who summoned me? Really? 'Ma! Ma?' I touch her to release her from terror's grip.

'Is that you, Sheba? Where's my grandfather? I called Nana Gyata su.'

'I'm guardian of our village now.'

What I'm thinking is, why call for help, when moments before she was gloating over her prey?

'You? Aba! How things change. Take me home, little chick. Hide me. *Please.*'

When she realises that I will do no such thing, she asks in the voice of the girl I heard: 'Have I been very bad today?'

That's when it hits me: this is the girl Nana showed me through her hair; Ma's younger self.

I nod, uncomfortable at the change in her, that tug at my heart that makes me mother to her child. Emotion flows through her, dragging me towards her like the tide at full moon. Before I know it, I'm standing closer to Ma than I have for a long time. So close, in fact, her breath mingles with mine.

'Are you going to let them do away with me, Sheba?'

The lioness growls again. Ma steps back, and as she does so, the sky darkens, grumbling thunder.

'I'm going to give you a choice, Ma.'

'A choice?' The child in her lights up as if I've offered her a bowl of guava jelly.

Is this a game Ma's playing? A trick to convince me she's not as bad as I think?

Snake's suspicious as well. 'If you have to go with your gut again,' she warns, 'take the full measure of her before you act.'

I remove the mud-cloth pouch from my pocket and Ma bridles. Won't touch it. Indeed, she shakes her head, warding it off as I recite a part of the spell she cast over me.

'Blood of my blood,
In this pouch I place the cord that binds a child to its mother,
The cord that bound you to me!

'That's what you said, Ma. You tried to use me to hurt someone else. I won't do it. Instead, I'm giving you the choice you never gave me.'

My heart pitches. One moment I wish I could turn back time and make everything right between us. Next, I'm grieving at the impossibility of it.

Grey clouds scud the sky and as a drop of rain splashes my cheek, I hurry on. 'The cord in this pouch bound me to you. You forgot that it tied you to me at the same time. Now that I'm a guardian of our village, your hold over me is broken, your spell obliterated.

So, what you wished for me returns to you a hundred times over!'

I toss the contents of the pouch over my mother. Bits of dust and hair scatter over her dress, while the remains of the cord, which has shrivelled into a strip like a snake's discarded skin, brushes her cheek.

Ma shrieks as if I've thrown acid over her. Shrieks when I ask her to choose. 'Do you want to live as a woman, Ma, or a bird? Do you want to become a woman, no magic in your blood, or fly free as a bird?'

'Traitor!' she screams. 'Is this the thanks I get for giving birth to you?'

The girl who called to me for help has disappeared, submerged by the fury of Mother Crow.

'*I carried you nine months. These breasts suckled you...*'

The lioness at my feet roars as a gust of wind dribbles droplets on my hands.

'Choose, Ma. Quickly,' I tell her. 'Or I'll choose for you.'

'Bird! Bird!' she cries. 'And I'll take my flock with me – all of them!'

What my mother has already set in motion is about to happen. I've no control over that. But as things stand, as a guardian of our village, the girl who walks with lions, I recite an incantation. The spell she cast on the night she introduced me to Mother Crow will now set her free.

> 'Be wild, Mother Crow.
> Wild as the wind.
> Be the beating heart of every storm
> The calm eye of a hurricane
> The fiercest flame of a forest fire
> Fly free, Ma! Free as the wind!
> Fly till the forest hears your cry,
> And takes you in.'

As I say the words, Ma's transformation begins. Her features twizzle. There's a stirring of noses and mouths; a kaleidoscope of lips and foreheads as her prey surface for one last look of the world through human eyes.

'We are many,' they mumble. And yet one face appears again and again as if reaching out to me.

Is that my father, I wonder. Is that the face of the man I've been desperate to know more about, or another of Ma's tricks? My

gut tells me this is an
ingenious attempt to
confuse and outwit me.
Too late to stop what I've
begun, I wait until Ma's traits settle
into features I recognise.

'Join us,' she pleads. 'Come with me, Sheba.'

I shake my head, and Ma's hair and skin spasm,
feathering.

Mouth hardens, stretching to a beak.

Toes curl into talons. Ma shrinks. Her white kaftan
overwhelms her, and she caws.

That's when I whistle, and as the lions gather around
me, snuffling my scent, as I thank my grandmother, in
particular, for all she's done for me and say: 'Goodbye,
Nana, we'll meet again soon,' I untangle Ma and

release her. She flies, taking her murder of crows with her. They soar into the sky and then tumbling and turning, zig-zagging through dark, wind-tossed clouds, they disappear.

Those left behind awake as if from slumber and, dumping stones still in their hands, wonder what they were doing beforehand.

The wind drops.

The lions fade.

I take Maybe's hand.

And as his eyes kiss mine, the clouds above us open, and rain falls at last.

Glossary

Aba! *an exclamation of shock and surprise*

Achumo *biscuits; often sold as street food*

Adire *indigo dyed cloth produced by Yoruba women of south western Nigeria. The texitile is decorated using the stitch-resist and tie-dye method*

Adjei! *an expression of severe pain, occasionally used when laughing hysterically*

Agbada *a matching gown, trousers and hat or head wrap; originally from Nigeria*

Aggrey bead *a type of decorated glass bead from Ghana used in necklaces and bracelets*

Ago *Is anyone in?*

Akofena *a symbol of a sword of war in Ghanaian Adinkra, in which symbols represent concepts and aphorisms*

Akpeteshie *the national spirit of Ghana, made by distilling palm wine or sugar cane; also known as kill-me-quick*

Akuffo *a small, bottled beer; short, like Ghana's president, Akuffo-Addo*

Akwaaba *Welcome*

Amie *Come in*

Ampe *a game usually played by two or more school girls, which requires no equipment. The leader and another player jump up at the same time, clap, and thrust one foot forward when they jump*

Araba *young woman*

Asemane! *What a situation!*

Basaa basaa *untidy*

Batakari *woven cloth from Northern Ghana which can be sewn into dresses for women and smocks for men*

Boflot *fried, sugared flour-dough buns*

Bou-bou *a long, colourful, loose-fitting garment worn by both sexes in West Africa*

Broni-wawu *second-hand clothes; literally dead, white man's clothes*

Eto *a celebratory dish of yam mashed with palm oil*

Fufu *an essential food in West Africa made from boiled yam, cassava or plantain pounded into a dough*

Fulani *the usual Ghanaian name for Fula people, cattle pastoralists found throughout West Africa*

Gidi-gidi *giddy, restless; a busybody*

Gonja *woven fabric from Northern Ghana*

Haba! *a variant of Aba! An expression of surprise or amazement*

Harmattan *a season in West Africa between the end of November and the middle of March; characterised by the dry, dusty north-easterly trade wind of the same name, which blows from the Sahara Desert over West Africa into the Gulf of Guinea*

Ju ju *magic*

Kaba *a skirt and blouse made in matching material*

Kai! *an expression of extreme disgust*

Kanga *a colourful, light fabric worn in East Africa*

Kenkey *fermented corn dough; a staple food in Ghana*

Kente cloth *richly woven colourful cloth from the Asante or Ewe regions of Ghana, traditionally worn on special occasions*

Kobi *the name of fish used to flavour stews. Only a tiny portion is used so the term can imply that someone is mean*

Konkonsa *slander, rumour; back-biting, idle gossip*

Krachi *young man*

Kyenkyema *useless*

Lawato! *Liar!*

Mallam *wise man, usually Muslim; a teacher of the Qur'an*

Naija *a nickname for Nigeria*

Neem *a tree with delicate, sweet-smelling flowers*

Obronie *light-skinned; outsider; European*

Onigi *a Nigerian, threaded hairstyle which literally means 'sticks'*

Pesewa *a coin*
Pickney *pidgin for child*
Prekese *a type of tree with a delicious perfume*
Ragga boy *a ragamuffin; street-wise boy*
Sakora *a term often used as an insult to describe someone with a close-shaven, practically bald head*
Sasabonsam *a blood-sucking monster*
Sheda *shiny cotton material from Nigeria often used for sewing agbada and bou-bou*
Sika *gold, money*
Sobolo *a drink made from hibiscus petals and ginger*
Tatale *plantain, ginger and chilli pancakes*
Toma *love-beads, waist-beads*
Waakye *a meal of rice and beans*
Wahala *chaos, commotion*
Wawa *an African hardwood tree*
Yama-yama *pidgin for disgusting, repulsive*

Adinkra Symbols

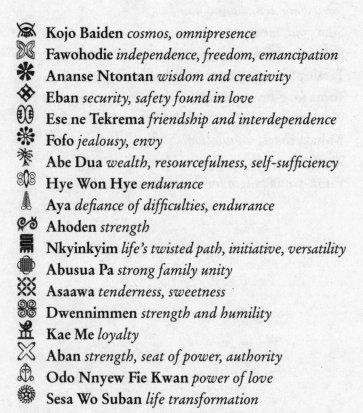

Kojo Baiden *cosmos, omnipresence*
Fawohodie *independence, freedom, emancipation*
Ananse Ntontan *wisdom and creativity*
Eban *security, safety found in love*
Ese ne Tekrema *friendship and interdependence*
Fofo *jealousy, envy*
Abe Dua *wealth, resourcefulness, self-sufficiency*
Hye Won Hye *endurance*
Aya *defiance of difficulties, endurance*
Ahoden *strength*
Nkyinkyim *life's twisted path, initiative, versatility*
Abusua Pa *strong family unity*
Asaawa *tenderness, sweetness*
Dwennimmen *strength and humility*
Kae Me *loyalty*
Aban *strength, seat of power, authority*
Odo Nnyew Fie Kwan *power of love*
Sesa Wo Suban *life transformation*

Adinkrahene Dua *chief of Adinkra symbols, greatness, leadership, charisma*

Nsa Ko Na Nsa Aba *help and support*

Duafe *beauty*

Dame Dame *intelligence, ingenuity*

Nokore *truth*

Osram ne Nsoromma *love, faithfulness, harmony*

Owia Kokroko *vitality*

Akoko Nan *nurture*

Sankofa *revival, wisdom*

Ti Koro Nko Agyina *co-operation, teamwork*

Ani Bere *diligence, perseverance*

Obaa Ne Oman *womanhood, femininity and feminism*

Okodee Mmowere *strength, bravery, power*

Tamfo Bebre *awareness of ill will, jealousy, enemy*

Nteasee *understanding, compassion to one and others*

Otumfuo Wuo Ye Ya *honour and nobility*

Yebehyia Bio We Shall *farewell*

Akoben *call to arms*

Bi Nka Bi *peace, harmony*

Tabono *strength, confidence*

Nyansapo *intelligence, patience*

Okuafo Pa *diligence, hardwork*

Kokuromotie *cooperation, harmony*

Acknowledgements

Thank you to the incredible team at Zephyr led by my brilliant editor, Fiona Kennedy. Thank you for your patience, Fiona, and for giving me the time and space to let this story emerge at its own pace. Thanks also to Leo Nickolls for the stunning cover and design of *Lionheart Girl*, which takes my breath away every time I see it. Leo, you've totally aced it with this one and I shall forever be in your debt. A huge 'thank you' to my agent, Matthew Hamilton, whose advice and feedback I rely on. And to friends and family in Ghana and London, especially Colin Izod, thank you for being present even when I'm immersed in another world.

Yaba Badoe
London
July 2021

Now enjoy reading

A JIGSAW of FIRE and STARS

Out Now

I

There's only one thing makes any sense when I wake from my dream. I'm a stranger and shouldn't be here. Should my luck run out, a black-booted someone could step on me and crush me, as if I'm worth less than an ant. This I know for a fact. And yet once or twice a week, the dream seizes me and shakes me about:

'Kill 'em! Kill 'em! Take their treasure!' The order goes out and a dilapidated trawler in a stormy sea shudders. An iron-grey vessel, lights blazing, rams it a second time. The iron monster backs away, then with engines at full throttle, lunges again.

Faces contort. Old ones, young ones, men and women, brown and black faces. Screams punch through the air. Fishing nets tangle, spill over. A fuel tank explodes and the sea glows, roiling with blood and oil.

Below deck, a stench like an over-ripe mango oozes

from a crouched woman. She shrieks: 'My baby! My baby! Save my baby!'

A tall man responds with a command: 'The sea-chest. Fetch our treasure. Quickly. For the child's sake. Move.'

A figure tumbles into the sea. Then an old man, a girl in his arms, leaps. A deafening jumble of sound and sea swallows the cries of the drowning. The slip-slip-patter of bare feet on galley stairs ascend. Anxious eyes flit in faces bright with fear in the flame-light.

The hand of the tall man pummels a pillow of yellow dust, then a footrest filled with glittering stones for the baby's feet. Someone folds a cloth, a fine tapestry of blue and green, into a blanket.

'Give her this,' says a burly, bald-headed man. 'My dagger to help her in battle. May the child be a princess, a true warrior, valiant in the face of danger yet merciful to those she defeats.'

'May your spear arm be strong, my daughter,' the tall man adds. 'Your legs swift as a gazelle's, and your heart the mighty heart of a lioness protecting her cubs.'

The petrified woman scribbles a note and hides it beneath the pillow, whispering a prayer. 'May our ancestors watch over you, my child. May the creator of all life guide you and make you wily in the ways of the world we are sending you to.'

The grey vessel, a trail of carnage in its wake, surges forwards with a splutter of gunfire. Bullets splinter the deck, tearing it open, and the trawler erupts in flames.

The tall man grabs the baby and bundles her into the chest. He holds it aloft and flings it into the sea. It lurches and almost capsizes. The baby gurgles, entranced by the rough play of water as a wave steadies her boat. She smiles, a jigsaw of fire and stars reflected in her eyes, and she stretches a dimpled hand to touch the moon.

Burning timber from the trawler's bow crashes down and splashes the baby's face. Enchanted by flying embers, she coos. But when the sobs of the dying reach her, and waves stifle their gasps, she begins to whimper.

And, flung to and fro, bobs up and down, crying in the night.

2

It took me a while to realise the baby was me. Even now, when I wake in a sweat, chest heaving, hands clammy, and Cobra tells me to relax – I'm just having another nightmare – I still can't quite believe it's me in the water.

What I know to be true is that, for as long as I can remember, we've been on the move: Cat, Cobra and me. We roam from place to place, spending more time in the spaces in between than in the cities. Yet when I wake up frightened and confused, all it takes is Priss to hiss in my ear, to twist my hair around and make a nest of it, to calm me.

It's thanks to Priss that I've figured out as much as I have. The first time I tore myself out of that dream and found enough words on my tongue to tell her about it, she suspected who I was straightaway, because she knows what happened next.

She found me in the water. There was a mist next morning. One of those whirling sea-fog days that makes it hard to tell where shoreline begins and sea ends. A sort of blurring where time seems to stop. It was like that when Priss, flying beneath a cloud, sees this big chest. She sees it, then hears a baby crying. Swoops to take a closer look. Lands on me, almost tipping me over, so tries again.

Second time round, she steadies herself, and settles just below my feet. Talons scratch me and I squeal. She could tell I needed feeding, 'cause after I squeal, I start shrieking louder than a banshee. Priss doesn't know what do. She's a bird, a bright golden eagle. Eats rabbits and rats, and, when she's lucky, small flying creatures on the wing. There's a whole heap of things she can eat. Could have eaten a baby, I suppose. Fact remains she liked the look of me: black face, big eyes. Just couldn't figure out how to feed me. So she brushes a golden wing over my face. The musty scent of her feathers, the soft swish and tickle of their kiss, quieten me.

There are two of us now, Priss and me in the chest, as it drifts to the shore. The tide recedes, wedging us on a slipstream of seaweed. Priss watches over me while, rattled by hunger, I cry myself to sleep.

A little later, a spaniel scampers up the beach and starts sniffing around the chest. Priss squawks, flapping her wings. She's so fierce the dog cringes and scrambles away. I wake up and begin to howl.

The owner of the dog hears me, a fat giant of a woman. Black hair, rosy cheeks, hands as wide as a bat's wing. The dog leaps ahead of her and she follows, flipper feet pounding the shore.

Priss won't let anyone touch me. She just won't let 'em. Scraps with the dog, screeches at the woman. But the woman inches closer: 'Easy, my pretty. What have you got there? Easy, girl...'

By now I'm busting a gut with my howling, and because she's beginning to understand just how hungry I am, Priss yields. Hopping from one foot to the other, she stays close. Says she would have pecked out their eyes, the woman and the dog's, plucked them out and eaten 'em just like that, if they'd hurt me.

The woman lifts me up: 'Little one,' she says. 'My precious...'

Her dark, pebbled eyes loom over me. Sticky-out ears, stringy hair. She's no beauty, but Priss can see she cares. I stop crying as she holds me tight to her chest, the way mothers are supposed to. And when I snuffle up against her and dive down, rummaging for breast, something to suck on to take away the ache in my belly, Priss can see she was right to let her come near. I need to feed.

Not yet. The woman wants to know more.

'Quiet now,' she says. And slinging me over her shoulder, patting me all the while, stoops to inspect my sea-chest cradle.

She fingers the blue-green blanket, savours the silky-smooth waft and weft of its weave. Finds a dagger, a leopard-skin drum. Beside the drum, a thin bamboo flute. Then she lifts the pillow and sees the note. Reads it. Looks inside the pillow and her mouth opens wide. 'Buttercups and daisies,' she says. 'Well, I never! Who would have thought it, Mama Rose? Who would believe it?'

She drags the chest into a patch of tall grass and hides it. Takes me home and Priss follows. Won't let me out of her sight, not for a moment. It's been like that ever since.

Before I had memory, I had Priss.

She was with me before my dreams began.

And before I landed on the seashore and Mama Rose took me in, there was Cobra and Cat.

About the Author

Yaba Badoe is an award-winning documentary filmmaker and writer. Yaba was born in Ghana but now lives in England with her husband. She has been nominated for the Distinguished Woman of African Cinema award. Her debut children's novel, *A Jigsaw of Fire and Stars*, and her second novel, *Wolf Light*, are both published by Zephyr.

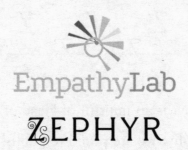

EmpathyLab

ZEPHYR

We are an Empathy Builder Publisher

- Empathy is our ability to understand and share someone else's feelings
- It builds stronger, kinder communities
- It's a crucial life skill that can be learned

We are supporting **EmpathyLab** in their work to develop a book-based empathy movement in a drive to reach one million children a year and more.

Find out more at www.empathylab.uk
www.empathylab.uk/what-is-empathy-day

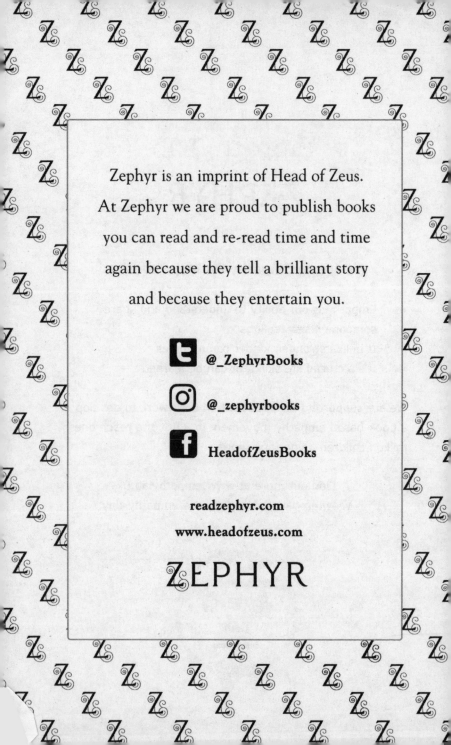

Zephyr is an imprint of Head of Zeus.
At Zephyr we are proud to publish books
you can read and re-read time and time
again because they tell a brilliant story
and because they entertain you.

@_ZephyrBooks

@_zephyrbooks

HeadofZeusBooks

readzephyr.com
www.headofzeus.com

ZEPHYR